Runes Beyond the Edge

RUNES BEYOND THE EDGE

LAUREL MEANS

North Star Press of St. Cloud, Inc.
St. Cloud, Minnesota

For Kenneth, Matias, Thomas, Maia, Jonas, Marcus, Sarah, and Christina

Companions to Harald

and

Kaia, for things Nordic

Copyright © 2010 Laurel Means.

All rights reserved.

This is a work of fiction. Any resemblence to any actual person, living or dead, is merely coincidence.

ISBN: 978-0-87839-389-3

Printed in the United States of America

Published by
North Star Press of St. Cloud, Inc
PO Box 451
St. Cloud, MN 56302

www.northstarpress.com

Table of Contents

1.	The King's Plan	1
2.	Harald's Runes	16
3.	High Seas	32
4.	The First Challenge	46
5.	On the Western Edge	62
6.	The Wilderness of No Return	81
7.	Heckla's Curse	96
8.	Through the Mists	114
9.	Runes Beyond the Edge	122
10.	Distant Drums	143
11.	The Mysterious Stranger	158
12.	That Pile of Whale Bones	180
13.	The King's Justice	196
	Historical Note	212
	Appendix: Norse Wordhord	216
	Futhark or Runic Alphabet and Numerals	218

Chapter One
The King's Plan

BANG! Harald nearly jumped out of his skin. Massive doors flew open. A giant king's guard filled them top to bottom, a huge warrior with a threatening sword. The silver on his breastplate shone dazzling bright, and over that a bearskin cloak was fastened with a jeweled pin to one shoulder. A two-horned helmet kept his face in shadow. It looked as if he had no face at all, just a hollow black emptiness.

Out of that blackness came a booming voice. "Come, now!" Harald jumped again. "Now! It is time."

Yes, it was time, and Harald's heart beat faster. It was hard to breathe. The time had come at last.

"Quick, stand up, son," Father hissed into Harald's ear.

Harald felt a painful wrench to his arm as he was jerked to his feet. He'd been sitting so long on that hard, wooden bench that his feet had grown numb. "Are we really going in now?" he whispered.

"Quiet!" hissed his father, "or we'll be in trouble. And straighten your tunic!"

Holding his breath, Harald tugged at the bottom of his tunic, glanced at his hands to see if they were still clean. *Erroowll*—his stomach gave a loud growl, and he squeezed his elbows in tight to stop it. *Erroowll* again. It wouldn't stop. Now his knees were shaking.

It'd been such a long, anxious wait in the ante-room to the king's great hall. They arrived at early dawn, now it was mid-day.

Harald had been so nervous about the king's command summoning them to his castle. There'd been little thought about food when they left, but now it was long past time for the dinner he'd been promised. Back at Grandmother's house it waited—cod with cream sauce, his favorite, and current cake. At the thought, the hunger pains increased—worse, they grew louder. Hunger and nervousness made him dizzy. This time it was good to feel his father's firm hand on his shoulder, steadying him. Embarrassing, too, for he was now almost as tall as his father and certainly no boy anymore.

The king's guard boomed out impatiently, pointing his sword for emphasis. "Come with me, Bjorn Erikson, known as Fierce-as-a-Bear, and you also, Harald son of Bjorn," he added even more sternly, "You must leave your weapons here. Only the king's guard is allowed weapons in his majesty's presence."

Harald's father dutifully unbuckled his long sword and laid it on the bench, with Harald's dagger soon beside it. The guard kept his right hand in readiness on the hilt of his own sword and, with his left, gestured menacingly for them to follow.

Harald caught his breath as they entered a small, half-lit ante-room. The intertwined ravens embroidered in gold on the front of the guard's sash around his waist, the king's royal emblem, caught the flickering light from the one torch on the wall. They seemed alive, those ravens, threatening, ready for the *ravens' feast*—men slain on the battlefield. The guard led them through wide double doors into the great hall, opened by a servant on each side, dressed in tunics with the king's royal crest.

"Mind your manners, now, " he heard his father hiss, with a painful squeeze to his shoulder.

"But father—it's not *that* I'm worried about," he hissed back. "It's—" but a dark look from the guard silenced him. No it wasn't manners, he was thinking about. All that instruction about court manners over the past month—he was sure some of it had stuck. No, it was his appearance. Did that red woolen cloak look fine enough, with its black and white checked border? His best one. Grandmother had insisted he wear Grandfather's deep-blue tunic, but now that he was taller than his grandfather had been, it was a little on the small side. He hoped the gray rabbit fur around the bottom and the ends of the sleeves would cover that up.

And what about his hair? For sure he'd combed it before he left, but there was a lot of it refusing to stay slicked down. He started to check but instantly thought better of it. And his fur cap—his sister Anna had made it herself from a wolf's head, putting in glass beads for the eyes, keeping its sharp teeth. Good thing he was wearing it today, because he always made him feel stronger—fierce as a wolf.

"Take off that hat, young man! Off, I said!" a servant hissed in his ear as he passed through the main doors.

Well, so much for the wolf cap, thought Harald.

"And don't forget to bow as you approach the king's throne, and kneel at his feet," the servant added with a painful jab to Harald's ribs. Of course, his father had already told him that. But he seemed to be forgetting all the rules under stress of the moment. Things were not going well, not at all like he'd expected.

The great hall was larger and lighter than the ante-room, with three stained-glass windows down each side. To Harald it still seemed dark and mysterious. For one thing, it was filled with smoke from the fire-pit in the center of the room. There was so much noise and confusion, so many people were standing, sitting, talking. Some soldiers were eating at a long trestle table set off to one side. The smell of roast pork sent off another hunger pang, another *erooool* in Harald's stomach.

"Come. Move respectively forward," ordered the guard with a prod in the middle of Harald's back. "His majesty is beckoning to you. You may approach the throne."

King Erik Thorgeirson sat on his throne on a raised platform at the far end of the room. There was no mistaking his as *the king.* Awe made Harald stop in his tracks, but before he knew it he was being pushed forward, then forced down on his knees at the bottom of the steps.

"Well, well," said the king, his deep voice filling the hall. "Finally you've come. I didn't think you'd ever leave that farm of yours. One would think the province of Telemark was on the other side of the world from Bergen, Bjorn Erikson." The king's voice echoed as in an enormous cave. "In our language, Bjorn, bee-yorn, *bear.*" The king chuckled. "Indeed, you are well-named *the fierce one,* like a bear." He pointed to Harald. "Your son, Harald?" The king spread his arms wide. "You are my kinsman, and I welcome you!"

Kinsman? He was related to the king? Harald raised his head cautiously, hoping it was all right to look up. He was startled to meet the king's piercing, gray eyes and immediately lowered his gaze. He'd almost forgotten what his father had told him many years ago. The king and his father were distant cousins of some sort—the name *Erik* came down from his father's grandfather.

The king was a big man like Father and like he—Harald— had every intention of being. But he'd never seen a man *that* enormous before. The king's size matched his powerful voice. In fact, his body filled the whole throne, and that throne was big—a huge wooden seat, elaborately carved all around the sides and arms, even up to the overhanging canopy at the top. Some of the carvings were gilded and the golden dragon figures seemed to move in the uncertain light, their bead-like eyes watching him suspiciously, their tongue flicking out at him. It looked as though they were guarding the king. The king, though, looked powerful enough to defend himself.

Yes, it was true what they said about King Erik, Harald was thinking. He couldn't take his eyes off the man, no matter how many times he'd been told not to stare. People marveled at how fierce a warrior the king had been. His own father had seen it for himself, when he'd fought at the king's side at the battle of Orkney. And people said the king could cut off a man's head with one slash of his sword. That's how he got the nickname *the slasher*.

With a gasp, Harald realized he was staring and that the king was noticing. He looked down at his feet, knowing full well his face was turning red.

"Taking me in, are you, young man?" boomed the king. "By the god Thor, young son of Bjorn, you look indeed like your father—same shaggy golden hair, same far-seeing gray eyes—eyes that could see up into the stars, as they say about you. How old are you, now? Well, well, it won't be long before you can grow a big golden beard like your father's." He laughed a big, deep-down laugh and motioned for them both to come closer.

Harald and his father came up as commanded to the lowest step on the raised platform, spread over with a big white polarbear rug. "Do you know why we have summoned you here, Bjorn and son of Bjorn?" the king then asked. Before Harald could get up enough courage to answer—he hoped Father would answer first—the king continued. It was obvious the king would do most of the talking. "I have a commission for you. An important one. I have selected you to carry it out. Are you willing to do as we command?"

Harald knew the king did not expect an answer. They were not being offered a choice. Father simply bowed his head in agreement. Harald was puzzled as to what a *commission* was. Must be related to *mission*, a job of some sort, a plan maybe. The whole summons, the whole command to come as quickly as they could to Bergen, had been mysterious. And why had the king really chosen *them*?

"You will be wondering what this plan is and why we have sent for you, eh? Out of all the others in our kingdom, eh?" asked the king.

Harald took a deep breath. How could the king have known what he was thinking? Was he able to read his mind? Maybe he should be more guarded in his thoughts. He wished he could somehow put a cloud of smoke around his thoughts like it was said the old Norse god Loki could do. That slippery Loki was always playing tricks. He could hide in any shape. He could deceive men's minds. But now he must pay attention because the king was beginning to explain what this was all about.

"There's no time to waste," King Erik continued, "so we'll cut right to the heart of the matter. I need you to go on a journey, a long journey to the Western Edge of the world as we know it. We recognize you as a loyal subject, a kinsman, a man of trust, and a great warrior, Bjorn. My *jarls* also tell me good things of your son. These noblemen say the lad has performed feats well beyond his years already. But for this task, we need more than someone good with sword and spear. We need someone we can trust. Most of all, we need someone who has a good head, who can deal with dangerous and unexpected situations in unknown lands, with unknown enemies. And there are many at the Western Edge, we're told."

Harald was a little taken back by the king's words *unknown enemies* and the *edge*. Who were the enemies? And what did he mean by *edge*? The edge of the world? Did the world drop off into space after that? Wasn't the world supposed to be round? For that matter, what had the king really heard about himself? Surely people had exaggerated! He didn't feel ready for some dangerous enterprise, not yet at least. There were older, wiser, stronger men in the kingdom. "But—but your majesty—" he started to protest, but instantly broke off when his father elbowed him hard and gave him a dagger-like look.

"No, our hopes are not set on those older or wiser, son of Bjorn," the king went on, again as if reading Harald's thoughts. "We have many reasons for our choice. You will not disappoint us. We know, for example, that you have studied the stars. We also know you are good with words, even in the old speech of our ancestors. And we know you are your father's son. So, then, do you agree to accompany your father on this enterprise?"

Again, Harald realized the king was not really offering a choice. Like Father, he could only nod his head. His mind surged with emotions he hoped the king—with his strange mind-reading powers—could not detect. The enterprise was beginning to sound very dangerous. Not to mention the fact that it would take a long time, a *very* long time. He would have to leave Norway, for years even. Maybe both he and his father would be killed and never return, and his sister would be left all alone with their grandmother. His mother and grandfather had died in the plague two years back. His sister Anna was only eighteen with no husband yet to protect her.

It was true, however, what the king said. Harald did know a little about the stars and the constellations. He had learned how to use an astrolabe and a bearing dial. With an astrolabe, you could sight the sun or the moon and tell the time of day. You could line up the stars and determine directions, find your latitude. With an astrolabe, you didn't really need a bearing dial, which had a stone pointing the way north. He knew such knowledge was useful for mariners. But he'd only made one voyage in a long boat around the south coast, from their old homestead in Telemark on the Oslofjord way up to Bergen city where his grandparents lived and the king had his main castle and his court. And, yes, come to think of it, he *was* fairly good with letters, too, even the old-fashioned runic letters called *futhark*, which his grandfather had taught him.

"Now, now, young lad," boomed the king. "You look doubtful. You have many questions, I see."

"No, your majesty," stammered Harald. "That is, I—" Another dagger-like look from Father. Well, no harm in raising doubts in private. What the king said about his skills? Would these be enough for the king's expedition? As for fighting—well, he'd only just mastered the art of using the heavy broad sword Grandfather left him. Now here, in the king's great hall, Harald's self-confidence was rapidly draining away.

He took a deep breath and tried to ignore the fact his father was squeezing his arm in a painful warning. "Well, you see, sire, I'm wondering if you have the right person. There may be a mixup—with all due respect." Another gulp. "You see, your majesty, there are so many named Harald in the whole of Norway. With all due respect, sire, perhaps you have sent for the wrong person. Too many Haralds, ever since the days of King Harald Hárfagri—Harald *Fair Hair*—some four hundred years back. With the greatest respect, your majesty, you must be thinking of some other, older, smarter, stronger Harald, not me!"

"Harald!" father turned to him in disbelief. "You should not even dare challenge the king like that!"

"Well, Kinsman Bjorn," laughed the king, "I admire the lad's daring and his courage in speaking up. Who knows, it may stand him in good stead in the days to come." He turned to Harald. "Harald Bjornson, we know you by that name. No mistake. Kings make no mistakes. That is *your* name, and your name alone. We indeed recognize you as your father's son and my kinsman. We accept that you are willing to do as we command. Good, very good."

Oh no, thought Harald, *he's reading my mind again! There's no mistake. The king* does *know who I am. He* does *know he has the right Harald. I'm* the right Harald.

Suddenly the king rose huge from his seat on the throne. He gathered his fur mantle around his massive body. "Come! Now that we're certain of your allegiance and loyalty to the throne of Norway, we shall begin to put it to the test. Let us adjourn to another room, both of you and several of our *jarls* here. We'll go over the details of this commission in private. There's much to speak of—and only behind closed doors."

With that, the king and several of his courtiers headed for a modest door opening off the back of the throne platform. The same guard who ushered them into the hall now motioned for Harald and his father to follow.

Entering the room behind the throne platform, Harald saw it was almost entirely filled by a large round table and about a dozen carved wooden chairs. An iron stand with candles stood in the middle of the table. There were a few shelves on brackets high up on one wall, a large wooden cupboard on the opposite wall. One small window let in just enough light to see without the candles being lit, but now the sea fog was rolling into the city from the fjord.

"Ho, there, Swein, light some candles," King Erik ordered a servant standing by the door, and then fetch those maps from the wooden cupboard." He pulled out a chair with a scrapping sound and sat down at the table with a wave of his hand for all to be seated.

"Well then, my good men—for you must be considered a man, now, Harald—let us begin," and he untied the ribbon around a leather roll, then slid out a large piece of parchment. As he unrolled the heavy parchment across the table, he told one of the *jarls* to hold down one end so it wouldn't curl up again. He reached down to pull out a jeweled dagger, which he carried in a sheath attached to his broad, leather belt. "Here is Bergen, the seat of our kingdom," he said, using the dagger's tip to point to a spot on the map. "Now, Harald, look carefully at this map. Come over here so you can see better, since you are going to be the navigator."

This took Harald by surprise. He had no idea how being a navigator could possibly relate to that large circle with various shapes and wavy lines inside it. Harald watched, fascinated, as the king traced a line from the right hand side of the circle toward the left. "Here you see west of our Norway there are many islands. Going further west, after five days' sailing with fair winds, you come first the Shetland, then the Orkney, then the Hebrides islands off the northern coast of England. That would be about five days' sailing more." The dagger's point moved farther to the left. "Now, continuing westward after a few more days, we come to a group called the Faeroes. Another week's sailing, and we find a big island called Iceland. All these are our fiefs, Norwegian lands, all Norwegian conquests. But Iceland is now our biggest fief, with hundreds of settlers there already."

A wave of excitement came over Harald. He'd heard so many stories about the early Norwegian settlements in Iceland. His grandfather had told him about the heroes Erik the Red and Lief the Lucky, about the many escapades of the rebel Egil Skallagrimson and his neighbors. His favorite story was about brave Njal and his wife, Bergthora. But the name *Iceland* really didn't sound too inviting. "An island covered with *ice*?" he blurted out. Another sharp, silencing look from Father.

"Not exactly," the king answered with a half-smile. "You will see. But meantime, keep your mind on what I'm saying."

Embarrassed, Harald quickly shifted his mind back from the idea of a land of ice and the scene of Njal's tragedy to the map spread out on the table. He'd never seen a map before. He'd never imagined that it was possible to see all the places on the earth at once, drawn out like that. How was it possible to see whole countries, islands, seas, without getting way up high in the air and looking down on them like a bird? Who could have made a map? Fascinated, he drew so close to the map that he suddenly realized he was leaning on the king's arm. He stepped back, his face turning red again.

Fortunately King Erik hadn't noticed. "You'll see," he continued, focused entirely on the map, "that there's a great land mass coming down from the north to the west of Iceland, shaped like a spear point. It was first discovered about four hundred years ago by Gunnbjorn Ulf Krakason. Ha, ha, now that's a story for you—an accident! Old Gunnbjorn just got lost in the fog off the coast of Iceland. Lots of fog and mist there, and beyond to the west."

The king paused. Harald wondered what lay beyond Greenland, beyond the fog to the west. A huge unknown place, full of danger and mystery.

"Now, young Harald, you'll be wondering what lies in the fog west of Greenland, eh?" asked the king.

Harald gasped in amazement. Again, the king seemed to be able to mind-read. He wished he could fog over his thoughts like Loki.

"Well," the king continued, "directly across the straits from Greenland is Markland, farther to the north is Halluland, further to the south is Vinland. We know something about Vinland, from some voyages there several hundred years ago. We don't know much about Halluland except that it's full of glaciers and high mountains."

"But your majesty," Harald found himself asking before thinking better of it, "what's west of Markland, then?"

"To the west of Markland? Ah, that's a different story." The king paused again, resting the point of his dagger on a wavy line marking what must be a coastline to the left of Greenland. "Beyond this wavy line is one, big question mark. You see on the map only an empty space."

"Is there no name for this part? But what is there? " Immediately he wished he'd kept his mouth shut. One of the *jarls* looked at him with a disapproving frown. His father gave him a dark look and shook his head. The code determined that a subject could only answer, never initiate any questions to the monarch. And he'd already broken that code more than once.

But, again, the king did not seem displeased—was it because he considered him nearly equal to his father? He began to feel reassured that he was who he was and in the right place. He hoped that confidence, even fake confidence, would get him through. He'd need even more of the real thing for what lay ahead if what the king was describing was true.

"It is called *Markland* because that means the *edge*, the *boundary*," the king answered. "And that's where you come in, you and your father. Come, sit down in this chair here beside me and we shall explain."

Harald could feel tension growing in the small room. The *jarls* obviously knew what was coming. And from the set expression on his father's face, Harald sensed that his father knew, too.

"Yes, Markland," King Erik continued. "The boundary land, the Western Edge, as it's called. And you must also know that, at that boundary, the Greenland colonies have been thriving for several centuries now, ever since Erik the Red first established the eastern settlements around Eriksfjord—a distant kinsman of both of us," he said, as he nodded toward Harald's father. "Since that time, we've depended much on their trade—we'll wager, young Bjorn, that the very cloak you're wearing is made from Greenland wool."

Harald looked down self-consciously at the cloak's unusual woven border and to his horror noticed it was torn in several places. With his soft leather boot he secretly slid the trailing edge farther under his chair.

The king pointed again to the great circle drawn on the parchment. "But we have heard that the Greenlanders are experiencing some difficulties—longer winters, fewer crops, other problems," said the king. "There is need for more settlers in the west, more need for land. Not only for the support of the settlers, but also for the survival of our crown, or kingdom of Norway."

Harald saw his father look up in surprise, a look which the king apparently noticed. "Ah, Bjorn," exclaimed the king, "you're surprised at this news, eh? You've been away from court too long. Too long you've been hiding away down on your old farm. We must inform you of today's facts. Here they are, in brief. We need more land because we're being threatened by enemies all around us. The royal treasury grows lean through the cost of men, of arms, of weapons, ships, horses, supplies. But we should allow *Jarl* Anders Matteson to explain. He is my *stallari*, in charge of our garrison down on the Oslofjord. He'll know the latest developments."

Jarl Anders was an older man with long gray hair and a drooping mustache to match. Harald noticed that, although he was richly dressed in court clothes—a blue brocade robe reaching to the floor—he wore a steel partial breastplate buckled on over the robe. A wide, leather sword belt circled his waist, although it was lacking its weapon. He'd set down a steel helmet on the table before him. "I thank you for this opportunity to speak, your majesty," Anders began, with a polite bow of his head toward the king. "We all know about King Vald of Jutland. He is gradually overcoming all the territory around him. First it was the land to the south, beyond Haddeby, Saxon land. Then that southern part of Sweden called Vastergotland. Now he has his eye on the rest of Sweden, and even the Baltic islands."

"Yes," interrupted King Erik, "the island of Gotland would certainly add to his crown. It has one of the most important trading ports in the whole area, the Hansa league, which includes all the countries surrounding the North Sea—all goes through there."

"Thank you, your majesty," said Thorleik, "for mentioning Gotland. It is indeed an important piece of the picture. But also important as you well know, your majesty," here he bowed his head again toward the king, "is the fact that he also has his eye on Greenland, even Markland beyond. Rumor has it that he is even contemplating a *landnáma*, a land-taking expedition across the western sea."

"So, my loyal subjects," said the king, slamming his big fist down on the table and causing Harald to jump in his chair. "That is the heart of the matter. Valdemar might very well take Gotland. His *landnáma* thirst is so great that he won't stop there. We must beat him into Markland," the king said defiantly, beating the table again. "We must expand our territories as far west as possible.

Should he succeed before us, he could swallow up all of Greenland—and who's to say he would stop there?"

The king paused, as if hesitant to say more on that subject. Then he added, "But it's more than just land. It's also people. You see, we have already sent two Greenlanders to explore and claim that territory to the west, that territory called Markland." He frowned with a dark look. "That was two years ago. Neither Thorkel Liefson nor Karlsefni Thorson has returned—good, brave, loyal subjects both. They have vanished without a trace. We would like you, Bjorn Erikson, to try to find out what happened to them, to rescue them if necessary, even to bring back their remains if—"

He looked thoughtfully toward the little window, but it seemed to Harald that it was the kind of look that saw nothing because feelings were running too high. No one spoke. All waited for King Erik to continue. At last the king gave a big sigh. "Time is running out. We must act soon, now, in early summer, while the seas are still open."

The discussion which followed between the king, the *jarls*, and his father seemed to last forever. It was full of details about boats, money, crews, provisions. The thought of provisions reminded him of food. *Erroowll!* The groans and the hunger pains were the only things keeping him awake.

Father was now asking the king questions about who would go with them, when they would leave. He and the *jarls* were talking about numbers, supplies, sea routes. "Will we go through the Faeroes? Who will replenish our ships in Rejkavik, Iceland's main harbor?"

"You'll learn all that soon, Kinsman Bjorn," said the king. "We shall have more meetings, be assured. There is much to decide. And many, many decisions will be a matter of life and death."

These last words got Harald's attention, and he snapped instantly out of his daze. He didn't like that answer at all. Up until then the discussion had been merely a blur of words. Now it sounded like things were beginning to take on more meaning. *Life and death*. No, he didn't like the sound of that. His feelings about being brave, fierce and a great navigator were beginning to fade. Maybe his wolf cap would have helped. Surely there'd been some mistake. He was surely the wrong Harald.

No, he'd rather stick to the other plans he had. They were important. They were safer. He'd start on them tomorrow, no matter what the king said. If the king could read his mind, then the king would understand. Yes, he'd understand and find somebody else for this commission. Another Harald. No question about his father, Bjorn. Obviously the right man for the job. But not *this* Harald—no, sire, thank you very much. It wasn't his thing to be part of all those boring meetings about ships and supplies, maps, or whatever. And for sure, he wasn't ready to drop off the edge of the earth. Much better to go out fishing in the fjord while summer lasted. Or get back to something he needed to finish. He wasn't going anywhere until it was done. His big project—and his runes!

Chapter Two
Harald's Runes

At last! The meeting with King Erik was coming to an end. Harald jumped from his chair, knocking it over with a loud—and most embarrassing—crash. There was a sharp look from *Jarl* Anders, a cough from his father. Then bowing from everybody all around, some private words, secret kinds of signs. Harald heaved a sigh of relief. Not long now. *Just let me out of here*, he thought. All that talk, talk, talk. And on an empty stomach, too. He couldn't take any more of it. Besides, it was getting harder and harder to cover up his stomach's moans and groans.

What a relief, the walk home from the castle, down the winding streets of Bergen and up the steep mountain path to Grandmother's log house. The fresh, sea air felt good and cleared his brain a little. And the walk offered an opportunity to ask his father more about the expedition. "What did the king mean by *life and death?*"

"Hmm—how important the commission is, I guess," Father answered vaguely.

But Harald suspected something worse. "Don't you mean, we might all be killed?"

"Hmm—maybe."

"Never come back?" No answer. "Well, when will everything be ready, then?"

"Can't say, exactly, son."

This wasn't getting anywhere. "But how long do I have?" Harald insisted.

"To do what?"

"My project."

"What project?"

"Well, it's—"

"Let's not talk about that right now. I've a lot on my mind." And that was that.

What a relief to reach the house. Thankfully Harald threw off his cloak, unbuckled his belt, laid his dagger on the shelf, and pulled off his boots. Best of all—hearing his sister Anna from the kitchen, "Dinner's ready. Kept it warm for you. Edge of the fireplace. Sit down, make yourselves comfortable. Grandmother and I will bring in the plates and dish up."

After two helpings of cod boiled in cream sauce, three large hunks of oat bread spread with soft cheese, a couple of spring onions just come up in the cold frame in grandmother's garden, and a very large slice of currant cake, washed down with ice-cold whey milk, Harald felt much restored. He curled up in Grandfather's big leather armchair, feeling sleepier by the minute. They'd had to get up so early—before dawn. So far only half a day and already it seemed like a hundred years.

Father stretched out his legs in front of the fire. He looked more relaxed than he had during their visit to the castle. Flossi, the furry, gray cat, jumped up into his lap, and Father absently began to rub the soft fur behind her ears.

Now! Harald thought. Good time to bring up the subject of the king's commission. If it *was* a matter of *life and death*, he needed to learn more. He shook himself awake and tried to collect his thoughts. "Father," he said, "please, can you tell me when the expedition will start?"

"Soon, my son," he replied. "Very soon. But now that I think about it, you mentioned on the way up your project. What is it? Why so important?"

Harald hesitated. How was his father going to take this? He'd probably laugh. But then, maybe not—Could he risk being humiliated? He took a deep breath and began.

"You know Grandfather?"

"Of course, of course," he smiled. "Know the man well. He was *my* father, remember?"

"Well, your father—my grandfather—taught me a lot of things."

"Grandfathers tend to do that, you know. Maybe even fathers." He smiled again as he rubbed Flossi's ears.

This wasn't going well at all. Harald might as well plunge in. "Well—humm—well, you may know—well, I've been working on something out in the shed. Some woodwork."

"Yes, glad to see you keeping busy." He paused, thinking about something else, but then came back to what Harald was saying. "What kind of woodwork?"

"It's a chest. An ashwood chest. I'm making it for Anna's dowry. She'll surely be marrying somebody fairly soon—you know that Tomas fellow seems to be hanging around a lot."

"Noticed that. He seems a very nice fellow. Stone mason, isn't he? But I'm pleased about the chest. It'll mean a lot to her."

"Would you like to see it?"

"Not now. Maybe later." Father paused. "No, now's as good a time as any, I guess. I'm going to have a lot to do in the coming weeks. So, go on, go out to the shed, bring it in—or whatever you've got finished so far."

Actually Harald had nearly finished it. Coming back into the sitting room, the chest held in both arms, he set it down proudly before the hearth.

For several moments, Father studied it. Finally he burst out, "Harald! What on earth? What kind of a design is that? Those old-fashioned-looking interlocking circles all around the edge? And that scene at one end from the story of the old Norse goddess of love, Freyja, with—can you believe it—a scene showing Christ's nativity—the baby in the manger, the shepherds—at the other end?"

"But Father, both scenes are about love. And this is a dowry chest, it's about love, it's for Anna's marriage. Look—I've nearly finished it, that is, everything except for her name—Anna Bjornsdattir. See, that's what the runes say." And he pointed to the letters chiseled into the lid.

ᚷᚾᚷ : ᛒᚠᛟᚱᚾᛋᛏᚷᛏ

"When she gets married, I'll just add the date."

"Harald, Harald," sighed Father, shaking his head. "Why on earth runes, of all things?"

"But that's what I learned from Grandfather, you know, starting back when I was about ten. He taught me the Old Norse *futhark* (another name for the old alphabet)."

"Why would he do that? What possible use are they?"

"He thought they had magic powers. They were used all over Scandinavia before the priests brought the Roman alphabet. It was always put on inscriptions, or tombstones or such. To remember heroes, to honor them. But I guess I was more interested in magic charms."

"Charms? Oh, really Harald. And in this day and age. How could just words make things happen—or cause bad things to go away?"

"Oh, yes. Grandfather claimed that, if you knew the right combination of runes, if you said the right words over them, they'd work. Then we'd practice tracing the letters on the window pane, steamed up from Grandmother's boiling soup kettle."

Father rolled his eyes. "He probably filled your head with a lot of other nonsense, too. Stories about Freyja and the like. Right? All those wonderful pagan gods, hundreds of years ago. A lot of them weren't so wonderful—like Loki. And I'll bet your grandmother didn't want to have much to do with them—or runes—either, for that matter."

So Father did know about Loki, the mind-reader, the shape-shifter! But he was right about Grandmother. He and Grandfather had to work on their runes in secret. Actually, now that Harald thought about it, the word *rune* meant *secret*. "But you know, Father," he felt compelled to add, "I do know all about St. Olaf's bringing Christianity to Norway and how all the old gods were outlawed. Don't you agree they had some exciting stories?"

His father laughed. "I suppose so, Harald. But all that on Anna's dowry chest? You'll embarrass the poor girl."

Harald hesitated to say what he really felt, why he was doing it—even if it meant embarrassing Anna. The truth was, that bringing the old world together with the new world gave him a sense of—he didn't really know the word for it. Maybe something like—unity—harmony. No, he didn't dare confess that to his father.

Now his father was gazing solemnly into the dancing flames. He said nothing for a long time. Harald hesitated to add anything. But finally, his father spoke, not looking at him—only at the flames, each word heavily weighted, " Finish your carving, my son. Finish Anna's dowry chest, her *heimanfylgja*. And finish it soon. When Anna marries, she must take her *home-follower* with her to her husband's home. Time will tell when that will be, but she must be ready then. Who knows how long this voyage will be—or—" He stopped abruptly, paused, took a deep breath. "Or whether you and I will come back at all."

This didn't sound good. The commission of *life and death*. "But it's all finished, Father," Harald replied, trying to put aside the frightening suggestion in his father's last words. "Yes, all done except for the date on the lid. And maybe the runes will bring her good luck. For us, too."

At this his father smiled, abstractly stroking Flossi's ears. "Let's hope in your sister's case it will be good—a good husband, a good home, many children. In our case, as well." Suddenly he pushed Flossi off his lap and leaned forward, becoming more serious. "Now, you asked about the king's commission, his plan for us."

At last Harald was going to get some answers. He leaned forward eagerly.

"First, you see, there is much to get ready—boats to load with food and weapons, crews to select. We must be very careful in selecting the crew: our lives may depend on them. Yet time is short. Now it's already the beginning of May. The seas are opening up, and we have much water to cross before the winter's ice locks them up once again."

"But, Father," Harald insisted, "when will we set sail?"

"We'll set sail soon, Harald-the-Impatient-One," replied his father with a faint smile. "Yes, very soon."

Harald didn't know whether to regard this answer as good or bad. He still felt uncertain about the glory of it all. If they didn't survive, where was the glory? And what about all those skills he was supposed to have? Someone had obviously played them to up King Erik, and now he was roped into a serious and life-threatening commitment on false pretenses. At least, if he never came back, Anna would have that chest to remember him by.

Several days later, the *soon* was nearly there. It was a bright, sunny day, the first real warmth of summer soaking through his clothes and deep into his skin. Harald felt like lying out on the rocks above the sparkling waters of the fjord, letting heat from the rocks and the sun warm him to the very center of his being, driving the memory of the winter's cold away. How wonderful to be just sleeping and dreaming up there—yes, dreaming about all the adventures this expedition was going to bring him. There had been nearly a week of warm days there in the harbor. The snow and ice of winter seemed very far away.

But lying out there on the rocks had not been possible for a single day, no, not one. There had been so much to do. Loading up the three boats with provisions—food, weapons, even a few live goats and chickens. The big *knorr* or cargo boat with its high decks fore and aft would hold most of what they'd need for the voyage, stowed away down in the cabin built amid-ships. The small cabin also contained an iron ring for cooking, with an iron kettle suspended from a tripod over it. A single mast, rigged for a large, square sail, rose up from its socket before the front end of the cargo cabin. The sail was a special gift from the king, his own royal emblem of inter-twined ravens painted on it. Just at the base of the mast was a small pen for the animals. There were three sleeping closets under the aft deck and a lean-to shelter on the fore deck, where some of the crew could eat and sleep. The other two boats had no cabins, no decks, only some small chests for stowage. They were open, most of the space taken up by rowing benches, with four oarlocks on each side. They had high-carved prows which curved around like dragon heads, with sharp teeth and bulging eyes.

The dragon prows reminded Harald of what Grandfather had told him about the old Viking longboats of long ago. Those dragons could cast evil spells on the lands they approached and help to overpower enemies. Maybe they'd had rune charms carved on them to help that work. When the ships came to a friendly place, his grandfather had once explained, the crew would cover those dragonheads with special hoods to check their power. Then the *landvættir*, the guardian spirits of the land, would know the boat had come in peace.

Harald and his father were standing on the dock where the boats were moored. "We'll certainly need those longboats," Father said, pointing to the two smaller dragon-prowed boats. "They're fast and light, with shallow drafts. That's why the Viking raiders found them so useful. We're sure to be navigating some rivers, where the water isn't so deep. Maybe even some shallow lakes. We may have to portage." He shrugged his shoulders. "We just don't know what to expect, Harald, but we must be prepared for anything. And if we meet any hostile natives—well, son, then we must be ready to fight."

Could these be the *unknown enemies* the king had mentioned? This was an exciting thought to Harald as he watched all kinds of weapons—swords, shields, spears, bows and arrows—being loaded aboard. It sure looked as though his father was preparing for every kind of attack. There were also extra sails, extra tackle, small kegs of flour, salt fish, dried currants. There were goat-skins filled with milk curds, many kegs of fresh water. There was even a small rowing skiff tied upside down on top of the *knorr's* storage cabin in the center of the boat.

The king had charged his father with selecting the twenty-eight men who, besides his father and himself, were to go. Each of the three boats would have a crew of ten, with a total company of thirty.

Harald was amazed at the great crowd of men who wanted to go. Word had spread that it would be a voyage of discovery, full of excitement and adventure for all those who went, full of rewards for any who returned. The noise and confusion around the dockside was deafening, with some men actually fighting to get ahead in the line forming at the sign-up table.

After several more days of hectic activity, a strange incident took place. Harald happened to be down on the docks, curious about the enlistment process. His father sat at a long table with one of the king's scribe, charged with writing down names and other information on a long parchment scroll. "Name?" His father repeatedly asked. "Experience?" "Why do you wish to take part in his majesty's commission?" Some men he turned away quickly, to Harald's relief. No way would he like to be stuck on a long voyage with *that* man—or *that* man. Others were asked more questions and eventually had their names written down on the scroll.

Harald began to notice that there seemed to be a large group of strangers wandering around, especially near the docks and the lower part of the city. Although Harald could make out most of what they said, they sounded a little different—funny-like, their accent sort of flat and cut-off, not like his own southern Norse, which went more up and down, like musical notes. And their dress was a little different, too. Maybe more like what you'd expect from some merchants he'd seen trading down in the city marketplace from France or Germany.

Harald's curiosity got the better of him. "What kind of people are these?" he finally asked his father.

"They're Goths," Bjorn answered. "Men from the Island of Gotland out in the Baltic Sea."

"But why are so many coming here?" Harald asked in amazement.

"You might not understand all the reasons, my son," Father replied. "As King Erik mentioned, their country is under siege—being threatened with war, and they don't like the man doing it."

"Do you mean what the king said about King Vald of Jutland?"

"Exactly. But they are brave, strong men and exceptionally fine seamen—living on an island, they are used to the sea. And there's one among them I spoke to yesterday. He might be particularly useful—a blacksmith named Ufila. We'll need much iron work—repairing swords, mooring wedges and the like. I'll make sure today that he's on our list."

Harald thought this was a strange decision on his father's part. Could these men really be trusted? That one name Ufila, the one his father pointed out, certainly looked suspicious. A little shifty-eyed, he shuffled his feet. He only hoped his father had made the right choices. But who was he to challenge his own father? Or King Erik Thorgeirson?

As he stood near his father later in the day, listening to each man's story as he came forward, he noticed a strange-looking old man in the group. He did look quite old, with a white beard and a long, drooping mustache, and gray bushy eyebrows under an old, brown felt cap. He walked a little bent over, leaning on a staff, his other hand clasping the shoulder of a companion. That one seemed much younger, about his own age. Hard to tell, though, as he just wasn't very tall. The old man and the boy bowed slightly as they came up to his father, sitting at the enrolment table.

"Not sure about these two, Lars, " Bjorn commented to the scribe. "Take down their names, ages, and homeland anyway."

The scribe dutifully dipped his quill pen in the inkpot and held it poised over the long parchment scroll, which by now was several feet long.

"Please, sir," said the older man, taking off his weird-looking brown cap, "my name is Jonas Arneson. We are from the island of Gotland. We've been driven out of our home. It was burned to the ground in one of the raids from Jutland."

"I'm sorry for you," Bjorn replied tersely, "but I'm more interested in your qualifications for this enterprise than in your loss."

"I can tell you of my qualifications, truly," Jonas replied, "I'm a good seaman. I've sailed all around the Baltic, even down the Volga River into Russia. I know much of sailing, both with longboats and cargo boats. The waves tell me much, how to turn the steering oar to meet them. The wind sings to me also, how to turn the yard arm to meet it, how to trim the sail to foil its strength." He bowed more deeply this time. "Please, sir, are you willing to sign me on for the king's commissioned voyage over the western sea?"

Harald's father looked closely at the man. He hesitated, then said crisply, "I wonder if you have the strength for this voyage. Clearly, at your age it would be too difficult for you. Besides, we have almost our full complement. Look behind you! So many others standing there—younger, stronger men—all waiting their turn. To me they look more fit. Stand aside now, make way for them!"

"But sir," the old man persisted, refusing to move. "My son here is more than capable, capable enough for both of us. And—

and we must stay together. We have no other family, no home, nothing."

Bjorn hesitated. Then he asked the boy, "How old are you, boy, and what do you have to say for yourself?"

"May it please you, sir," the young man said, "I'm no longer a boy, although I may not be very tall. My name is Snorri Jonasson, the son of the Jonas who stands before you. And I think I was was nineteen or twenty, last birthday. Can't remember exactly. I can wrestle, climb trees, ride a horse, swim—not many know how to swim. And I'm very strong and quick on my feet." At that he leapt up into the air and turned a backward somersault, landing with both feet on exactly the same spot.

Harald's eyes opened wide. He'd never seen anyone do that before.

"A long list of accomplishments, indeed. But boats, young Jonas—have you ever handled a *boat*?" Bjorn asked. "What do you know about seamanship?"

Snorri hesitated. "No, sir. I must tell the truth. I have only sailed with others from Visby in Gotland to the Oslofjord. From there my father and I made our way around the coast to Bergen. But that was—that was with fishermen." He paused, embarrassed, and looked down at his feet. Harald followed his glance and noticed that Snorri's leather boots were so worn that his big toe stuck out of one of them. Then Snorri added quickly, "But I can shoot. Yes, I can shoot arrows as well as any archer. I can shoot an arrow and hit the mark as far away as from here to the top of your boat mast there." He pointed to the *knorr*, moored over on the other side of the harbor.

"Well," Bjorn replied slowly. He looked closely at Snorri, taking him in. "That might be useful. Who can tell? I might be willing to sign you on. But, make no mistake, *only you, without* your father."

"No!" Snorri exclaimed emphatically. "I won't leave my father alone here among strangers. We'll sail together, or not at all. We'll find work somewhere. On a farm nearby if nothing else. I'd rather clean out the filth of cow stalls, as degrading as that may be, than leave my poor father here alone, without a *krone* in his pocket!"

Harald felt drawn to the young man, although he couldn't explain why. It was true, he seemed small for his age. Yet he had a determined way about him, a strong kind of look with his short, black hair curling heavily about his face and thick, dark eyebrows rising up into peaks on his forehead. His dark eyes seemed kind of sunk in, yet when he looked at you, they seemed to throw off sparks. His skin was darkened from the sun—he and his father had obviously journeyed far and lived out in the open for several months at least. He set his mouth in a firm line as he spoke, the last remark to Harald's father with clenched teeth and a clenched fist brought down right on the scribe's scroll, making the scribe jump.

I sure wouldn't like to get into a fight with him, Harald thought to himself. But, on the other hand, he'd sure make a good friend, someone who'd stand up for you.

It would seem that his father liked the young man, too. At least, he didn't immediately turn both father and son away. "I'll have to think on it," Bjorn said thoughtfully. Then he smiled. "We have no need for men who can do a backward somersault. However—" and here he grew more serious, "I can see this young man's skill with the bow might be useful. So far, most of the men signed on are skilled only with daggers and the broad sword. And who knows what enemies we may encounter?"

Then he raised up his hands and shrugged his shoulders. "But there is really no place for the father," he continued firmly. "His days of voyaging are long past."

Should he say something? Harald hesitated. He wanted his father to reconsider. There was something about Snorri Jonason—Yet he knew he had no business to interfere with his father's decision.

Much to Harald's surprise, however, Bjorn now turned to Jonas. "Perhaps, old man," he began thoughtfully, "perhaps there is a solution after all. Come back tomorrow and we'll talk again. Meanwhile, I'll leave this list open tomorrow morning." He told the scribe to make a note of it. "But at the time when the sun is at its highest in the sky and the cathedral bells toll for the noon-day mass, then this parchment sheet will be rolled up, and taken to the king for his approval and final seal."

And Harald's father seemed to be trying to find a solution. Long into the night Harald heard his father and grandmother talking before the fire in the little parlor. He didn't know what they were saying, but he heard the names of those two Goths, the old man and his son, mentioned several times.

Next morning, as Harald drank the last of his hot whey milk to wash down the third oatcake, he was surprised when his father handed him his red wool cloak. "Here, put this on, son," he said. "A cool morning down by the docks."

"The docks? You want me to go with you?"

"Yes, I want you to look around town for that young man Snorri and his father, Jonas. They could be anywhere—the market place, even out into the nearby countryside. They mentioned going out there to look for work. It's rumored that Farmer Gunnarson needs a hired hand. It's doubtful they had enough money to stay at an inn."

After about an hour's walking around the streets of Bergen and just before heading down the road north out of the city toward the Gunnarson farm, Harald at last found father and son wandering down a little alley-way beside St. Mary's chapel. Out of charity, the priest had let them sleep in the chapel overnight, then given them some bread and cheese for breakfast.

"You must come with me now," Harald insisted, without explaining why. They looked surprised, as if they hadn't at all expected Harald's father would follow through on his promise. They whispered back and forth to each other for a minute or two, then hesitantly followed Harald.

As Jonas approached Bjorn on the dockside, he bowed and removed his stained brown felt cap, turning it around and around in his hands. "We are here, sir," he said, "as you request. We await your final decision. Again, we beg you to take us on King Erik's expedition, but we will consider humbly whatever you propose."

"Come, sit down here on this bench," said Bjorn, "and I'll tell you what I propose." The two men sat down together on the bench alongside the enrollment table, while Snorri perched himself on one of the nearby wharf posts. Harald went over to stand beside him, but wasn't sure what to say. Snorri didn't seem to know either, and stared off into the distance.

"I'm willing to take your son, Snorri Jonasson," Bjorn continued to Jonas. "Something tells me he'll be very useful to us, considering his skill with the bow. But I regret that I cannot risk giving a place to you. Space is limited, and every man must count."

Jonas rose stiffly from the bench, looking crestfallen. "Come, then, Snorri," he said quickly to his son. "We must find something else." They turned to go.

"No, wait," said Harald's father. "I haven't finished yet." Snorri and Jonas hesitated. "You see, I *do* have a place for you, Jonas. Now, come back, sit down, and listen to my proposal."

Harald listened with amazement as Father outlined what he and his grandmother had discussed the night before. Snorri would be taken on as part of the crew. To keep an eye on him, his father would place him, along with Harald, in the big *knorr*. Before Jonas could protest, Bjorn continued. "Now we also have a place for you as well, Jonas Arneson," he said, "but on land, not at sea You would remain here with my mother and daughter, Anna."

"I won't accept your charity," Jonas cried out, "I would rather—" But Bjorn once again motioned him back to the bench.

"Let me finish," continued Bjorn. "Here's my proposal. There is a little cabin in back of my mother's house, where a caretaker, a servant or two, have always lived."

Yes, Harald remembered, while Grandfather was alive, they'd needed a hired hand to look after the few acres of barley Grandfather grew in the fields just outside Bergen. Then, after that terrible epidemic, the Black Death, struck the city—it hit Grandfather, then the hired hand, eventually his mother after she'd come up from Telemark to help Grandmother care for them. First the hired hand died, then his mother, then his grandfather. Shortly after that, Harald's father had hired a man named Ole as general caretaker for the house and Grandmother's kitchen garden. But Ole had died several months ago, and that's when Father had sent Anna up to Bergen to live with her grandmother. The caretaker's little house was still empty.

"You may live in the house if you're willing to work," Bjorn explained. "Being caretaker for my mother and daughter will be easier for you than life at sea. It'll offer you more peace and security, and, for one of your age . . ." He broke off, thinking better of what he'd intended to say.

"But, sir," Jonas began, "I cannot—"

Bjorn cut him off. "I'll be frank. You'll be doing my mother and daughter a great service. They need someone to look after them during my long time away." Then he added, as if by afterthought, "And, of course, I'll rest easier in my mind, knowing they have a man's help and protection."

Jonas Arneson still looked bitterly disappointed at not to be allowed to take part in the expedition. He slowly rose and turned away. Going off a little distance, he held another whispered discussion with his son. After a few moments he returned, defeat mirrored in his face. "I'm sorry not to be able to serve you on the voyage, Bjorn Erikson," Jonas said, looking longingly far down the fjord. "Yet my son and I will agree to your proposal. And may God reward you for your generosity!"

"Now, Harald," Bjorn said in a stern voice, "I still have some business to do down here at the docks. You take this boy."

"I'm not a *boy*, sir!"

"Take this young man and his father up to Grandmother's house, tell her to make a place for them out in the servant's cabin. Hurry up now. Time is running out—every minute, every hour brings us closer to setting our sails toward the west. Don't dawdle—didn't you hear me?"

"Well, Snorri," Harald remarked, somewhat surprised at his father's sharp words and sudden change of manner—after being so kind to the two Goths. Yet he knew the pressures of preparation, the responsibility, the decisions his father was having to make. Obviously they were taking their toll. "Well, I guess I'll have to call you that, even though it's such a strange name."

"Not strange to me," Snorri answered curtly. "Pity yours is so—so *common*."

Harald felt his anger rise. *Harald* was a great name. And he was related to the *king*. He tried to think of a good response, to put this Snorri in his place. But he couldn't think of one off hand. Best let it pass. He'd get even with him later. "Follow me," he said instead. "Both you and your father. It's a long, steep walk up to my grandmother's house. Hope it's not too much for you."

A strange look was exchanged between Snorri and his father. Snorri started to say something, but his father motioned him to be quiet.

The three of them began heading up the path. Harald turned to Snorri. "Well, then, does this mean we're to be shipmates together? And for a long, long time?" Going through Harald's mind was concern about how it would be to live at close quarters aboard the ship with this person. "And don't you forget. My father's in charge, but the king commissioned *me* as well. So you've got to take orders from *me*, right?"

Snorri smiled a funny, twisted sort of smile and looked off into the distance. He wiggled his shoulders slightly, then muttered half to himself, "Well, Harald-of-the-Common-Name, that's what *you* think!"

Chapter Three
High Seas

The day arrived! "We're ready to leave—hurry, get your boots on," Harald heard his father shouting. Welcome words! Or were they? Harald had had time to work through many conflicting thoughts. He wanted to take part in the king's great commission. He wanted adventure, to prove himself. But yet—What exactly *did* he want? "Harald!" His father was growing more impatient. There was no choice.

Anna and Grandmother came out of the house to walk down to the dock with them. "Such a beautiful, bright sunny morning, my son," Grandmother said to Bjorn. "It bodes well for your journey. Now, Jonas, watch out you manage that wheelbarrow carefully!"

Jonas, as Grandmother's new caretaker, pushed a large wheelbarrow overflowing with provisions packed by her for the voyage. "Yes, ma'am," he said, clearly not at all happy about being left behind, having Snorri chosen for the voyage and not also himself.

"The dried fish and smoked reindeer meat will keep well," Grandmother continued in her high, cracked voice as she hobbled alongside the wheelbarrow. "The pickled beets in those crocks will provide a little variety—and they're good for curing the cough and the catarrh in your lungs." She wagged her finger at Bjorn. "And make sure, son Bjorn, you pad those crocks very well, though, so they won't break. And bring them back, mind you—all in one piece!"

Harald's father laughed and said, "well, Mother, we'll try. But it's a long voyage, there and back—do you think you can manage a year or so without your crocks?"

"The king! The king's here!" Anna exclaimed, pointing. "Oh, what a sight!"

Harald could hardly believe that King Erik himself would come down to see the boats off. He was surrounded by his guard of honor and a group of courtiers, some of whom brought departure gifts for all the men.

"Where is Harald, son of Bjorn?" one of them shouted. Hurriedly Harald was brought before him. "His majesty presents you with this gift in his name. He bids you use it well."

Opening the silk bag, Harald gasped in surprise. It was a new brass astrolabe, its beautiful mother plate engraved with his name. But before he had time to examine it more closely, there was a flutter of banners and flag bearers, and a beat of drums surrounding them.

"His eminence, the Bishop of Bergen," whispered Harald's sister in awe. "He's come in person, with all the priests and acolytes from the cathedral. Look, they're going to bless the ships. Doesn't he look splendid?"

Harald agreed. He'd never seen anything quite like this before, and it certainly emphasized the importance of the king's commission. The bishop wore flowing white robes, with a green brocade vestment over it and his tall, miter hat with the long silver ribbons down the back. He carried a long staff with a curved hook on the end, like the kind shepherds use on their sheep, except that the bishop's was made out of gold and set with precious stones. Harald couldn't help but feel more important than he'd ever felt before, certainly much older, certainly not the youngest member of the crew.

"Ho, there! Tide turning!" called out the watchman in the tower near the docks. "Water in the fjord now turning, flowing back out to sea."

"Here, men, get those last items aboard!" Bjorn shouted. "No, don't take time to stow them now, just get the stuff down into the storage areas—and watch out for those chickens, there! We'll organize more at sea."

"Goats won't go up the ramp . . . what'll I do, sir?" They were giving Snorri a hard time.

"Pick them up and carry them if you have to, but get it done!"

Snorri and another man struggled, finally got the animals into the pen on deck amid-ship. Such a squawking of chickens, flapping of wings, bleating of goats! Harald would have thought it funny if he didn't already know what fate awaited those chickens and goats. The crew's survival depended on them for food during the long voyage, milk and eggs for a start, but later . . .

Shouting, cries, a roll of the drums, blaring of trumpets. "Farewell!" "Safe voyage!" "Fare you well." "Return safe!" "The Lord keep you!" came from both the docks and the boats, as all thirty adventurers took their places, ten on each of the three boats and their families and friends bid them good-bye.

"Hey, you there! Piek! Let go the last bow lines holding the boat to the dock!" Bjorn shouted to a man positioned at the bow of the *knorr*, called across he dock to men on the two longboats to do the same.

Harald and Snorri stood together on the foredeck, watching two crewmen men coil the thick cables, made of twisted walrus hide, into the bottom of the boat. "There go our ties with home," remarked Harald with mixed sadness and excitement. He immediately wished he hadn't said this, realizing that Snorri didn't have a home anymore.

"I'll miss my father, but I'm not sorry to leave," commented Snorri. "But what's that noise? That supposed to be *singing*?"

"The men heaving up the sail to the mast? Don't you know a sea chantey when you hear one?"

"That's supposed to be music?"

Harald grinned. "Of course—it's a work song. It must go back all the way to old Viking times. It keeps the men pulling together. Like this, see—yo-ho heave, yo-ho heave."

"Oh, stop, stop! Sounds like sick cats to me," Snorri commented dryly. "I do know that until the wind catches that big square sail—on our boat and the other two—we're not going to move very fast. It seems so ignoble to have those pitiful fishing skiffs towing us out into the fjord. They're just crawling."

"Don't worry, Snorri, we'll be out on the high seas soon enough. Then we'll see what your stomach feels like." He regretted this remark, too, because he wasn't sure about his own.

Harald watched his grandmother and Anna get smaller and smaller, way back there on the dock, and felt a sudden pang of homesickness. He saw his sister climb up in the wheelbarrow to get a better view. Snorri's father was standing beside her and waving his tattered brown cap in the air. Now all Harald could see was the flutter of Grandmother's white shawl. He felt a choking in his throat, seeing them disappear little by little like that. His eyes stung—surely not from tears? Probably the salty sea spray. He didn't know when—or if ever—he would see them again. He hid his emotions by pretending to check the knots in some of the ropes. He hoped Snorri wasn't looking at him. He wondered how Snorri felt. A strange kind of person, did he have normal feelings? He didn't seem to.

The city was disappearing, bit by bit. Only the very tops of the cathedral towers in the far distance. Suddenly the wind caught the sails and they billowed out with a big boom. "Just look up there, Snorri," Harald exclaimed. "The king's crest of inter-twined ravens painted on them." The crest, newly painted, was beautiful, all shining red, black, and gold in the sun. "Doesn't that make you feel proud? And, see, there go the towing skiffs." He waved to the fishermen, who were also waving, standing in their little boats.

RUNES BEYOND THE EDGE

They were at the mouth of the fjord. Harald knew what would come. "Now, Snorri, you watch. Now we're really going to fly!"

THE FIRST SEVEN DAYS' SAILING brought fair weather. "Good thing for you, Snorri," Harald commented as they were set to cleaning the deck, a job they had gotten almost every day so far. "No telling what you'd be like if the seas weren't so calm. Brisk wind, though, we're really moving along. Just wish that salt spray didn't mess up the deck like this."

"Haven't noticed your sea legs yet," said Snorri, scrapping along the far edge of a plank. "Staggering around, looking green around the gills, if you ask me."

"Nobody asked you." But it was true. The constant motion made Harald feel queasy. Since it didn't seem to bother Snorri, he pretended otherwise. "Just not very hungry," he'd say whenever the food rations came around.

"Right, right," Snorri would comment, then make one of his funny, twisted smiles.

There were other problems. This voyage didn't seem as glorious as he'd expected. For one thing, space was cramped, everybody falling over everybody else. And he hated that his clothes were damp all the time from the salt spray, even when he was assigned to some duty on the aft deck, where the sun and wind could dry them out. And there was so much to do—scraping the deck, trimming the sail, or raising it, depending on how strong the wind was, standing watch during the long night hours when he was desperate for sleep.

"Look after the two goats and the chickens? Why me?" he asked his father incredulously a few days out. "Couldn't I be assigned something more . . . more dignified? This isn't a farm. It's a boat—the king's boat!"

"That's your regular duty onboard during this voyage," Bjorn crisply replied. "You're under my command. Don't question my orders, hear? You are not my son—you are only a member of this crew."

The tone of his father's voice came as a shock. He seemed a different person while captain of the *knorr*, not his father at all. Harald swallowed hard, feeling more miserable than ever.

Nevertheless, as it turned out he rather liked this duty. He and the goat named Whitebeard were getting to be good friends. The goat would rub his head against Harald's arm when, each morning, he'd reach into the pen to put in fresh water and a little dried grass, hay. "There you go, old Whitey," he'd say. "Eat your fill—while you can." Harald tried hard not to think Whitey's future. But, sooner or later, the ships' food stores would begin to run low and Ole, the cook, would have to start preparing goat and chicken stews. Sometimes Harald lay awake at night, trying to think of some way Whitebeard could be spared. He could try arguing Whitebeard wasn't fat enough yet. Maybe he could catch enough fish off the side of the boat to provide enough food. In fact, one day he'd seen some whales nearby. Maybe they could harpoon one of them—that would give them enough food for the whole voyage, hide for new ropes, oil for the lanterns!

On the third day out, Harald was excited by the sight of the Faeroe Islands, faintly to the north. He expected the helmsmen to change course toward them, but they seemed to be sailing right past. He asked his father about that. "No, Harald," said Bjorn, "we must keep those mountains on the northern horizon at half their height and keep sailing due west. We measure our course from those islands, you see, by how high the mountains appear to be from this distance—the width of a finger."

"But why not put in there, Father?" asked Harald, very disappointed.

"We can't spare the time," Bjorn answered impatiently. "Those islands are a day or so off course—we must make landfall as soon as possible, and that'll be Reyjavik in Iceland."

"How long will that be, then?" He thought again of *iceland*—surely a land full of *ice*, didn't sound very inviting. The Faeroes looked like a nicer landfall.

"Oh, with a good wind, fair weather, not too much tacking, that should be another six days or so."

When he had a chance to talk to Snorri, he told him about what his father had said. "Another six days, Snorri!" That seemed so far into the future, Harald wasn't sure he could wait that long and told Snorri so.

"Do you have a choice?" Snorri asked, with his usual dry sense of humor. "You could always jump overboard and swim back to Bergen. That is, assuming you can swim, which I doubt. And riding on a whale's back looks rather risky, don't you think?"

But the wind held and, although mainly westerly and against them, they made quick time with short tacks. The longboats sped through the foam like birds, the *knorr* not far behind. Each day Harald found his assigned duties—whether with the animals, the sail, the ropes, the deck, or the watch—becoming easier, although he still considered animal keeping below him.

"Well, I see you're not staggering around so much," Snorri commented one day. "You see, the trick is, just move your body with the motion of the boat and then you can keep your footing, even on the slippery deck."

"How come you're managing so well? Thought you'd never been much on boats before."

"I just learn fast."

It was true, it was getting better, the turmoil in his stomach almost forgotten. And when the day's provision were handed out, Harald's keen sense of hunger made even the leathery reindeer meat taste delicious. Grandmother's pickled beets, though, were another matter. Luckily Snorri relished them, so Harald passed that part of his rations on to him. How could anyone like that awful, sour, vinegary taste? Yuk! But Snorri *was* a bit weird, he had to admit.

Each day meant one less day before they reached land. On the fifth day, with an enormous sense of relief, Harald heard the cry, "Land ho!" from the lookout up on the mast. In a snort while, entering Rejkavik harbor, he could only think how wonderful it was going to feel going on shore—even if there *was* ice all over the place. "Just think, Snorri, solid land underfoot, dry clothes!"

"Can't wait to eat some meat that wasn't tough and swimming around in a luke-warm strew," added Snorri.

"And this is the land of those famous heroes we've heard about—Njal and Egill."

"So—who are they?"

"You don't *know*?" Harald asked in amazement. "Maybe we'll hear more about them here. Maybe we'll even meet some of their descendants, handle their old Viking weapons. Just think, maybe we'll even be able to see the ruins of Njal's burned-out farmhouse."

"An old, burned-out farmhouse? Pah! And you're excited about *that*?"

"It's a terrific story, and true. A couple of hundred years ago, Njal Skallagrimson and his wife, Bergthora, with their little grandson were burned alive by their enemies. In their own farmhouse, too. Njal refused to give in to them. And when his enemies came to look for their bodies under the burned timbers and ashes, they found Njal and the others totally unburned by a thick cowhide that Njal had spread over them. Only the little boy's one finger was burned—he'd stuck it out from under the cowhide. What an awful death for a hero!"

"Those old stories are for children!" Snorri retorted. "Come on, act your age. If you can handle a broad sword, like you claim, they aren't for you!" He turned away in disgust. "Come on, Peik, you and I are supposed to straighten out these mooring ropes."

This remark stung. How could Snorri say that? Such men were heroes, served as examples. Harald felt put down, resolved

RUNES BEYOND THE EDGE

to avoid sharing his ideas with Snorri, at least for a while. He leaned moodily over the rail to stare out toward the approaching harbor.

"Harald! To your duties!"

No time for such thoughts—there was father. He didn't want to be reminded about his assigned duty with the anchor.

The *knorr* and two longboats sailed into the big Rejkavik harbor. Only after the boats were safely moored and the necessary arrangements made for their provisioning, was Harald able to look around. To his surprise, Reykjavik was a town almost as big as Bergen, with bustling streets and many shops around the harbor. It was summer, and there were some green trees—but not many—but no ice except on the peaks of some distant mountains. In fact, behind the town steam rose up into the air. *Steam*? Unbelievable!

"What's that, Father?" Harald asked in amazement as they stood together on the dock where the *knorr* was moored

"That's coming from the big hot springs behind the town. There are volcanoes underground here, they heat up the water until it comes boiling out of the ground—just like a kettle over the fire, if that's easier to understand."

Hot water? *Volcanoes*? Harald's original notion about a land full of ice obviously had to be revised. The spire of a large church rose up from the middle of town. Log and sod houses were scattered far up into the hillsides surrounding the harbor. Maybe Njal's house had been like one of them.

He found Snorri in the act of carrying a large cask of salt fish aboard the *knorr*. "Snorri," he said, "let somebody else do that! We've got to have a look around." He didn't dare tell Snorri the real reason he wanted to go up there.

"Listen, you. Where's all your talk about being *commissioned by the king*, eh? There's work to do here. The quicker we get loaded up, quicker we can get on with it. And weren't you supposed to look after more hay for the goats?"

With a pang of guilt, Harald turned away and went to check on the goat pen. It saddened him that, several days before, Whitebeard was sacrificed for food for the crew. He did have to admit, though, that Ole's stew sure tasted wonderful after that old, tough reindeer meat. It had warmed his stomach all the way down. Maybe—just maybe, there would be time enough later to explore. He'd start with the hot springs. "Do you know," he heard himself saying to the remaining goats—since Snorri wouldn't be interested, "do you know that Grandfather once told me about strange creatures, like trolls and elves, who live in caves under hot springs? And listen, old One Horn, Snorri and I, when we're both free, we're going to take some weapons out of the weapons chest and go look for them. And then, One Horn, we're going to capture a troll—just a small one—and take it home in a cage as a pet for Anna. She would certainly like that. Flossi, the cat, might get jealous, though. Do you think trolls eat cats?" But One Horn offered no opinion, just kept munching the new-mown hay.

Unfortunately, their few days in port left no time for such exciting plans. Harald and the others were kept constantly busy. It happened, shortly after they'd passed the Faeroe Islands, that salt water seeped into several water casks, and they had to be scoured out. There was a shortage of dried meat in town, which meant someone had to be sent out to nearby farms. Some of the walrus rope rigging needed replacing, a few rowing oars had been lost and needed replacing—not so easily done, with wood so scarce in Iceland.

"Don't worry, Harald," said his father reassuringly by the end of the third day in Reykjavik. They stood aft on the *knorr's* deck, watching the last water cask being rolled up the gangplank and lowered down into the storage cabin. "You may have some time to explore once we reach Greenland. We still have a long expedition ahead of us, and must leave here on the morning's first tide."

Harald could not suppress a sigh. Already the voyage was beginning to seem endless. At least the name *Greenland* sounded more promising than *Iceland*. He imagined dense green forests, deep pools of fresh water, green pastures. "When will we reach Greenland, then?" He hoped his father wouldn't sense his disappointment. That wouldn't be appropriate, considering how important his role was in the king's commission.

"Now, don't get so impatient," Father said, shaking his head. "Consider who you are."

Well, his father had seen through him, all right. He'd try a different approach. "Can you tell me more about the rest of the voyage, sir?" He tried to sound more professional.

"It all depends on the weather and the winds. Between here and the east coast of Greenland should only be about four days' sailing. Sailors tell many stories, though, about the treachery of those waters."

That did not sound reassuring at all. Was fear beginning to creep into his brain? His brain, he kept telling himself, had room only for thoughts of courage, great adventures, big war swords, finding and capturing trolls and other such creatures deep in the earth. Of course, there might be rune charms to back these up.

"There can be terrible storms, blowing a boat off course," his father went on. "Fog is normal for the first part of each day at least. Then we won't be able to take any bearings by the noon-day sun from the astrolabe—if we ever need to. Nor can we always trust the bearing-dial, as you know."

Harald could not suppress disappointment. Even the king had recognized his ability with an astrolabe. It didn't sound as though it would be of much use when they needed it most.

"And, of course," Bjorn continued, "there are icebergs, sometimes lying bigger under the water than on the surface. You can't always be sure. You could tear out the bottom of your ship. Those whales and walruses, too—can ram a boat and sink it in a split second."

Worse and worse. Harald sighed again. Why did his father have to be so specific about all those dangers? Maybe this whole expedition was a foolish idea. More than likely they'd never get where they were going, let alone back to Bergen. Depression and doubt began to set in. His thoughts, however, were rudely interrupted by some shouting, an argument going on down the deck near the storage cabin.

"What's going on there?" Bjorn strode over to the men, his hand on the dagger carried in a leather sheath attached to his belt.

"Caught this Goth trying to steal one of the swords out of the weapons chest, sir," said Ole, the seaman who also served as cook. He'd thrown the Goth named Ufila down on the deck, his foot on the man's throat. Ufila was gasping and choking from the pressure.

"Get up, you," Bjorn demanded, still holding his dagger ready. Ole released him, and Ufila struggled to his feet. A large war sword, which he'd been concealing under his cloak, fell to the deck with a loud clatter

"What's the meaning of this? It's against the law to steal from the king, on penalty of death. You know that."

"But, but sir," Ufila stammered. "Oh, please, sir," he pleaded, "so sorry—won't ever steal from you—from the king—again. Only needed a weapon for self-defense—some people . . . there are some out to get me on this boat," and he looked directly at Snorri.

"A *war* sword for self-defense?" Bjorn asked incredulously. "Don't make me laugh!"

Harald hadn't liked Ufila from the start, couldn't understand why his father had signed him on to the expedition. He had a suspicious air about him—"Watch out, he has thief's eyes," Snorri had warned Harald even before the boats were out to sea. Snorri had little use for him, despite the fact they were both from Gotland and spoke the same language. "A really creepy person," Snorri said the second day out, "besides being jealous of you, he thinks your father's giving you an easy berth. No telling what he might do to you—or him."

"Bind that man's hands and take him ashore," Bjorn now ordered sternly. "I'll have the authorities in Iceland put him under arrest and in irons. They'll know how to deal with him—and it won't be nice, I can assure you!" The usual punishment for a thief was to cut off his hands. "And Harald, I'm assigning you guard duty with Awair. Take a long sword out of the chest, don't hesitate to use it if Ufila tries to get away."

Harald felt immensely proud. It was a real step up from feeding the goats and chickens. He and Awair hustled Ufila down the gangplank. Ufila tried to resist, once almost broke away, but Harald tripped him, then grabbed him by the arm after he fell to the ground, then sat on him to keep him there. After a few minutes, they were joined by four tall Icelanders carrying heavy swords and a battle axe. They threw Ufila into one of the storage sheds on the dock, placed a heavy bar across the door. Harald heard him shouting and whining inside, even as he and Aiwar went back aboard the *knorr*.

As his father and the crew readied the boat for sailing early the next morning, he remarked in a low voice to Harald, "Maybe just as well we caught the rotten apple before we'd gone any farther. Something about the man—could he be a spy from Jutland, I wonder? Somebody sent by King Vald? We know Vald is anxious for that territory to the west. It's possible he's got instructions to locate, then bring the information back to Jutland. Or, it could be that he's out to—"

"Out to do what?" Harald asked in alarm. He knew his father was about to say, *out to destroy us, end the commission*, but thought better of it.

"Well, just be glad he's no longer on board. Rotten apple out of the barrel means the rest of the apples are saved." With that last comment, Bjorn turned to inspect the new ropes, which lay coiled on the deck. And that was that.

LAUREL MEANS

Well, what about me? Harald said to himself, looking *disappointed. What about my own brave and daring actions? Didn't I just keep Ufila from escaping? Was the rest of this voyage going to be like this? Put down like that? It wasn't fair! No, a plague on the king and his old commission!*

Chapter Four
The First Challenge

"Hey! Hey!" Harald shouted. He'd gone to feed the goats a day out from Iceland and made a shocking discovery. Ufila was hiding under a pile of hay.

"Oh, please, sir," he pleaded with Harald's father, stalks of hay sticking out of his hair all over his head, "I'm so sorry—won't ever steal from you—for the king—again. Not ever. I swear to you. I could be so useful—you know I'm a blacksmith by trade, reason you signed me on, isn't it? I can hammer swords on the forge, make iron wedges for your mooring rocks." He mumbled and snuffled. "Oh, please sir," he whined, throwing himself down prostrate on the deck and trying to kiss Bjorn's feet. "Oh, kind, honored sir, I have skills you'll some day need." He raised himself to his knees, seized Bjorn's hand and tried to kiss it.

Bjorn face contorted in a way Harald had never seen before. He kicked Ufila roughly away with his boot, then ordered Harald to stand guard with his dagger over the man. "If he makes one false move, don't hesitate to use it." Turning away, he said between his teeth, "Now I must consider carefully what to do. For this wretched creature—life or death?"

After a half-hour or so in his private cabin with Awair, he emerged, still very angry. "Ufila, you're fortunate I don't order you thrown overboard, pulled by rope through the water until you drown. That's what we do with criminals at sea. But we can't afford to be short even one crew member, not even one as worthless as you. Nor have we the time and resources to return you to the authorities in Iceland. Therefore, you're to be released into the custody of Awair, and two more men of his choosing. You'll be constantly watched. If there is even a hit of suspicious behavior—the rope and the sea!"

Harald hoped the second chance his father had given Ufila was justified, but he had his doubts. "Doesn't Ufila remind you of the trickster god Loki?" Harald asked Snorri while they and Peik were working together on the rigging.

"Well, that's a good one," laughed Peik. Harald had discovered that Peik, who was about his own age, knew a little about the old ways.

"Loki? Who's he?" asked Snorri.

"You don't *know*?" Harald never ceased to be amazed at Snorri's ignorance. Where'd he been brought up? Didn't they know about those old gods anymore back in Gotland? "Well, for your information, he's a slippery character and a shape-changer who managed to wriggle out of one bad situation after another and was never to be trusted.

"Sound to me like the perfect name for Ufila."

It was strange that the following days did not seem as long to Harald as they did when he first left Bergen. "Well, my son," his father remarked by the end of the third day out from Iceland, "I see you're ready to take your turn at the port side steering oar, back there on the aft deck. Arne, here, will be at the starboard oar. He'll show you how to keep the boat steady by heading into the waves, keep us from being broadsided by a wave and overturning. Yes, indeed, the helmsman's job is a very important one, and you're hardly a boy anymore."

Yet that same day brought a dramatic change by the time the cabin's hourglass marked the tenth hour. The winds from the west had become stronger, with tall waves pitching the ship up and down, each time on the plunge downward sending a cascade of spray over the entire boat.

Harald was kept frantically busy, first constructing a heavy canvas cover over the goat pen and the chicken coups, then bailing out water from the boat's bilge under the deck. Repeatedly he was called to help Ari or another helmsmen at one of the two steering rudder oars. The men had to put all their weight against them to keep the oars steady. The four-hour watch at the rudder keeping the boat on an even keel against each on-coming wave left him exhausted.

"Your watch is up now," his father finally announced. "Go below and get some rest."

He fell into his swaying hammock in the sleeping cabin and almost immediately sank into a deep sleep, which lasted all through the next day. He was disappointed that his father had not roused him. He was, after all, a member of the crew—of the commission—and should not be shown any favors.

"Don't worry," his father reassured him. "A good rest will put you in better shape for what's to come."

His last remark worried Harald. It sounded full of foreboding. In fact, for the second time on this expedition, he was feeling something like fear. But he forced himself to deny it. The king, after all, had chosen him, Harald Bjornson, for a good reason. Just exactly what that reason was, Harald was still uncertain. Nevertheless, it encouraged him to know that reason existed, in his head, in his heart—somewhere.

In the middle of the night, the storm hit. Never before had Harald been in a storm like this, neither at sea nor on land. They were now four nights out from Iceland. The boat tossed and reeled, sometimes rising up into a dizzying height, then plunging down so fast into the trough of a wave that it seemed they would keep going down to the bottom of the sea. They had tied down everything they could. Harald roped the one remaining goat to the side of his pen and covered the chicken coups with a large cowhide, then ran a rope through the bars and secured it to one of the mooring rings along the boat's railing.

Laurel Means

Each time a giant wave struck them broadside, the boat shuddered and pitched to starboard. But for Finn, the port helmsman, and the two other men putting their weight against the second steering oar, the next wave to hit them broadside would surely have rolled the boat over. Then all of them would spill out into the freezing cold, turbulent water. People, weapons, provisions—all would plunge down to the bottom of the sea—the final end of their commission.

Harald had never learned to swim. Snorri's guess had been correct, and he didn't think any of the men could either. Except for Snorri, of course, who told him it was easy. Still, in seas like these, even Snorri wouldn't stand a chance. He wasn't sure about One Horn. Surely the goat would drown, too, although he reckoned that might be preferable to being meat stew like the rest of them.

Harald tried to force this picture of universal drowning out of his mind. He put his arms around the base of the thick mast in the middle of the boat, so as not to be washed overboard into the foaming water. He turned his face away as each wave crashed over him. His mouth and nose seemed to be filled with salt water anyway, and his eyes burned from it. Holding to the mast with only one arm, he tried to wipe his eyes with his jacket sleeve just as a mammoth wave came down on the boat. Its force weakened his one-armed hold on the mast and he felt himself being pulled away, sliding down into the water swirling around in the scuppers of the boat, then slammed against the fore bulkhead.

He tried desperately to find something to hold onto, but he could hardly see for the burning of his eyes and the cascading water. "Father, Father!" he screamed. He knew he was going to be swept overboard, knew he would drown. Just then he felt something grab hold of his long hair, then his jacket, then a strong arm went around his neck and held him fast up against the railing.

"Hold on, here," a voice shouted in his ear, "onto this railing. Use both hands and wedge your feet against the side of the cabin."

It was Snorri. He was very strong, and Harald knew Snorri's strength had saved him. But now his father was calling out for Snorri to go back to help with one of the rudders.

"Here," Snorri shouted, "I've got you. Grab hold of this rope after the next wave hits, and then you'll be all right." Then Snorri slowly, resisting the repeated force of the waves, carefully made his way aft, gripping the railing hand over hand until one of the helmsman grabbed him and guided him to the rudder oar.

"Harald!" His father yelled. "Bail! Bail for your life, for all our lives!" His father was trying to pull down the shredded remains of the big square sail, which were blowing and flapping in the wind. "We must save the sail, repair it later!" he cried. It was their only main sail, and they would need it. But Harald's bailing bucket had just been washed overboard: he'd had to let go of it in order to hold on.

"Look sharp, there!" His father was shouting something to the three men huddled together up there in the bow of the boat. "Grab hold of that tackle—no, not that one. Grab the one over . . ."

Harald could not hear the rest for the howling of the wind and the violent waves rushing over him. It was clear they were trying to rescue some of the tackle that held the mast steady. "Fine, now the . . . watch out . . . you're going to . . ." One of the men got his neck caught in the rope. "Catch . . . end . . . going to hang himself . . . no, not that . . ."

The wind cut off most of the words. With relief Harald watched his father leap forward and free the man. The two ropes they'd managed to tighten hummed and vibrated in the wind. Harald crawled into the storage cabin to see if he could find something he could bail with.

Two men were already in there. One of them was Grimm, the other *Loki*, who immediately stopped what he was doing as soon as he saw Harald. "Ufila," Harald demanded, "didn't I hear my father assign you with Awair to the watch on the rigging?"

"Oh, no, young Bjorn, with all due respect, you must have heard wrong. I'm supposed to check things in here. Can I help you, young Bjorn?" he asked in his whining voice. It reminded Harald of honey being poured out of a jar, but he knew that, around honey, bees could sting.

There was no time to worry about Ufila now. He had to find something to bail with before waves swamped the boat. "Well, Goth," Harald shouted, after the next wave had allowed the boat to right itself, "you can help me find something to bail with." He was kneeling on the planks and holding on desperately to the rope handle of the small cabin door.

Grimm, the other man, was trying to keep the barrels and Grandmother's pickled beet crocks from breaking loose by reinforcing the rope nets holding them in place. They could act like cannon balls and break the ship apart as they slammed into the inner walls. Or, if water got into them—well their food, their extra clothing, even the leather parts on their weapons as well as the arrow feathers would be ruined. This would mean that, if they didn't drown, they would have nothing to hunt with ashore. Or, if they should meet with enemies in that unknown land, they could not protect themselves.

Nevertheless, Grimm stopped what he was doing to look around for a bailer. Ufila looked too and finally unhooked the iron kettle from its tripod. "Here, little Bjorn," he whined, "take this." *Little Bjorn*—how Harald detested the man putting him down like that. The kettle was heavy and unwieldy, but Harald looped the handle over his arm and dragged it along as he crawled back out of the cabin on his hands and knees. He began scooping up the foaming water as fast as he could, throwing it over the side. It surged back in as fast as it went out. He despaired of ever getting ahead of it. Was there an old Viking charm, a *seiður*, he could say to protect them? Grandfather hadn't said anything about storms at sea. Oh, what were some of those magic words? The first rune should be "s" for *sikkerhet* ᛋ like so. But what comes next? Then—and then—Frantically he tried think of what might work, but the next wave washed over him, and that rune was lost, and with it any charm for safety.

The wave nearly swept away the kettle as well. He grabbed the handle just in time, and frantically resumed his bailing. As he did so, his thoughts flew briefly back to the day, so long ago it seemed, when he'd seen this very kettle loaded onto the boat. What a contrast! He remembered that sunny day, back in Bergen harbor when they were preparing to leave. And the day before that lying on the fjord rocks watching the white clouds form into fantastic shapes. He had imagined sunny days and blue seas, skimming across the water under a full sail, a sail emblazoned with the king's glorious crest. He'd imagined all sorts of wonderful sights and adventures to come. Now where were they? Was this terrible storm their last adventure?

No, he thought glumly, it sure isn't turning out as he imagined. Bailing with one hand and clinging desperately to whatever he could with the other, he prayed to the blessed Virgin Mary, to the god Thor, to anyone who was listening, not to let him be washed overboard. Not to let his father be washed overboard. Not to let the waves turn the boat upside down, and then all would be lost, even for the other two boats. They could not continue on to Greenland and beyond to the unexplored lands of Markland without his father. The expedition would be over for all of them. The king's great commission would have failed before it even started.

Suddenly there was Snorri beside him again. "I was sent back here to help you bail," he shouted against the wind. "Here, I've found a goat-skin flask—a little hard to scoop water up with, but it'll hold a lot." And he immediately demonstrated by filling the flask and quickly emptying the water back over the side into the sea, repeating the process over and over again.

Harald was grateful. Together they were beginning to make progress. The water sloshing around in the bilge had gone down from two fingers' length to only one. But a *goat-skin* flask—he thought of Whitebeard, and the thought bothered him greatly. Then something else gave him a start. The swirling water in the bottom of the boat was turning red!

Noticing it, Snorri cried out, "Harald, Harald, are you hurt then?" He put down the goat-skin flask and took hold of Harald's arm.

It was only then that Harald remembered hitting his head on a corner of the storage cabin, and on the railings, and the mast—he'd been banged around a lot in the storm. He put his hand up to the right side of his head, where the pain still throbbed. "Must be bleeding," he said. "Yeeii, ow, ow, it hurts," Blood ran into his eyes. He feared he was bleeding to death. "Snorri," he shouted, "do something!"

Snorri looked more closely at the wound. "But it's not bleeding," he said. "In fact, there's no blood there at all. Hey, look! What 's that down there?"

Pieces of pottery swirled around in the reddened water. Pieces of Grandmother's pickled beet crocks! It wasn't blood, it was *beet juice*! A crock had broken and allowed the juice to mix with the sea water. Harald wondered what his grandmother would say about the broken crock. But then she would probably have had more to say if he'd had a broken head. Snorri began to laugh loudly at the joke as he continued to bail, at the same time yelling at Harald to take up his kettle once again. Harald, however, failed to see the humor of it. If the joke had been on Snorri, he wondered whether Snorri would have laughed. He was reasonably sure Snorri would have, the Goth—the *good* Goth, that is, not like the Goth Ufila, was like that.

Harald head was nevertheless still hurting as he lay exhausted in his hammock that night. He could feel a change in the motion of the boat. The wind was lessening, the motion becoming a gentle forwards and backwards, rather than side to side. Maybe some fresh air would help his aching head, so he went up on deck. By the light of the horn lantern, Awair, who claimed he was good with a needle—he'd once been a weaver by trade, he said—was repairing the torn sail.

It was a peaceful scene, in contrast to earlier that day, when he and then later with Snorri had bailed out the boat with the help of the big kettle and a goatskin flask. They'd managed to keep water from of most of the provisions, except for a barrel of dried beans. The beans had swollen up from the water and burst the barrel. Then, of course, there was the matter of Grandmother's crock.

Now, standing at the prow of the boat, Harald could see that the waves were reduced to low, sweeping white caps. There remained only a few high banks of clouds, occasionally racing across a crescent moon. Even at this hour it was not really dark—being so close to mid-summer's eve, or St. John's Eve, as Grandmother called it. At that northern latitude it remained twilight most of the night. Harald's father ordered the boat's main lantern to be lit for Awair's repair work on the sail, and the flame, flickering behind the horn panes, cast a warm, comforting aura around the boat which penetrated the grayish twilight.

"Harald," said his father, who'd also come up on deck, interrupting Harald's thoughts, "we need to know where we are. We were surely blown off course—with all those days of heavy fog, not being able to take a sighting."

"But father," Harald asked, "couldn't we use the bearing dial? The lode stone will point north, won't it?"

Bjorn held up a fragment of wood. "I'm afraid this is all that's left of it," he said. "A wave smashed against the dial box, tore it loose, and washed it overboard, everything except this part of the base where it'd been fastened down." He threw the splintered wood overboard in disgust. "For all I know, we may be heading due north or even back to Iceland."

In Harald's opinion, that wouldn't have been such a bad thing. Back in Iceland he could go after that troll. Instead, he said, "But father, look, the skies are clearing now. You can see the moon and just very faintly a few stars near the southern horizon."

"How do you know that's due south? We have to be more precise."

"But, Father, I can't really locate the pole star, we're too far north to see the stars clearly in the summer sky."

"But there's the moon—if your astrolabe can get a bearing from the sun, can't it do that from the moon?"

"I've never tried that."

"Well, you've got to try. Go below and fetch it. Good thing we haven't needed it before, but let's see now if you can unstuff some of that astrological knowledge crammed into your head and put it to use. Even the king heard about your star-gazing ability, your ability to figure out the influence of the planets and the stars." He smiled as he added, "Let's test now if the rumor he heard is really true, whether the king's naming you our navigator was justified."

What was he to do? Harald was being put to the test. Not the time for any kind of a rune charm, either. He rushed down into the sleeping cabin to get his gift from the king, the new brass astrolabe, which he kept stowed in his small wooden sea chest.

With the ring of the large brass disk of the astrolabe in his right hand, Harald climbed atop the skiff tied upside down on top of the storage cabin. Hooking his left elbow around one of the mast ropes to steady himself, he held the mother disk up to take an altitude reading through its small hole in order to determine their approximate latitude.

"What do you see up there? Where's the pole star?"

"Can't get a sighting from the stars," Harald answered. "Impossible to make out in such a light sky. We're too far north."

"How about that moon, then? Nearly full tonight."

Harald waited for the exact moment when the full moon emerged from behind a cloud. That was the bearing he needed. He turned the disk until the moon appeared through the little hole. By the light of the lantern tied to the mast, he lined up the pointer to the latitude markings on the inner disk. He knew it was the fifteenth day of June. Now he needed to know the time of night. "What time is on the hour glass measuring stick?" he called out.

Awair put down his work on the canvas sail, unhooked the horn lantern from the mast, and ducked down into the sleeping cabin entranceway. "Nearly the twelfth hour," he called up. From measuring the moon's distance in degrees above the horizon and comparing it with the time indicated on the hour glass, Harald knew then that they were heading northwest.

"Good, that means we're only a little off course, then," his father said with a sigh of relief. "Finn, you at the steering oar, veer slightly to port, taking us a little more southerly. And you, Awair, take the lantern and signal the other two boats to follow course. By rights, if we've not been blown too far north, tomorrow early we should see the coast of Greenland along our starboard bow."

"How long? When?" Harald asked eagerly.

"Maybe, if the wind is with us and the Lord is with us and we don't have to tack too often, just maybe we'll round the cape of the eastern settlement and reach Eriksfjord by midday the following day."

Never had Harald heard such welcome words, although, at the same time, it was scary to realize they'd arrived at the western edge, the very edge of the known world. He was both excited and yet afraid to imagine what might lie beyond that edge—cities of gold? Giant animals? Trolls? Witches and ghosts? Strange-looking people? Or just darkness and empty space? He shivered at that last possibility, even though some people were saying the world was round, not flat and that, if you went far enough around, you'd come back just where you started.

He hoped they would indeed sight the snowy peaks of Greenland when the dawn came. He would very soon feel land, real land, under his feet. He hoped beyond hope that they would be able to complete the first part of their journey, at least. Beyond that—well, who could know?

That night he and Snorri slept out on deck, for the weather had turned mild. The great dome of the sky stretched out far above them, far above the swaying topmast of the boat. He knew that, even though the sky was too light to actually see them, the sky was studded with stars, layers and layers of them. Harald propped himself on his elbow. "Look up there, Snorri," he said in wonder. "Do you think there's another world up there? Imagine if, some day, people could figure out a way to sail up there, like we sail down here. Have to be in some kind of sky boats. They could sail to the far away edges of that space and prove whether the earth is round or flat. Just imagine that, Snorri! What do *you* think? Snorri?"

No answer.

"Snorri, wake up!" He shook Snorri's shoulder. "Come on, you can't just lie there, snoring. This is important, wake up!"

Still no answer, except for a few groans, deep snores.

Then Harald burst out laughing. "Ha, ha, that's very funny—Snorri is *snoring*!" Lying back down on the deck, his arm for a pillow, he became more serious. "Oh, Snorri," he sighed. "What if I can't talk to you, depend on you anymore? You're a weird character, all right, but I don't have anybody else—except maybe Peik—and that goat."

Morning came with fair skies but stiff winds. And it brought the coastline of Greenland in sight, and far behind that, steep ranges of snow-covered mountains. Almost the first to sight it, Harald was up onto the boat's prow.

"Can't do it!" Harald yelled against the wind. Clinging frantically to the long curving prow, he struggled to pull the red wool hood over the carved dragon's head. They didn't want the bad charm to place a curse on the land they were approaching. Somewhere on that dragon's head were the original rune charms, but no time to find them now.

"You must—try again! Start with the shorter edge and pull it over the dragon's snout first." It was hard to hear Aiwar below him, even though he was shouting with hands cupped around his mouth. "If we don't cover up the dragon prow, the Greenlanders will think we come in war. They've got to know we're coming in peace and mean no harm to the land. He signaled to the crew of the two long boats following them to do the same.

With one final desperate tug, Harald pulled down the long, fringed end of the hood and passed the cord around the dragon's neck to secure it. He was glad to climb back onto the deck, although soaked through with salt spray. The *knorr* and the two long boats were steering due east into Eriksfjord. Once on deck, Harald concentrated on the sight ahead.

"Oh, Snorri," he cried out, unaware that he was working up above on the mast ropes and couldn't hear him. "Will you look at that! Just look—land at last!" And he waved his arms in pure joy. What a welcome sight, especially after the terrors of the last storm. "Never thought we'd see it. Not very green, though. Sort of gray and pinkish. Thought we'd never, ever make it! Did you think we would?" He gave a shrug of disappointment to find Snorri still out of earshot. "Would have been such a great moment to share," he muttered. "Just like the other night under the stars."

Another disappointment. Looking ahead, then to port on the left-hand side and starboard on the right, he was shocked. Not only was the country most definitely not green and fertile, like he'd imagined, but the town of Brattahlid wasn't at all what he expected. "Not at all like—like—"

He felt Father's firm hand on his shoulder. "Not at all like the great fjord turning in from the sea toward Bergen, back in Norway, is it, son? No steep rocky cliffs rising up sharply on both sides? But see, notice how broad this inlet is—could sail in a thousand boats like ours all at the same time."

"Except for all those nasty islands all over the place," Ufila snarled in his heavy, Goth accent. He came up behind them, and Harald instinctively drew away. "Just ugly rocks," he spat out. "Some big as houses. Wreck a boat in no time, drown the crew." He pointed ahead, waving his hand. "A bad place, a place full of evil. I know evil when I see it."

"I'm sure you do," Harald's father answered sharply, his double meaning obvious to everybody except Ufila. "Get back to your work there—you were assigned to one of the sail ropes." Ufila ambled over to one of the port-side ropes, muttering under his breath. Ufila was not to be trusted, and Bjorn was not sure Ufila would stop only with theft.

Some pale greenish hillsides came in sight, sloping up from each side of the wide inlet and dotted with outcroppings of pink sandstone. Rising up far behind them were the sharp crags of mountains, the highest covered with snow.

Snorri climbed down from the masthead and joined Harald on deck. "This fjord seems endless," Snorri commented, disgust in his voice as he looked ahead. "We've been sailing east for the whole morning now. It's past midday already, and no port in sight yet. And look over there—those weird black blobs on that island over there? What's that strange noise?"

"Seals, of course," Harald replied, rather pleased that here was something else Snorri didn't know. "A whole colony of them, looks like, all barking like dogs. You've never heard seals before? And look—over there to starboard—a big whale. What we couldn't do with all that oil—Not sure about the meat, though."

"Not very good, unless you're starving," commented Snorri dryly, shuddering. "I do know about whale blubber!" Suddenly he pointed directly ahead. "Hey, hey—ho there, helmsman! Look out, look out!" A second whale was surfacing within a foaming patch of water just yards ahead of the boat. Ari jerked the starboard steering oar sharply to the right and the *knorr* cleared the foaming patch of water only seconds before a large whale surfaced with a great spout of water.

"Whew! That was close," Harald said. "That monster would have broken the boat apart, for sure!" He was thankful for Snorri's sharp eyes and a quick reaction on the part of Ari, the helmsman. Maybe he would have to revise his opinion of Snorri.

At last the fjord began to narrow. Steep outcroppings of rosy-colored rocks on both sides looked as though about to plunge into the sea. By late afternoon the three boats were entering a small harbor. Protected as the harbor was from the wind, the boats' sails began to flap lazily and their speed reduced to a slow movement through calm water.

"There's the town, Brattahlid!" his father called out, pointing straight ahead and signaling to the two long boats following behind in their wake. "Strike down the sail, you men. Get down to your rowing oars! And you two, there, Harald and Snorri—take your places!" There were three long oars on each side, one pair fewer than on the longboats, and Harald and Snorri both put their backs to the number one and two on the port side. "Now let the boat drift into the dockside—watch out there. Snorri, you're pulling too hard, getting us off course. Peik—pull harder to starboard! Ari more to port on the rudder there. You men at the prow, get ready to cast out the ropes. Then one of you jump ashore and secure it!"

Harald glanced back at the two longboats following them. They, too, had struck sail and were using their banks of oars. But they weren't heading toward the docks, but rather toward a rocky beach. "Easier to just beach them on shore because of their light weight," explained Ole, who was manning the starboard oar beside them.

The thought of being able to leave the cramped boat at long last, to get out and explore the town, filled Harald with excitement. He wasn't going to take Ufila's dire predictions seriously. Yet, how disappointing! That town down there at the end of the fjord certainly looked nothing like the city of Bergen. Only a cluster of low, log houses built around a small stone church with a wooden bell tower. A river flowed down from the plain above, and some docks had been built where it met the sea. Very few fishing boats were moored there.

Still, even this place was welcome after the long crossing. With the storms and the fog, the near drowning, salted fish, goat stew, and tough, smoked reindeer meat, it seemed to Harald an eternity since they'd left. In his mind's eye he could still see the white flutter of Grandmother's shawl, the tall towers of Bergen cathedral getting smaller and smaller. But remembering Bergen reminded him of King Erik. And remembering the king called to mind the reason for their voyage, the purpose of their mission. Its importance. His duty. *Well, let's forget about exploring Brattahlid*, he thought to himself. *We must move on*. He turned to Snorri. "Say, how long do you think before we set sail again?"

"Soon," Snorri replied with a shrug and his twisted kind of smile. "I hope very, very soon! Let's get some teeth into this expedition. Let's get some real excitement, some real danger! That is, oh Harald-of-the-Common-Name, if you think you can take it!"

Chapter Five
On the Western Edge

Bjorn stood at the prow, addressing the crew. "Now listen, men, let me warn you. It could be we'll encounter some problems, even if we are commissioned by the king and carry his seal. But we must make sure we're well prepared and provisioned. There's an even longer and more dangerous journey ahead! When we go ashore, don't show any weapons. No long swords, spears. You may carry your personal daggers somewhere concealed, just in case there's trouble. The longboat captains will have already instructed their men. All right, now. Look lively, get ready! Dock coming up on the port bow!"

By the time the *knorr* was secured at the dock, hordes of townspeople were gathering around it. A man broke away from the crowd and came forward the moment Harald's father stepped off the boat. He was tall, yet stooped, with a long white beard and white hair showing beneath his wide felt hat. He wore a full-length striped surcoat with silver clasps on the shoulders, a broad leather belt around his waist from which hung a massive broad sword.

"Look at all that gilt on the sword," Snorri muttered to Harald as they watched, leaning on the aft rail. "Must be somebody real important."

And, sure enough, they heard the man introduce himself as headman of the town. "Welcome, sea voyagers," he said. "I see that your dragon head prow is covered with red hoods and you do not hold weapons in your hands. Therefore, come in peace." He held out his right hand in welcome. "My name is Lief Thorkelson. I am the direct descendent of the first man to discover Greenland some three hundred years ago. You will know of him."

"It is indeed an honor to meet the descendant of so famous a man," Bjorn said. "We are of Norway and Gotland. My name is Bjorn Erikson. This my son, Harald. The others you will meet in due time."

"Peace be unto you also, then, strangers from the sea." He embraced Harald's father warmly and bowed slightly toward Harald. "We Greenlanders are eager for your news—news of our countries to the east, news of our families. Yes, we still have many family ties to Iceland and Norway. But, we are so very, very far away. We see so few strangers here, and then only during the short summer months when boats can cross the sea."

And so, after a number of introductions and other formalities, which seemed to Harald to go on forever, the three boats were properly secured. One crewman was left as a guard on board each. "Take this man," Bjorn said to Lief, as he pointed to Ufila, "and keep him secure until we sail again. He's a criminal according to King Erik's laws."

"I shall not ask what he's done," Lief replied, "but trust your decree in this matter. Here, you two men," he motioned toward a group of men standing by, "see that he bears no weapons and lock him up in the pig barn behind the church."

Harald could hear Ufila whining, protesting, as they moved away. "A pig barn, eh Snorri?" he said. "Serves him right." He was relieved no longer having to keep close company with him—at least while they were here in Greenland. What would happen to him later—well, who could tell. Something about the man—what was it? Harald's brain triggered a warning each time he thought about him.

Lief bowed toward Bjorn, motioning him toward the narrow stone roadway which led up to his house. "If you will follow me,

Bjorn Erikson. You and your son, along with the two captains of the other boats—you will lodge at my home. I have instructed that your other men be distributed around to other families in town and the nearby farms. Come, now, you will be welcomed most warmly."

Bjorn stepped forward, and Harald did as well, with Hakon and Svein, the other captains, just behind them.

"What about Snorri, Father? Harald whispered.

Lief apparently heard him, for he said, "That young man will be with the Egillsons on the other side of the harbor. They will treat him well, be assured."

That evening, Lief's wife, Gudrid, produced a most satisfying feast of roast duck, dumplings, red sauerkraut with caraway seeds, and apple tarts with clotted cream. She kept pressing Harald with second helpings of everything, especially the apple tarts. He could not get enough. He ate and ate, until he noticed his father staring at him very pointedly. With a sigh, he put down his wooden fork, then left the table to join his father and the others as they went to sit around Lief's big stone fire ring in the middle of the great room.

It was already turning cool in the late afternoon, and the log fire was comforting. Harald was fascinated by the circles the smoke seemed to make as it curled up and disappeared through the opening in the roof. From time to time Gudrid came in to throw another log on the fire with a loud crash, and the sparks flew up through the hole with the smoke.

"We haven't always had to build a fire here in the main room this time of year," Leif explained, somewhat apologetically. It was just past the middle of June, mid-summer's night. "Winters here seem to be coming earlier, the summers shorter."

"Yes, indeed," added Gudrid, returning this time to pass around a wooden platter full of what looked like deep-fried honey cakes. "It's getting harder to grow crops, flowers, for the bees to make honey."

LAUREL MEANS

"That means," Lief said, with a wink at Harald, "we don't know how much longer we'll be able to have those apple tarts you liked so much, these honey cakes. But there's another problem, too. Because of the change in weather, Brattahlid has grown over the past few years."

"Grown?" Bjorn asked. "Where are the people coming from? Isn't that a good thing?"

"No, not in this case," Gudrid explained slowly. "So many settlers are now moving down into town from the settlements farther north. That means more mouths to feed. And with the shorter growing season, less food, it means the cost of food is going sky high!"

"All because the climate's changing?" Bjorn asked.

"Only partly," Lief answered in a more solemn mood. He gazed into the fire for a few moments. "Unfortunately there's another reason, a more serious reason."

"What's that, sir?" Bjorn asked.

"Do you know about the *skraelings*?"

"No, I can't say as I do," said Bjorn. Harald paid more attention. He didn't know what *skraelings* were, either, but the name had a nasty, scratchy sound to it.

"The *skrælings*," Lief went on, "are a group of native people we settlers originally found living in this land. They were here centuries before us. Small people they are, use mainly short spears, heads made from stone, that is, since they don't seem to know how to work iron. We haven't been able to learn what they call themselves."

"You haven't had much interaction with them, then?"

"Yes, at least at first. They seemed friendly, glad to trade furs and the like for what we had—food, red cloth, little metal buckles, especially milk from our cows and goats, which they seemed to be very fond of. But then things changed."

"What happened?" Harald found himself asking as he moved forward on the edge of the wooden bench. The story was getting more interesting. He smelled danger, adventure.

"We're not sure. The milk seemed to make some of them sick, and they got angry. They also appeared to regard us as taking too much of their land, too much of their game, fish. Part of that problem had also to do with the weather."

"How's that?" Hakon looked puzzled.

"It was like this. Just as their hunting grounds to the north began to experience longer winters, so they, too, moved farther south. To gain more hunting grounds for themselves, they began to attack some of the more remote farms up in the western settlement, killed the settlers, burned down the buildings."

"Oh, I begin to see now," said Bjorn, rubbing his chin thoughtfully.

"Yes," Lief continued, "and then the settlers got more afraid, started moving south down here to the eastern settlement villages."

"But surely you could resist those attacks," exclaimed Bjorn. "You have better weapons, iron weapons. You descend from generations of warriors, do you not?"

"That's so, " said Lief. "But, you see, we have fewer men. Our over-all population is not what it used to be. You must know that many settlers have given up their lands here because of conditions, moved back to Iceland, even back to Norway. A few of us, however, refuse to give up our land here—we've worked so hard for it. It's our home—over three hundred years, since the time of my ancestor, Erik the Red."

Harald could tell he was very proud of this connection, for he mentioned it often.

Lief continued, "We are determined to survive. If only we could move farther west, farther south, into that country they call Vinland. They say it's so warm even grapes grow wild there."

Although Harald was intrigued by the description of lands farther away, even beyond the western edge, he'd heard enough talk. He couldn't sit still. He couldn't focus his mind on wherever Vinland might be, or whatever was happening in Greenland these days. Mention of those people called *skraelings* caught his interest, but after that his mind began to wander. He heaved a great sigh, shifted his body several times on the hard wooden bench, and wiggled his feet. He tried to catch his father's eye. *Oh, please, Father,* he thought, *give me some excuse for getting out of here! Please, oh, please!*

As if aware of Harald's discomfort, Bjorn finally turned toward him and said, "You needn't stay, Harald." Harald gave a sign of relief. "I'm sure you're eager to stretch your legs after all those weeks at sea. Go on, now, off with you, my son. It's still close enough to mid-summer to provide enough light to explore the town before time for bed."

"Yes, son of Bjorn," Lief Thorkelson added. "If you will go knock on the door of the house just across the road, you'll find my granddaughter, Astrid. She's about your age—she'll show you around." Then he added, "but mind you, my lad, be back when the sun dips down to one hand's width from the horizon. The *skraelings* like to attack as the dusk deepens."

Harald welcomed the invitation but ignored the warning. Meetings and talk—he'd leave those boring things to others. Besides, he was anxious to meet this Astrid—a real Greenlander, great-great granddaughter of those famous explorers. Well, although you couldn't expect a girl to know much, she might have heard some pretty good stories. And then maybe they'd go see if they could find Snorri. This girl Astrid would surely know where the Egillsons lived, where Snorri was to stay until they set sail again. They'd explore together. Maybe they'd even encounter something exciting—or one of those *skraelings*. He checked to see whether his dagger was still attached to his belt, well concealed under his cloak.

Astrid proved to be a tall, slim girl with one long, thick braid down the middle of her back. Her hair was so blonde as to be almost white, and her cheeks reminded Harald of rosy apples. She had a short, snubby kind of nose, which seemed about right for a girl like that.

"Come in, come in," she said, and her bright blue eyes crinkled up in a smile as she welcomed Harald into her house. This is my mother."

"I'm Karen," Astrid's mother said. "We've been expecting you." Karen looked like an older, plumper version of Astrid. "My father-in-law sent word earlier. And this is my little son, Njal. It's unfortunate my husband, Thorkel, is not here to welcome you as well. He is—well, he's not here at the moment." She looked rather strange as she said this, and Harald wondered what the problem was. He dared not ask out of politeness. But the fact that Astrid's brother was named *Njal*—now *that* was interesting.

Astrid eagerly began to ask Harald about Norway, if he had any brothers or sisters, what the king's court was like, about the voyage. She could not seem to get enough information, nor did she seem the least bit shy. Harald wasn't sure why he seemed nervous around her.

"Come," Astrid said at last as she took a gray-and-brown knitted shawl down from a set of wooden pegs by the door, "I'm sure you're wanting to explore a bit. You've been cooped up on that little boat so long—can you still walk? Let's see if you still stagger from the way the boat moves with the waves! All sailors do that." She laughed and her eyes crinkled up. "I know what we can do," she said suddenly. "We'll go out to my friend Thora's farm—it's just out on the edge of town. She's got some ponies we can ride."

"My friend Snorri—can't we—"

"All right, we'll go find him, take him with us. Can he ride?"

They soon found out. Harald and Snorri straddled small ponies, descended from ponies which original settlers had brought with them from Iceland. No saddles, just bridles. They rode up the slopes behind the town along with Astrid, Thora, and Thora's brother, Ivar. Harald had never seen a pony like that before, with a light-colored mane and shaggy forelock.

"What's the matter—haven't you ever ridden before?" Snorri asked, with one of his weird smiles, followed by a smirk. "You keep sliding around on its back."

The truth was, although he was not going to admit it, that Harald had never ridden a pony before, let alone a horse. His father kept a few cows and goats on their farm in Telemark, some plow and cart horses, but no horses for riding. Sure, his father had had a powerful warhorse when he went to battle, but he'd given that up. *Suppose I fall off?* Harald worried. *How do I make a horse stop? Go? Suppose the pony refuses to go?* Snorri appeared to be doing all right, but then that was Snorri for you. He could even swim.

"Your friend rides well," Thora remarked to Harald. Then, to Snorri, "How come?"

"You see," Snorri explained, "my grandfather had a big farm and he used to let me sit on his great plow horse during the spring plowing time. No saddle then as now, either. Hey, Harald, race you to that pine tree down there!" And off he galloped.

Snorri was already way ahead by the time Astrid showed Harald how to dig his heels into the pony's sides and flick the reins. The pony immediately lunged forward and Harald found himself bouncing around on the pony's back, clinging desperately to its thick mane. He seemed to be catching up to Snorri, though. That pine tree was coming closer.

And then it happened. Harald's pony stopped suddenly, right in the middle of the trail. Harald found himself flying over the animal's head and landing in a thicket of bramble bushes beside the trail. Astrid and Thora burst into giggles. But Astrid must have seen the look on his face, for she stopped laughing almost immediately, dismounted, and rushed over to help extract him from the thorns.

"Ow, ow," Harald cried as the thorns tore at his hands and clothes while Astrid took one arm, Ivar pulled on his leg. By the time Astrid, with Ivar's help, had gotten him out, he had scratches on his hands and face and rips in his jerkin and the sleeves of his tunic. How would he explain those to his father? But Astrid's hand, brushing back his hair and straightening the collar of his jerkin felt cool and comforting. He wished she could do it for just a bit longer. Fortunately his heavy leggings and thick woolen stockings had protected his legs from the thorns.

But where was Snorri? It angered him that Snorri, his so-called good friend, hadn't bothered to come back to help.

"Ho, ho, ha ha, hee hee—look at Harald, will you?" There was Snorri at the pine tree, sitting smugly on his pony with his arms crossed across his chest and laughing his head off.

"Well, well," Astrid giggled as she helped Harald back onto his pony, "it must be true what they say about sailors—that they can't ride. Except for your friend Snorri, of course. But you have a good excuse—that Bruni you're riding will throw anybody who's a stranger. I'm sorry—should've warned you. Want to go back? We still have about an hour's more light."

Harald refused to admit that what he really wanted was go back and maybe sit in the hot tub his host had offered earlier. There was what they called a *fire room* out in back, or a *sauna*. They built a fire in a rock circle in the middle of the room, then when the rocks got hot they threw water on them to make steam. They also filled a big wooden tub with hot water to soak in. Or you could lie on shelves around the room, let the steam take out your aches and pain. Hmmm, all that hot water and steam would feel so good! The scratches stung his face and hands. His legs were already sore from squeezing the pony's sides. But, swallowing hard, he forced himself to say, "Go back? Not on your life! Let's ride up to the top of the bluffs. I want to see as much as I can."

They started the steep climb up a narrow rocky trail. Bruni, having done his worst to Harald, appeared to have come to terms with him by keeping to a more comfortable gait.

Suddenly a large hawk screamed overhead and swooped over them. It dropped down so close to Astrid's head that its talons tore out a lock of her white blonde hair. Still screaming, it reeled, circled far out over the harbor, headed down the fjord, then disappeared while its screams became fainter and fainter. The group watched for a moment, not quite knowing what to think of this encounter, then continued a little more cautiously up the steep trail.

Once they'd turned a sharp angle in the trail, Harald saw a tiny, log cottage set back into a cave. In fact, the cave seemed to be the house, with only a peaked log wall built across its entrance and a low, black door in the middle. In the center of the black door was a small, square window, its glass pane catching the glint of the setting sun. It looked as if it were winking at them and made Harald shiver. Smoke was rising from a hole up near the peak of the entrance wall, a strange smelling smoke. It seemed to Harald unlike the customary smoke coming from kitchen or house-warming fires. It made him feel giddy, almost fall off the pony.

Astrid, leading the group, slowed her pony and turned back toward the others. "Sshhh!" she whispered, placing her hand on her lips. "We must be very quiet as we pass this cave."

"But why? Who lives here?" Snorri asked loudly. He was actually shouting, since he was now some distance back, bringing up the rear of the five riders.

"Sshh!" Astrid whispered again, motioning him to be quiet. Without a word, she then turned and urged her pony more quickly up the trail.

Tempted out of curiosity, Harald looked back. The door of the cave-house had opened, someone was coming out. It was difficult to see who, exactly. That strange-smelling smoke from the chimney and the pockets of dust on the road from the ponies' hooves together created a kind of shimmering, shifting veil between Harald and the figure. What he could see, however, before he was forced to turn away lest he lose sight of Astrid, was a bent, old woman, dressed in a gray fur cloak. Instead of a regular woman's headcloth, she wore a black fur hood with horns on it. She shook a crooked staff at them, then pointed it directly at Harald.

Harald shivered again. A strange feeling of uneasiness came over him, a sense of foreboding. He could not explain it, for he had never felt anything like that before, not even when he'd almost drowned in the storm at sea. What could it mean?

Once past the cave-house, they rode fast for another ten minutes or so, Harald getting more and more uneasy about the strange house, the old woman. Astrid's caution was puzzling, too. He'd actually seen fear in Astrid's face. She hadn't seemed the kind of girl who'd be afraid of anything. Harald wasn't sure whether it was fear he felt himself. Probably only curiosity. There sure were some strange things going on here. What had Ufila said about this place? That it was an evil land? And if anybody could know that, it would be Ufila.

Before Harald could give Ufila another thought, there was a roar above them, a loud rumbling which sounded like a hundred carts going down a cobblestone street. What Harold noticed first were small pebbles rolling across the path just in front of Bruni. The pony whinnied and balked, refusing to go on. The others, with Snorri bringing up the rear, stopped. Astrid in the lead looked back at the group, then up toward the mountain towering above them.

"Hurry," she called out, "make those ponies gallop! Come on, follow me!"

The roaring grew louder, the pebbles rolling across the path had turned into rocks, then rocks mixed with chunks of ice. Harald saw Astrid kick her pony in the flanks and he did the same. He didn't dare look back, because his only concern was keeping Bruni on the path, galloping as fast as possible. He heard the crashing of larger rocks, boulders behind him, Snorri yelling to look out, Thora screaming.

With the ponies snorting and foaming around the bits in their mouths, the group finally reached a large meadow at the top of the bluff. There, beside a stunted pine tree, Astrid drew her pony to a halt. She motioned the others to gather around her.

"That was a rock slide," she announced, still out of breath. "We were lucky to get just ahead of it, lucky to be alive.

"I've seen rock slides before," said Snorri, "but there sure was some thing very strange about that one."

"You're right. It wasn't a natural rock slide." Astrid pointed back down the trail. "Back there, that little house, built into a cave? Remember?" It seemed to Harald that a shadow crossed her face. "An old woman lives there," she continued, lowering her voice to a half whisper. "Her name is Heckla and she is thought to be a witch, maybe even a *draugar*—a ghost."

Harald felt a strange prickly in his scalp. "My grandfather once told me something about such things, about spirits or ghosts who come back after life to take revenge for something that happened to them in life. I think he even used that word—what was it? *Draugar*?"

"Oh, come now," snickered Snorri, "surely you don't believe in those old superstitions? They went out with those old Vikings, long time ago!"

"But no, Snorri, not all—my grandfather—" Harald began, but was interrupted by Thora.

"Yes, not all," Thora broke in. "There's something to it here—some of those old beliefs still survive, brought over with Erik the Red. We've been cut off from Norway for a very long time, you know. Old beliefs stick around. They become kind of fossilized."

"Yes," said Astrid. "That Heckla has some sort of magic power, all right. My father—" she broke off. "No question but what she caused the rockslide. And didn't you see that hawk fly over us, screaming, nearly pulling out my hair? Well, Heckla sent it as a warning to us—to me to keep away. That hawk was Heckla's *fylgja*."

"What's that?" Harald asked. His grandfather hadn't mentioned that word.

"Some people call it a *fetch*—a personal spirit, it can leave the body, take any shape it wants. Sometimes Heckla's fetch is a hawk, sometimes a sea gull, other times a wolf. I know I've seen it as rat once or twice, nosing around our grain store."

Harald found this hard to believe, as much as his grandfather had told him about the old stories. Yet the thought of a ghost did disturb him a little. "You said the woman might also be a ghost . . ."

"Yes, a ghost that takes the body of a human," Astrid explained. "People used to believe they were restless spirits, sometimes bad, sometimes even good—they could either cause people harm or warn them of danger."

"Well, which is Heckla, then?" Snorri jeered as he leaned over his pony's back to poke Harald in the ribs. He was clearly skeptical, not believing a bit of it.

Astrid turned very serious, that shadowy cloud once again coming over her face. "Harm," she said simply, "the cause of much harm. But let's ride on. I know another trail back into town. We can't go back the way we came, the path will be wiped out by the rock slide." She turned her pony, and, motioning the others to follow, headed north out of the meadow and toward the top of the ridge.

Harald urged Bruni forward so as to catch up with her. At that point the trail was just wide enough for two to ride side by side, and from time to time the side of Astrid's pony, Grann, brushed against his right leg. "Now look here, Astrid," he said. "You don't seem quite like the type of girl who'd fall for what some people called sheer superstitions. What's Heckla actually done to you?"

Astrid hesitated before she answered, seemingly intent on guiding Grann through some loose rocks which had rolled down on the trail from the hill above. At last she spoke, but in a hard voice, different from what she'd used earlier. "That witch has done much. It's a long story, and I can't tell you everything."

"But can't you tell me *something*?" Harald asked. "I really want to know." He found it difficult to understand why the affairs of Astrid's family were beginning to be important to him. There was something about her—her pony brushing against his leg . . .

"Well," she answered, "I can at least tell you how it started. About five years ago in the spring my father was out in his fishing boat, way out beyond the fjord, hunting for whales. Many had been sighted out at sea, in amongst the floating icebergs. Heckla's husband, Kolbein, was one of the crew. They'd harpooned two large whales and were towing them back to the harbor. As my father told it, an argument broke out between Kolbein and another man over who'd killed the larger whale. It was worth more money, you see. Kolbein pulled out his knife, and the two began to fight there in the bottom of the boat. My father tried to stop them, and Kolbein slashed my father's shoulder in the process, whether intentionally or not, we'll never know. Just at that moment, the boat hit an iceberg. The jolt sent Kolbein overboard, and he landed on the floating ice. At that point the wind came up, forcing the iceberg to drift quickly out to the open sea." She paused, as if it pained her to repeat the story.

"What happened next?" Even Snorri seemed interested.

"My father tried to maneuver the boat close enough to rescue Kolbein. Then he discovered his own boat was beginning to take on water—the ice had crushed part of the hull, you see. By that time, Kolbein was almost out of sight, so my father had to make a hard decision: whether to return to harbor as fast as he could and lose Kolbein, or continue to chase after the iceberg and possibly lose his own life, the boat, and the rest of the crew." Here she stopped and looked intently at Harald. "What would you have done, Harald? Snorri?"

Harald was glad she gave them no time to answer. "There was no question on my father's part. He was thinking of his crew, the other men with families back in town. He returned with the rest of the men, just barely made it into the harbor. After my mother had taken care of his knife wound—although he'd lost a lot of blood—he went over to Kolbein's house to inform his wife, Heckla, of the tragedy. She took it very hard."

"Was Kolbein ever found?" Harald asked.

"No, no trace of him. He must have died of exposure on the iceberg, or drowned. My father offered to help Heckla with whatever he could, in fact, Leif Thorkelson and the whole town offered. They brought her food, made house repairs."

What happened next?" Harald asked.

"The next thing we knew, Heckla had disappeared. The following spring someone discovered she was living in that cave. She'd built herself a kind of cabin inside of it. And then all sorts of strange things began to happen, strange stories floating around about her."

"But why does she seem to have it in for you, Astrid?" Harald asked.

"Don't you see?" Thora had ridden up beside Astrid, forcing Harald to rein in his pony behind them. "Don't you see? She blames Astrid's father for her husband's death, has put a curse on the whole family—a *seiður*. That's a secret magic rite, meant to cause harm. And if she wrote it in runes—which she probably knows—it'll be even more powerful. As for Astrid's family, if you must know, a lot of harm has come to them—hasn't it Astrid? Tell him, so he'll believe!"

But Astrid turned away, not answering. Harald noticed that her shoulders were shaking, as if she were crying, although she made no sound. *Runes*—they were still using runes here in Greenland. He wanted to find out more about that.

"You must excuse her," Thora's brother Ivar said. By this time the whole group had surrounded Astrid and her pony in the one wide spot in the trail. "It has been hard for her and her family to bear. You see, her father has disappeared and they think—most of the town believes that it was Heckla's *seiður* that caused his disappearance."

"Yes," Astrid said, now more in control of her emotions. "Two years ago he was sent by Leif and the Elders—by command of King Erik himself—to explore Markland and beyond for future settlement. My father, Thorkel Liefson, left with another man named Karlsefni. That was two years ago when they sailed to the western edge. They never came back."

Harald gasped in surprise. Leif had said nothing about losing his son, Astrid's father, in this way. And, for the moment at least, Harald failed to recognize the danger this news implied regarding his own situation. "Why, to find those men was one of the king's charges to us," he said instead. "We were sent not only to claim new territory, but also to look for them, to bring them back."

Astrid brightened. "Oh," she exclaimed, "if only that might be true." She edged her pony over closer to his and threw her arms as far around Harald's neck as she could reach. He was not sure how to handle this. He drew back a little, almost falling off the pony. He felt his face turning red. He didn't like that Snorri noticed this and smirked. "But Harald," she added as she turned to continue down the trail, "there are so many other things. My baby sister died after Heckla put the spell on us. The rats came and ate up a whole winter's supply of grain. My mother fell ill. Surely you can believe me, now!"

Yes, thought Harald, *it could be true. Perhaps a* seiður *does have some kind of magic power.* He shivered again, remembering how Heckla had pointed her staff directly at him. But whether it was from fear of Heckla, anxiety about the coming exploration, or chill from the north wind coming up along the high ridge, he was not sure.

Suddenly Astrid spoke. "Come here, all of you," she called out. "This we must do!"

The group drew their ponies up closer. "Make a circle, now, around me." They edged in still closer. "We must form a protection for ourselves," she said. Harald noticed that she seemed to have become very serious, pale even. Her voice shook a little as she said, "We must form a circle of protection around us. We must make between us a *föstbræðralag*."

Harald thought he'd heard that word before, in some story his grandfather had told him. But no matter how hard he tried, he couldn't remember. Should he show his ignorance and ask her?

Fortunately he was saved that embarrassment. "Never heard of that," Snorri commented wryly. "More of your old Viking stuff?"

"No, no," Astrid quickly replied. "It's very real. It's a way of bonding together for protection. The evil spirits might harm one person, but when a number are bonded together—well, then, the spirits are afraid someone else will take revenge. Come now, all of you," she said. "You must hold out your hands—reach them all out around the circle so our fingers are touching together in the middle."

"Then what?" Harald asked.

"Then you, Harald, because I see you carry a little dagger, you must make a small cut in each of our thumbs, then we press them together one by one, so each of us becomes blood-kin to the other. Then nothing, no one, can harm any of us."

Harald hesitated. Couldn't anyone else draw the blood? To draw blood from Astrid, from your friends even? It appeared he had to do it. So, unsheathing his dagger, he carefully made a small cut in each person's thumb as they held them out: Snorri, Ivar, Thora, then Astrid. Thora and Ivar flinched a little, yet Harald noticed Astrid did not even close her eyes but kept looking straight at him. Snorri laughed a little, claiming it tickled. Then each pressed his or her thumb against the person on the left, until all were joined in an exchange of droplets of warm blood. Harald wondered whether he felt any different. *Yes*, he decided, *I do feel different. Larger than myself. Something important has happened.*

They were all silent as they rode on for another mile or so. "The other trail back to town begins to descend up ahead," Astrid called back to the riders, "just up there by that group of trees."

The trees, a small woods of pine trees, wasn't very tall but thick and dark. The rocky soil up there on the bluffs produced only stunted vegetation—small trees, thorn bushes, grassy undergrowth, and thistles. Without a word, suddenly Astrid and Ivar both urged their ponies into a gallop. "Come on," she called, "let's hurry. Quick, make for that big rock, where the trail begins to go down."

They all followed. There was something about her urgent manner that prevented questions. Harald barely managed to hang on to Bruni's thick mane, with little thought for anything else. A quick glance over to the dark woods as he rode past it, he was sure he saw something move. A dark shadow, a movement, something light in the darkness, a human face. He couldn't be sure. But Astrid and Ivar had already seen something there in the deepening dusk, something to make them afraid. Riding nearly headlong down the first half-mile of the steep trail, he could not ask. In fact, he did not want to ask. He saw relief on their faces as the group came within sight of the town, nestled down there at the head of Eriksfjord.

"Wait," he said, "stop for a moment, will you? Look, Snorri, look at that, will you?" They could look down at the town and the harbor, even down the length of the wide fjord and out to the sea beyond. The view took his breath away. The sight reminded Harald of the king's map, with its outlines of land and sea. The sea was now blood red in the low, suspended sun.

"Yes, a wonderful view here," Astrid said, turning her pony back to stand beside Harald's. She pointed far out across the water. "Look over there to the west, Harald. What do you see?"

Against the sun Harald shaded his eyes with his hand, but even if he squinted his eyes, he could see nothing but the dancing sparkles of the sea and a band of mist along the western horizon.

"Look hard, now. Look very hard over there. Try to look just above the mist."

Harald squinted his eyes even more. Then, sure enough, he could just make out, rising above the mist and not very distinct, the pale gray outline of a jagged bank of mountains, far off in the distance. The sun cast red glints on a few of the snow-capped peaks.

"Do you see it, then?" Astrid asked, excitement rising in her voice. "That, over there, is Markland. The Western Edge."

Harald forgot about the bramble bush. He no longer felt his stinging face and hands, or the aches and pains. He pushed Heckla and her spells, the rock slide which almost killed them, the frightening pale face in the dark woods far, far back into one small corner of his brain. Instead, he felt a surge of emotion, racing through his body from his head down to his very toes. Those pale gray mountains over there, surrounded in the haze of a setting sun suspended in the western sky—*that* was where their voyage of discovery would take them!

Chapter Six

The Wilderness of No Return

"Can't understand this strange wind! Seems to shift abruptly from west to north," shouted Bjorn on the aft deck of the *knorr*. He and Ari were instructing Harald how to handle the port side steering oar against the force of the wind. Since they'd left the harbor of Brattahlid early the morning before, they'd been struggling to cross that arm of the sea separating Greenland from Markland, the Western Edge.

Bjorn pulled his fur-lined hood up around his head for warmth and braced himself against the wall of the sleeping cabin. "This unnatural wind keeps pushing us backwards, no matter how often we tack. We aren't getting anywhere, at this rate! Watch out, now, Harald. Here comes another big wave! Move that steering oar to the left—the *left*, I said!"

Harald threw his whole body against the shaft of the steering oar and held it there until they'd gone down into the trough of the wave. Ari had to lend a hand to steady it. Could this terrible wind be Heckla's doing? Harald wondered. He hadn't dared tell his father about that strange series of encounters up on the cliff above town. He knew his father would have just laughed it off as superstitious nonsense. *Head too full of old Viking stuff*, he'd say. Still, it wouldn't be too farfetched to assume that Heckla had cast a spell to draw the boats back toward Greenland to prevent their going beyond the Western Edge. Quite possibly something was there that she didn't want them to discover.

Harald tried hard to focus on handling the big steering oar—he knew the safety of the boat depended upon him and Ari. He needed a clear mind and strong arms. At the same time, he could not help thinking about Astrid's revelation. Astrid said that Heckla was convinced her father, Thorkel Liefson, was responsible for the whaling accident which killed Heckla's husband. Two years after that, King Erik sent Astrid's father and another Greenlander on a discovery voyage into Markland. They never came back. And strange things kept happening to Astrid's family. Was it all Heckla's doing? What if Heckla had directed her curse toward them, too? What if they would meet some disaster in the Markland wilderness and never come back? Heckla had pointed her staff directly at him. He had a prickly feeling all over his scalp and up and down his spine.

Old Viking stuff, his father would call it. Well, maybe. He tried to remember some of the things Grandfather had taught him about counter-spells. There were some verses one could say, some rune letters you could write down, which might protect you against witches like Heckla. But he couldn't be sure of that, either, even if he remembered them exactly.

"Harald, Harald!" Father shouted against the howling wind. With a start, Harald came to. "Stop your day dreaming! You're not paying enough attention to the rudder—leave yours to Ole and lend a hand over here!" His father and several crew were trying to trim the big square sail. One corner had come loose and was whipping around, its rope dangerously slashing at anyone or anything in its way. Harald looked up toward the top of the mast. The intertwined ravens of the king's crest painted on the canvas sail looked as though they were flapping their wings, ready to fly off on their own. Harald had a fleeting thought—if only this boat had wings! He left the steering oar, making sure first that Ole had a firm grip on it, and made his way—hand over hand along the rail because of the wind—toward the mast. On the way, though, he stopped to put more dried grass in One Horn's manger, since he'd forgotten to do it that morning. The wind immediately picked up most of it, sending it swirling across the deck. Harald tried to save what he could, but most of it disappeared into the white-capped waves.

"Never mind about that goat," yelled his father, this time in real anger. "Let it go! This sail is more important than the belly of that old goat. Climb up on top of the storage cabin, grab hold of the middle of the sail! Then you there, Awair, hold down the next bit. We'll gradually work ourselves out to the end."

Fighting against the wind, Harald scrambled up to the top of the cabin, and climbing over the small rowing boat secured there up side down, seized the bottom of the canvas sail with both hands. It was hard to hold onto, so he wound the end of one of the loose, walrus hide ropes around his fist. The wind made it tear into his flesh with such force that he noticed blood oozing onto the rope.

"Hold it down harder. Tighten it more, Harald, " Father shouted.

"Can't tighten it much more," he yelled, forcing himself to disregard the pains shooting through his hand, up into his arm.

Gradually Bjorn and Awair struggled to work themselves out to the sail's bottom edge. Standing on top of the dangerously pitching boat's railing, they finally managed to catch hold of the end of the main rope as it whipped around in the wind.

It was only when they'd made it fast to the end of the yard arm that Harald was able to pull taunt his own rope, attached to the bottom of the sail's mid-section, and make it fast to the yard arm. He did so with great relief. The rope was soaked with blood—*his* blood, and his hand throbbed with pain. He didn't want Father to know, so when his father wasn't looking, Harald crawled over to the side of the boat and plunged his hand into the waves. The cold salt water stung like a hundred summer black flies. He clenched his teeth against the pain. Shortly afterward, however, the cold numbed his hand to the point that he could disregard the pain and begin remembering what he'd been about to do—feed One Horn. Since most of the grass had been lost to the wind, all he could do was give the goat an extra rub on the forehead. "That'll have to do for now, old friend," he said with a sigh. "As soon as we strike land, I'll find you something nicer, like lily stalks, or wild thyme."

By late morning the next day, the land off their port bow was becoming more distinct. Although they'd had occasional sightings of it since they'd left Greenland, it was now possible to make out distinct objects on shore.

Back in Eriksfjord, Lief Thorkelson had given Bjorn some detailed instructions about that shoreline. They'd all been standing at the *knorr*'s mooring on the morning of their departure. Harald had looked for Astrid, but was disappointed not to see her among the small group gathering to see them off.

"Just steer due north close along the coast of Markland until you reach a great opening to the west," Lief had said, and Harald tried to remember every single word. "Don't turn into any smaller bay or inlet, or you will come to a dead end, or worse, shatter the boats on rocks. That wide opening is not like a river. It will look like the way into another sea. You must then steer directly to where the sun sets. There will be sharp, black mountains on your left hand, few trees, only grass-covered plains. Beyond that—we don't know." Then, Harald rememberd, Lief shook his head and lowered his voice. "That's the way into the heart of Markland—and may God be with you! May God lead you once again out of that wilderness! May you have better fortune than my son, Thorkel, and his companion, Karlsefni! They have not returned, nor do we ever expect them to now."

Harald could tell that Lief's remarks about the two Greenland explorers disturbed his father, in fact, everybody listening. Especially him. No, they sure didn't bode well. For the first time a dark shadow of doubt crossed Harald's mind. Doubt that this venture would lead to anything except disaster. It was linked somehow to Ufila. To Heckla. To Astrid. After all, wasn't Thorkel Liefson also Astrid's father?

But at the same time, there was something in what his father had said in response to Lief's warnings. He'd pointed out that his expedition was better equipped than Thorkel's, and more men meant a better chance for survival. "Yet, to be truthful," he'd added, "we do not know—cannot know—what to expect."

Now it had two days and two nights since that departure from the docks of Brattahlid. During the last two nights as they'd sailed along the Markland coast and against the fierce, continually shifting winds, Harald had looked desperately for some stars to guide them. He reckoned they were slightly farther south than Iceland, but still, in summer the light of the northern skies during the night blotted them out. He had to depend upon sun sightings with the astrolabe during the day. And today he'd just made what he hoped was an accurate one.

"Fortunate we have you along, my son," Bjorn said, joining him on the aft deck. "There wasn't another bearing dial to be had in Brattahlid or indeed Eriksfjord. We'll have to rely on you, your astrolabe, the sun, and the stars—if we can see them—from now on."

But it was the night watches which Harald looked forward to. These gave him a chance to talk to Snorri, who'd asked for the same watch. That night they sat at the prow, watching the waves break away from the keel into foam. The foam dazzled white in the moonlight, and the sea around them seemed filled with mysterious, moving lights—blue, green, pink, yellow.

"Look! What are those?" he asked. Snorri seemed to know everything.

"Don't know," Snorri answered to Harald's surprise. "Seaweed? Fish? Mirror of the stars, maybe?"

"No, don't think so," Harald replied, reassured by Snorri's ignorance. "And you can't see the stars from here, besides, they're different shapes. Have to be something else."

"Well, maybe there's another world down there we don't know about," Snorri reasoned. "Those stars wouldn't always have to be in the same places, the same shapes, would they?" Harald was always impressed with Snorri's practical way of thinking, but he'd noticed Snorri didn't seem to have much imagination beyond that.

Yet Harald remembered thinking about the stars, way back before they'd reached Greenland, the night the storm was over. He hadn't been able to share that with Snorri, because Snorri had been *snoring*! Harald remembered wondering about the starry world up above him, what might be up there. He marveled how it filled so much space. It seemed to go on forever. Now, as they were talking during their night watch, coming so close to Markland itself, Snorri's suggestion about the possibility of another world, down in the sea below them, was interesting. Yes, he'd think about that.

"Look, Snorri," he said, leaning far out over the boat's prow. "Look down there. Those little lights are moving around, and there are different colors, too." He wondered whether they might be some sort of little sea creatures. At least he hoped they were not evil spirits sent by Heckla, although that was possible. Well, he sure wouldn't be putting any injured hand down into the waves again, no matter how much it throbbed. Some monster might grab him and snatch him overboard.

Finally, toward noon of the fourth day, there it was—the great opening from the sea described by Lief. Black mountains rose up on the left hand side, grassy plains on the right. "I must say, it does look like the tundra parts of northern Norway, parts of Finland," remarked Harald's father. "That's a surprise. We'll keep to the southern, leeward shore. It looks more hospitable. Besides, there's less danger of being driven against the rocks on the north side of this inland sea. More protection from the wind, too."

That leeward shore seemed to go on and on. For the first day or so, sharp rocky mountains rose up steeply on their left, and those way off in the distance were snow-capped. After a while, the mountains gave way to pine-covered hills. For days they followed the irregular shoreline, sometimes in a more southerly direction, where the pine forests became deeper and darker. Other times the forests were so dense that no underbrush could grow beneath them. From time to time the three boats turned due north along the shore for a half-day or so.

"I'm sure we're still sailing mostly west," he remarked to Snorri during one night's watch.

"How far do you think this Western Edge goes?" Snorri asked. "Do you think we'll know when the edge is *the edge*?"

Harald recalled the map the king had shown them back in the castle meeting room. After what Snorri had said the night before, Harald tried to imagine what the country might look like if he could draw a map of it, might give some kind of a clue where *the edge* was.

Asking Ole, the cook, for a piece of charcoal from the fire ring in the *knorr's* galley, he tried to trace on port-side wall of the storage cabin the outline of the shoreline they were following. Sometimes, when he could sight the sun with his astrolabe, he made a little note of his bearings on the wall. Other times he tried to sketch roughly any unusual landmarks he saw, like a rock cliff, or an island, or a really tall tree.

"Humpf, that's a funny-looking shape," snickered Snorri as he came to watch Harald make some additions just after noon on the fourth day. "What do you call that? It looks like, well, I dunno what!" He laughed as he stood back and folded his arms across his chest. "Well, I guess it looks like the front end of a big bear. See, there—" and he pointed to something looking like a paw.

But Harald didn't see it. "It's a map," he protested. "Like the one the king had. This one, on the wall here, is supposed to show us where we've been. No one's ever been here before. At least, we've never had a map of this part. And, besides—you don't know but what it may show us the way home. Then, who'll be laughing, eh?"

"No," said Snorri firmly, "it's not a map, it's a big bear. You've drawn a bear, a fat bear, with little numbers and pictures on its fur. See, there's his head, his front leg—and well, I'd hardly call that thing a back leg."

"But don't you see," Harald protested again, "what you call the head, that's the big inlet we turned into from the sea. Then we sailed down along his right shoulder, and there, what you call his front leg, that's the bay where we turned south. Went all the way down to his claws, we did, see, right there. I guess you could say all those little rivers emptying into this sea looked like claws at the end of the bear's paw."

Harald pointed to a place on the outline. "But you remember, my father decided not to follow any of the rivers—er, claws, I mean—flowing down out of the bay, just there. Then we went back up the bear's leg, now here we are—about here." He placed his finger at the end of the charcoal line he'd just drawn. "Yes, right here, just along what you'd probably call the bear's belly."

"Does that mean his hind leg is coming up next?" Snorri asked with another laugh.

Harald reluctantly recognized that, essentially, Snorri meant no harm. He was basically good natured. The best thing to do was not to take him too seriously. Snorri's been through a lot of bad things, he reasoned, lost his home, lost his family except his old father, left behind in Bergen. Maybe he acted the way he did in order to feel better, to sort of protect himself. Best to look only at his good points. And certainly, Snorri's jokes and sense of humor did get them through a lot of problems, like the time his *blood* had turned out to be pickled beet juice. But Harald couldn't forgive him for laughing when the pony threw him into the bramble bushes back in Greenland. Right in front of Astrid, too.

Strange, though, Snorri's joke about the bear's hind leg did come true. Early the next morning on the fifth day they sighted another large bay to the south, which, from Harald's outline, did resemble the hind leg of a bear, although much smaller than the front leg. Harald overheard Snorri making some joke or other to Peik about the leg's looking as though it had been cut off at the knee.

"We'll put in to shore in this smaller bay," said his father. "Looks like a number of rivers down there at the end of the bay. One fairly large, I can see. In any case, we need to replenish the water casks, hunt for some game. I'd like to explore a bit, too. If the outlet from the bay to the south looks promising, that one river deep enough, we may try to send a small, exploratory party inland there."

He signaled for one of the two longboats to move ahead of the *knorr* and beach on the shore, where there was a small, sandy slope leading gently down to the water's edge. The *knorr*, with its deeper draft, would anchor a little ways out, while the second longboat would come alongside to take the crew off and bring them to shore.

Harald watched as the first longboat crunched its keel against the sandy beach and several men jumped out to pull it farther up on shore. The second longboat was now drawing alongside his own.

"Now, Harald," his father said, "you go ashore with the rest of the crew. Ari and I will make everything secure on board here, then follow you in the skiff to the beach. We'll take enough supplies to camp there for tonight, maybe tomorrow night as well."

A tingling sensation surged through Harald's very being as he took his first step out onto the beach. Here was a whole new world! As far as he knew, no human being had ever set foot on this beach before! A new land, a wilderness unknown to anybody. King Erik had commissioned a voyage of discovery, and now they had discovered a way in, would discover what lay beyond—and he, Harald Bjornson, was one of them!

Yes, how proud Anna and Grandmother would be of him, their daring young explorer! Astrid, too. He could just see the expression on Astrid's fair face. He thought of the brightness of her hair, the way her eyes crinkled up when she smiled, the cool touch of her hand on his face as she helped him get out of the briar bush. She had wanted to come along, to help look for her father, but of course there was no place for a mere girl on this expedition. Still, if a girl had been allowed, she would have been the right one.

His thoughts were interrupted by some shouts. Svein, captain of the second longboat, had discovered something. "Here, look here!" he called out, standing on a large rock where the beach met the water's edge. Several men rushed over to see.

"Here, Bjorn," he said, pointing to a particular place on the rock. "What do you make of this?"

Harald's father knelt down on the sand and examined the rock. "No, no—it can't be," he exclaimed, incredulous.

"Why, what is it, Father?" Harald asked.

"Do you see this hole made in the rock?" he said, his tone expressing not a little wonderment. "A triangle-shaped hole, smooth-sided, chiseled into the rock about a half a hand's length?" But Harald failed to see why it seemed so important, just a hole in the rock.

"It's a special kind of hole," Svein explained. "Your father is surprised because this is a mooring stone, a stone used to moor a boat, and only used by Norwegian boats." He leaned over and traced the hole with his forefinger. "You see, this hole has been made with a special iron chisel. It's only used for mooring a boat. A rope from the boat is pegged into the hole and secured with a wooden stake. It's an old method used by the Vikings, but still often used by us today. Usually a blacksmith makes such holes. Maybe that's how Ufila can be useful, although—and pardon me for saying so, Bjorn—I don't agree that we should have kept him on. Should have left him back there in the pig barn in Brattahlid. But—that was your decision. For sure he'll mean trouble!"

The crewman named Grimm came over. "Wouldn't have noticed this, sir, if I hadn't been looking for a rock the right size, one heavy enough to be a mooring stone. Instead I found this one already here."

"So you did, Grimm," Bjorn commented, slapping him on the back. "It means some Norwegians—or Greenlanders—landed on this very spot. But it looks like it must have been a while ago, years at least. See that moss at the edge of the hole?"

It didn't take Harald long to realize the stone's significance. It meant someone had come this way before. "Someone from Greenland—maybe Astrid's own father—could he have been the one to make it?" he said.

"Yes, Harald," his father returned. "I'm thinking the same. It could very well have been Thorkel Liefson and his men. Look around. See if we can find other traces. They must have recognized this as a good landing site, just as we did. Someone followed Lief's description of the big inland sea, all right."

Further search, however, failed to reveal any additional evidence apart from the fact that a campfire had been made down at the other end of the beach, but a long time ago. Small saplings had grown up through the circle of stones. That was disappointing, especially for Harald, thinking of Astrid and her father. He and his men, if they were the ones, had at least gotten this far, but beyond this point—the trail would have grown cold by now. There was no hope of following it. Suppose they'd been killed by *skraelings*? Wouldn't that still be a danger for *them*? The end of their own expedition?

"At least we've found out something," Snorri later remarked to Harald as they sat around the campfire that night. Snorri had put his skilled bowmanship to good use that afternoon and shot several rabbits. The animals now roasted on spits resting between upright logs. Their succulent juices were spitting into the flames, and their delicious aroma filled the smoky air.

"Besides being able to eat something other than salt fish and leathery reindeer meat—not to mention those pickled beets," and here Snorri paused to bite off a large mouthful of rabbit handed to him. "Besides that, at least we know we may be at the right spot to get through into the Western Edge."

"Yes," broke in Harald's father, squatting down on the sand beside them. "We've hit it right, I'm certain. Thorkel and his men, if they were actually the ones who made this mooring stone and fire ring, must have seen this as the most suitable landing spot anywhere along this rocky shore. And they must have concluded, like we did, that this broad river promised a good way into the interior."

"Are we going to follow the river, then?" asked Harald.

"Yes," Bjorn replied, "as far as we can. We'll anchor the *knorr* here, leave ten men with her until we return. We'll take the two longboats with the rest of the men—these boats can navigate shallow waters almost up to swamp land."

He paused to accept the plate of steaming rabbit meat which Ole the cook handed him. There were some griddle cakes added, fried on an iron plate resting at the edge of the fire. Harald knew he had to wait his turn as the youngest, but the wonderful smell of the meat and the griddle cakes was almost too much to bear.

His father continued, after chewing thoughtfully for a moment or two. "As I said, we'll be leaving part of the crew here to guard the *knorr*, and that will include you, Harald."

Harald immediately forgot about his hunger, the roasted rabbit. "Leave me here? You mean, not continue on this adventure?" he exclaimed, incredulous.

"That's what I said, my son," Bjorn replied. "It's far too dangerous. You'll be safer here. Snorri will go. His skills with a bow may be useful. We're turning away from the sea and entering a land where we may have to defend ourselves. Yes, I'd like him along in one of the longboats." He picked up one of the griddle cakes, took a a bite or two. "I'm sorry, son," he said finally. "Your face tells me how you feel."

Lying out on the sandy beach under the stars that night, Harald could not sleep out of disappointment. He tossed and sighed from a crowd of thoughts turning over and over in his mind. Not to go—not to continue—to be stuck here on this little beach on the shore of this great inland sea. To be living off and on the *knorr,* with nine of the crew, also left behind. Day after day, while Snorri had one adventure after another. He wouldn't be able to look for Astrid's father. What would he tell her, if and when he ever returned? Snorri would lord it over him. Snorri would laugh at his being left behind as the youngest. Better to just die, here and now!

The next day the men provisioned the two longboats for their journey into the dark and hostile-looking wilderness. By midmorning they were ready.

"All stowed, food and weapons, sir," Hakon called out. Bjorn had made him captain of the second longboat. "Men all eager to shove off, sir."

Harald could see that the masts had been lowered into their fork-shaped supports standing in the center of the boat aft, just before the one rudder oar. The river could not be navigated by sail, his father explained, since it was too narrow and too winding. "Besides," Father said, "we may be going against the current for some time." Then he ordered the four rowers for each boat to take their places on the benches, Snorri being a rower in the lead boat. "I want you close to me, young Goth," he said. "At the first sign of trouble, be ready with your arrows. And I'm keeping Ufila close to me as well. I don't dare leave him here. No telling what he might do—commandeer the *knorr,* take off, leave us stranded—don't know what else." As he stepped over onto the rudder bench, Bjorn placed his hand on Harald's shoulder. It was that reassuring kind of pressure Harald had felt, going into the king's great hall, and he was grateful for it. "Good-bye, my son," he said. "May God be with you and protect you, as I pray he will us. Aiwar is in charge here now: I'm sure he is worthy of it. You must follow his orders."

The two longboats began pulling out into the center of the river, the men rowing harder as they encountered the current flowing against them into the great inland sea. Soon the forests on the banks closed in around them and they disappeared from view.

Harald heard Snorri's voice calling back. "Remember, Harald, don't fall into any more briar bushes! No pretty girls to pull you out, this time," and his mocking laughter faded away.

Sitting before the campfire that evening, poking absently at the embers, Harald felt angy and bitter. To be left behind, at this stage, after all that long way across the sea, to Iceland, through Greenland, left at the very edge of Markland! As if that wasn't bad enough, Snorri was the one allowed to go on. And his *own father* had made that decision! There was surely no justice in this life, he thought. Now if he'd only been the old Norse god, Loki—he'd follow them in disguise. They wouldn't know he was there until they were in deep trouble, then he'd surprise the enemy and rescue them. Snorri might help with that bow of his, but he, Harald, would be the one who'd do the most to save the whole expedition.

"Come now, son of Bjorn," said a voice. He recognized the slight difference in pronunciation which the Goths used. It was Aiwar. "Come, we must go out to the *knorr*. Your father left strict instructions that we are not to sleep here on the beach. We must all stay on the *knorr* at night for protection. No one can approach us out there without warning."

With his heavy calfskin boot he brushed sand over the embers until the red coals were no longer visible. "Come, now, the other men have already gone out there, are probably already asleep on the deck. See, Ole has come back in the skiff for us. Can you row? The effort of rowing may temper some of that emotion I see burning in you, some of that disappointment. You've grown into a young man already, it is true. Be comforted, though. Disappointment is not confined only to the young. I know."

The night was clear and bright moonlight was reflected in the moving ripples of the water. Harald couldn't remember ever seeing a half-moon so bright. It was almost like daylight. Looking toward the shore, he noticed that, although the moon transformed the tops of the tall pine trees into silver, there was band of intense darkness beneath them, all around the shore line. Somewhere in that darkness were his father, the other men, Snorri. A slight breeze rocked the *knorr* gently, the water slapping and sucking against its high, wooden sides. Sometimes the little skiff would bump against the side where it was tied to the *knorr* by a single rope.

These were the only sounds, apart from occasional snores and grunts from the men sleeping around the deck and in the two small cabins. Sometimes the call of a bird came across the water. Harald had never heard such a strange call before, a haunting call—rising, then falling into a sad, sad echo. What kind of bird could it be?

He shivered, remembering stories of ghosts and spirits, the ability of the *fylgia* Heckla to change herself into the form of a bird, like the eagle he'd seen up on the cliffs above Brattahlid. Could she have followed them to this shore? He shivered again, pulling his red woolen cloak up more closely around him as he lay out on the aft deck. He tried curling up on the small bench alongside the storage cabin. So many thoughts, until at last with the gentle rocking of the boat he drifted off to sleep.

"Go!" the voice hissed. *"Take the skiff and go!"*

Chapter Seven
Heckla's Curse

CRACK! HISS—SSS! *Go! Take the skiff and go—go!* Harald woke with a start. That noise! Who said that? He jumped to his feet and looked around. Bright moonlight revealed only the crew scattered around the deck, still asleep. The only sound was water lapping against the boat, the skiff bumping against the stern, the mournful call of that mysterious bird. Yet those words he knew he'd heard. They'd made their way through his sleep, dropped right into his head. He couldn't tell where they came from. But he understood their message. *Take the skiff and go.* TAP—BUMP—BANG! As if to reinforce the message, the skiff kept insistently bumping against the boat, trying to tell him something.

Suppose he *were* to climb down into the skiff? Suppose, just suppose, untie the single rope, take the oars and row toward shore? Enter the mouth of the river where the two longboats had disappeared from sight earlier that day? Follow them, catch up with them? It'd be too late to send him back. Harald would have to continue on with them into the wilderness. Carry out the king's plan as King Erik wanted him to. He'd show them, all right. Especially his father.

But to do that, he would need some things. Food, a sword from the weapons' chest in the storage cabin. His heart thundered as he quietly tiptoed around the sleeping forms on the deck toward the storage cabin. What he saw made him stop short. Ole, the cook, was half-lying, half-sitting propped up against the storage cabin doorway. He stirred. "Cough, agg, ahem, rrrrumph," he snorted in his sleep.

What could Harald do? He needed some provisions and a weapon more substantial than his short dagger in its sheath on his belt. Looking around, he saw a piece of roast rabbit and some griddle cakes left uneaten on a wooden trencher near Ole's outstretched hand. Must have fallen asleep before he'd finished his meal—the cook was always the last to eat, and he'd waited until getting back to the *knorr*.

A basket of apples from Greenland sat near Ole's right foot. Might do. A snuffling sound came from the animal pen on the other side of the cabin. One Horn, the goat! Harald had to keep him quiet. Thinking fast, Harald snatched up one of the apples and tossed it over into the pen, hoping that would work. Good, slight munching sounds.

Harald he took off his cloak and rolled the rabbit meat, griddlecakes, and a few apples up into it, but one of the apples fell out and rolled across the deck. Ole must have heard the noise, for he stirred again and called out. Harald froze, then dropped down behind the cabin wall and waited. No further sound from Ole except a slight moan. He must only have been dreaming. Harald crawled out from behind the cabin to see Ole roll over and stretch out further on the deck. When he began to snore, Harald knew it was safe to move toward the aft deck.

Harald looked down at the skiff, bobbing on the water about a man's height below the *knorr*'s deck rail. He now realized that it was too far to jump without making a loud thump in the bottom of the skiff. Surely that would wake up the *knorr*'s crew. To wake up Aiwar, whom Father had put in charge, was the last thing Harald wanted to do. Good thing Aiwar was down in the sleeping cabin. But he probably had a second pair of ears, listening for warning sounds of an attack on the *knorr*. Oh, no—the sleeping cabin! His astrolabe was in his sea chest down there! He'd just have to leave it.

Harald looked closely at the rope running from an iron ring in the skiff's prow to a mooring ring on the *knorr*'s deck. By wrapping his feet around that rope, maybe he could go hand over hand quietly enough down into the skiff.

But here was a problem. If he did that, then he couldn't reach up as far as the mooring ring on the *knorr* in order to release the skiff. And if he went down the rope into the skiff first and tried to release it from the skiff end, then he wasn't sure how he could do that. The rope at the skiff end was in a kind of lock. Whenever they'd used the skiff and wanted to secure it to something, the rope at its bow end was put through some kind of iron clasp, then closed with a lock and key. That evening, after arriving back on board the *knorr*, Harald had seen Aiwar put the key into his pocket. What was he to do?

Desperate, he came to a decision. It would mean a dangerous risk—but that voice in his brain—go! Go! Go! He couldn't stop it. As gently as he could, he tossed his cloak with the provisions tied up in it down into the bottom of the skiff. A muffled thump. Then he untied the skiff's rope from its fastening on the *knorr*. Tying the end around his waist, he quietly let himself down over the side of the boat, let go, and dropped into the water. Down, down he went, plunging way beneath the surface. He came up gasping for air. His teeth began chattering from the unexpected icy coldness of the water. He sank down again under the water, couldn't breathe, came up one more time.

At that point, to his horror he saw the skiff drifting away the full length of the rope and now out of reach. He would have to go after it, but how? He couldn't swim. He was about to go under again and swallowing water. If only there'd been time for Snorri to teach him! As he felt himself sinking down through the icy water once more, without quite knowing why, he tried kicking his legs. Amazing! He did not sink. Also he discovered that by moving his arms backwards and forwards, like the wings of a bird, he could just keep his head above water. And the skiff, drifting in a wind beginning to get stronger from the north, was actually pulling him by the rope tied to his waist slowly toward shore.

With relief he finally felt the rocky bottom beneath his feet and drew the skiff to where the encampment had been. Untying the rope, he pulled the skiff up over the sand and slid it under some bushes. It was good that his cloak was still dry, and he unwrapped the few provisions he'd gathered, laid them aside, and pulled the cloak around him. Fortunately Ole the cook had not succeeded in putting out all the embers of the cooking fire earlier that evening, and Harald sat as close as he dared. He hoped the little warmth would keep his teeth from chattering and help dry out his tunic, leg cloths, and boots. Clouds were forming, sometimes covering the moon and throwing the night into moments of total darkness.

Thinking of the moon, Harald suddenly remembered his astrolabe. Without it, how would he know where he was? In fact, how would his father know where they were going? How could his father make such a mistake, leaving his son behind? Hadn't Harald been given the role of chief navigator?

Yet in his heart, he had to admit that Father probably was thinking only of his son's safety. The thought moved him. At the same time, however, he was deeply concerned about his father's own safety. There was some comfort in the fact that, onboard the boat during their long voyage across the sea, he'd been able to teach Snorri something about the stars. Perhaps that would be enough to guide his father and the other men through the wilderness.

But what if it wasn't enough? All the more reason to follow them, try to catch up with them. They could be only one day ahead. Surely they had camped for the night somewhere along the river.

Now too dark for him to start. He'd have to wait for the first signs of dawn. Meantime, why not catch an hour or so of sleep? In any case, he must be long gone from this beach before any of the men onboard the *knorr* realized he was missing. With a start, he recognized the obvious. They wouldn't have the skiff, and they couldn't swim to shore. They'd have to construct another boat or a raft of some sort, and that would take time. Until then, they'd be marooned onboard the *knorr*. Harald felt some guilty pangs about this and he shuddered to think how angry they'd be, once they'd discovered their situation. At least he couldn't be followed, not immediately, anyway.

Falling into an uneasy sleep, he woke up with a start. What was that strange sound? He sat up and looked around. There was a slight stirring in the bushes on the other side of the dying fire, a faint growling. Two eyes were peering out at him like yellow fire. It might be a wolf, a small bear—he couldn't be sure. Snatching up a piece of wood still showing red embers at its tip, he aimed and threw. There was a thrashing in the bushes, a strange hissing sound, then silence.

What was it? He wondered what other creatures might be out there. The Western Edge must have different kinds of animals, as they had birds, and he thought of the strange, lonely call of the bird he'd heard back there on the water. He laid his dagger beside him. Curling himself up into the smallest possible ball for warmth, he tried to go back to sleep.

It was at one of those moments when racing clouds uncovered the moon and cast the world below into brilliant moonlight, that he heard it—and saw it. A large gray form against the dark woods behind, near where those yellow eyes had peered out at him. This time a strange, whispering sound. A human voice, but not yet quite a human voice, the words indistinct. He was frozen with terror, unable to cry out, even to reach for his dagger. His only thought was *Heckla*!

Mists swirled in from the water, partly hiding the form, then drifted away revealing it more fully. He saw a hand raising a staff, the staff pointing at him. More whispered, hissing sounds. In the next few seconds clouds again covered the moon, and in the total darkness Harald felt even more terrified. His heart beat wildly because he could not locate his enemy. No protecting himself from something he could not see, yet he could hear its hissing, its breathing coming closer. The rune charm for protection, for safety—what was it? He desperately tried to remember what he'd done on the boat during that storm. Yes, yes, it was—was—Yes, that was it, beginning with the old "s" rune. With his finger he traced in the sand beside him. The hissing sounds, the breathing stopped. Just as suddenly the moonlight returned. There was only the darkness of the forest before him.

The experience left him limp and bathed in the sweat of fear. Stirrings in the brush, other strange noises woke him every time he dozed off. After an hour or so, the chirping of birds high up in the pine tree and faint gray streaks of light in the sky warned that it was nearly dawn.

Before he left this place, however, there was one thing he had to do. Taking up his dagger, he looked for something to write on. Over by the edge of the beach, something shone faintly in the moonlight. Picking it up, he saw it was a piece of old whale bone. Just the thing! Harald crouched down and began to dig his knife blade into its porous surface.

How to begin? He had to keep his mind clear, had to search his mind for the right rune, the right combination of runes. Yes, he thought, here is the one for *evil*, here is the one for *protection*. He had no idea how to devise one to represent *Heckla*, so he scratched what he thought should be the runes for both *sikkerhet* and *fugl*, because *bird* was one of her shapes.

Then he buried the bone under a large rock and traced the rune for protection on its surface.

Re-sheathing his dagger and shaking out sand from his damp woolen cloak, he pulled the skiff out from its hiding place in the brush. It slid quietly into the water. No time to think of the meat, the griddlecakes, and the apples taken from the *knorr*. He wrapped them back up in his cloak and tucked the bundle under the skiff's rowing bench.

He seated himself on the bench and took up one of oars, using it to pole the little boat around the rocky shore until he could enter the main stream of the river. Then he seized both oars and rowed into the current, trying to keep close to the shore where it wasn't so strong.

Rowing upstream against the current proved harder than he'd expected. By noon the sun was getting very hot. Sweat ran down his face and stung his eyes. His tunic was soaked through, this time with sweat, not seawater. Swarms of insects stung his forehead, his exposed hands as he rowed. Some of the insects were like those back in Norway, others he didn't recognize.

Thirsty and exhausted, he didn't dare stop, even though he saw many tempting places along the shore. There were springs emptying fresh, cool water into the river, water with which he could wash down some of the food he'd brought. It seemed he hadn't eaten for ages. There were shady and fragrant pine branches overhanging patches of smooth sand where he could beach the skiff and rest his tired arms for a short spell, even catch some sleep. But he could not stop. He had come to realize that his father and the others in the two longboats could pull much faster, with four sets of oars in each. He wasn't sure he could ever catch up, they must be at least two days ahead by now. But there was no turning back.

Just before dusk he noticed something through the mist along the riverbank. A tree had been chopped down, its clean-cut edges gleamed golden in the fading light. Even more surprising, some of the branches looked as though they'd been fashioned into a spit for roasting meat over a fire. In fact, there was a real smell in the air of burning wood and roasted meat. A surge of joy ran through him. "It's them, it's them," he called out, turning the skiff toward the spot, "Father, Father! Snorri! It's me, Harald!"

No one answered. All was quiet. After beaching the skiff, he walked a little way along the bank, even back into the woods. But he saw no more signs of the exploring party, other than marks along the sand where the longboats had been drawn up. Tears filled his eyes, no matter how hard he fought them back. Men do not cry, but he could not help it. He was exhausted and hungry, his face and hands burned. He did not know whether the party had camped there last night or the night before. Since the ashes were quite cold, it would more likely have been the night before, their first night out, given the fast pace they were capable of going. In that case, it would be nearly impossible to catch up with them, unless—unless—surely they would have to camp for more than one night in the same spot in order to rest, to hunt for food, or even to make further explorations away from the river.

With this hopeful thought, Harald made camp there that night. Digging down deep through the ashes, he found enough live coals to kindle handfuls of dry grass, then bigger and still bigger branches. Warming up Ole's rabbit meat on the spit the men had made, he felt more confident in having something hot in his stomach. He drew the skiff well up over the bank, and, unsheathing his dagger and laying it beside him, drew his cloak over him and fell almost at once into a deep and dreamless sleep.

Next day promised to be better. Cloudy, it wasn't so hot. And, while the insects were still annoying, they didn't seem to bother him as much—too full of blood—his blood—to suck out more.

New problems, however, rose up. He hadn't been rowing more than several hours before the river branched out into two main streams and a smaller one. Which one to take? How could he be sure? The smaller one, probably not. Farther up it narrowed into no more than a creek. He rowed the skiff up and back a little way into both of the larger branches. Still, he was uncertain.

Then as if by some miracle, he remembered hearing Awair and Snorri talking one evening onboard ship about rivers. They were talking about the rivers in Gotland. Snorri was bragging about one which ran through his farm, a big river, he said, must be the biggest in the whole of Gotland. "Ah, yes, my young lad,"

Awair replied, "the biggest is not the most important. It's the deepest, with the strongest current, the one which runs into the sea which is the most important. All the others run into it."

Harald looked again at the two branches ahead of him. He noticed some leaves floating downstream past him where he'd pulled the skiff to shore and was keeping it steady by holding on to a branch. They were traveling fairly fast. But some pieces of driftwood floating down the other branch appeared to be going much faster. That had to be the main stream. "Well, Awair, I hope you know your rivers," he said aloud to himself as he headed up what he hoped was the main stream." If Snorri had listened well, he would surely have directed his father the same way, down this very branch. At least Harald hoped so.

As the day wore on and he became more confident that he was following the right path into the wilderness, Harald began to take more interest in what he was seeing. At one turn in the river he saw three elk drinking at the water's edge. They didn't turn away, but watched curiously as he rowed by, their antlers still covered in velvet and due to grow a great deal before autumn, but already quite large and raised up higher than a tall man could stand—even were he big King Erik himself.

Harald smiled, remembering that day in the castle. And so, here he actually was, carrying out the king's plan. Sometimes it seemed hard to believe, other times he thought he must be dreaming. Any moment he would wake up in his own bed in his sleeping closet, back on the farm in Telemark, the sound of the cocks crowing, the cows mooing while going out to pasture.

By late afternoon he'd seen a number of bears, so huge and black that he was glad he was out in the river. There were deer coming down to drink, and antlered animals bigger than deer or even the great elk. He'd never seen deer-like animals that big, with velveted antlers that seemed to fan out into great scoops. Several times he caught glimpses of color through the trees—red, white. Once a flash of something bright, like metal.

Puzzling. That didn't seem to make sense. But he soon focused his attention on some funny little brown animals with striped tails and what looked like a black mask over their eyes. He had never seen any animals like that before. Great, if he could catch one and bring it home to his sister Anna as a pet. Maybe a small bear cub for Astrid, fierce like her. Now if he could just get back to Iceland and capture a troll—His mind played with how delighted they'd be, how pleased with him for bringing home such gifts. Home? So far away.

Suddenly Harald realized why thoughts of home had come upon him so strongly. The air was filled with that old familiar smell of wood smoke and roasting meat! He'd reached another one of his father's campsites.

Disappointed, he again found it deserted, although it looked like quite a bit of activity had taken place. The ground was all disturbed, branches broken off the nearby trees. Kicking a big branch aside, he discovered an axe half buried under it. He picked it up, puzzled. It did not look quite like the ones from the *knorr*'s weapons' chest. The brass wire decoration on the handle was a little different from Bergen style decoration. Turning the axe over, he noticed that one side of the blade was covered with rust. Strange. He couldn't explain it.

He was relieved to find that, this time, as he knelt beside where the campfire had been and stirred the ashes, some of the ashes were still warm. They were from the night before, which meant he was getting closer!

In his excitement he wanted to continue on, push the skiff at once out into the river, but soon thought better of it. Dusk was growing deeper, and he really needed to rest. He would launch the skiff even earlier tomorrow morning and row even harder all the next day. Surely he would find them by tomorrow night.

That night he decided to sleep in the beached skiff in order to lose less time in getting off the next morning. He seemed to be a lot farther south than before—he could actually see a few southern stars, like Orion. Now if he could only find the pole star, he could tell what direction the river was now flowing. At least the current seemed less strong. As he curled up in the bottom of the boat, he could hear things moving around in the deep forest overhanging both banks of the river. There was the call of a wolf, the cry of some night birds, one owl echoing another, the snap of a twig. But neither those sounds nor the stealthy stirring of the brush from time to time bothered him. They didn't seem connected to Heckla usual sounds. Was it possible his rune charm had worked?

Besides, he was getting used to wilderness sounds. Encouraged by the thought he was getting closer and closer to the others, he felt stronger, braver. He'd eaten all the food he'd brought, but no matter. He was certain he could catch up with them at the very next campsite. Then they would all go on together, journeying southwest as far as this great river would take them, encounter bravely whatever dangers came their way.

At dawn he woke up to blood-curdling cries. They seemed to come from all around him—the deep woods, the camp clearing. He sat bolt upright in the skiff, shaking off sleep, and seized the dagger lying by his hand. In the gray light he saw that the skiff was surrounded by strange looking men. They were smaller than Norsemen, darker skinned, with black hair. Some had long black mustaches. Their faces were streaked with red and white paint and they wore high headresses made from feathers, pieces of bright metal, and bone. His first thought was—*skrælings*! They talked excitedly among themselves. Several pointed spears at him, poked at his clothes, raised up a lock or two of his hair. The spears had stone, not iron tips.

Harald got to his knees and pulled out his dagger. The nearest *skræling* knocked it out of his hand with his spear and the dagger fell with a clatter into the bottom of the skiff. Now how was he going to defend himself? What would Njal do—Egil Skallagrimson? But they never had to face men like these!

One, who appeared to be their leader, motioned for Harald to get out. What choice did he have, without a weapon, surrounded by at least a half-dozen fierce looking warriors? As he stood there on the sandy beach, they gathered around him in a circle. They examined his red woolen cloak with interest, especially its black-and-white woven border. To his dismay, they held it out and began cutting it into strips, which they distributed among themselves. His beautiful cloak, cut to ribbons!

The chief and two other warriors went off a way under the trees and began what was obviously an argument. All the while they kept glancing back at him, shaking their heads. Harald was reminded of something, but under the circumstances it was hard to think clearly. He associated the memory with Greenland, with Astrid, with their ride up on the bluffs above Brattahlid. Yes, their faces reminded him of that face he'd seen in those bushes. So that was why Astrid seemed afraid, why she so quickly led them back down the trail. Harald was sure the three warriors over there were planning to murder him.

He fell to his knees and began a silent prayer to the Virgin Mary. He began one to Thor as well, also to Loki to apologize for identifying him with Ufila. Maybe Loki could change him into a fast-running deer, or a bird which could fly away and escape what seemed certain death at the hands of these *skrælings*

At last the three came back to where Harald was kneeling in the sand. They said something to the others, then motioned for him to get up. Continually prodding him with their spears, they forced him to walk along the shore to a deep cove, where a stream emptied into the river. There, hidden by branches, were two curiously shaped boats made from birch bark and curved up a little at each end. The *skrælings* motioned for Harald to get into one of them. The chief and two warriors climbed into that one, along with another warrior who took up a broad paddle and moved them slowly out into the main stream. The *skrælings* in the other boat paddled back to where Harald had camped with the skiff. They tied the skiff to their birch boat and, towing it, soon caught up with the first boat. They continued down the river, one boat behind the other.

The boats entered first one branch of the river then another, until Harald completely lost any sense of direction or distance from the main stream. The fact that it was cloudy meant that he could determine no directional bearings from the sun. He was convinced now, in fact, that he was so deeply imprisoned within the heart of this wilderness that he would never see his father or the others again.

At last they came to a landing place and the boat lurched suddenly as it grated on the gravel beach. *Skrælings* seemed to come out of nowhere to pull it up onto a grassy slope. Harald was again prodded with spears. Clearly that meant *get out of the boat*. Soon he was surrounded by a large crowd of *skrælings*, including women and children, all running down from a sort of village. It had strange-looking round huts, smoke rising up from them, dogs barking, people shouting words he couldn't understand. They gathered excitedly around him, pointing to his hair and clothes. The *knorr*'s skiff the *skrælings* had been towing behind their second birch boat was also an object of curiosity, especially the iron lock which secured the tow rope to the bow.

Harald tried to imagine what the old Vikings would have done in this situation. Should he try to stand and fight, as they would have done? Should he try to run—he could probably run faster that any of these *skrælings*. But he had no weapon, not even his short dagger, knocked out of his hand earlier. He had only bare hands. Their spears could reach farther and faster. With a sinking feeling, he realized he was helpless.

The crowd surrounded him cautiously as he walked with an armed escort up the slope. They stopped before one of the huts as the chief called out something. Most of the *skrælings* fell back, leaving only a small group of warriors forming a circle around him, with the chief and himself in the middle. The chief motioned for

Harald to sit down on the ground, while he himself remained standing. There was much talk back and forth, sometimes angry, sometimes questioning.

"Oh, Loki," he said out loud. "Please help me understand what's going on! Who are they? Why are they so curious about my clothes, this skiff, keep pointing to my hair? You're the only one who can give me the words to explain I'm not their enemy." One of the warriors seemed to nod at this, which gave him the courage to continue. "I mean no harm—I'm just here exploring the land for our King Erik." And the warrior nodded again! Was Harald's appeal to Loki really working? Now the man was speaking to the others, pointing back and forth between himself and Harald. Now Harald could only wait to learn his fate. It was in their hands. And Heckla's.

After what seemed a lot of talk between the warriors, several shrugged and walked away. The one who was clearly their leader disappeared into the nearest hut. Two of the warriors motioned for Harald to get up and follow them. They led him to another hut, out toward the very edge of the village, and shouted something to someone inside.

In a moment or two, the deerskin flap over the door was raised and an old woman came out. Her surprise at seeing Harald was obvious. She said something questioningly, and the men gave her some kind of answer. Stepping out of the hut, she seized Harald's sleeve and roughly pulled him through the doorway.

There wasn't much light inside. Harald at first couldn't make out anything, especially because his eyes began to burn from the smoke, rising up from the fire built on a pile of stones in the center. There was the strong smell of food and a strange smell he couldn't identify. Whether it was the unfamiliar smell or a combination of fear and exhaustion which caused him to lose his appetite, he wasn't sure. In fact, his stomach heaved and gurgled. When the old woman pushed him over toward a pile of furs in one corner, it felt wonderful to lie down.

Once he got used to the smoke and the darkness and had rested a bit while the old woman was occupied with something near the fire, he began to look around. The hut was actually round, constructed with large timbers and stones. The timbers formed a circle, meeting up at the center of the roof, and supported by a series of upright beams around the outside of the hut. There were rugs made from furs all over the floor, except for the stone fire ring in the middle. Some woven tapestries—mainly red, black, and white—hung over the walls.

But it was hard to take it all in, so great was his thirst. When the old woman finally handed him a wooden cup of something to drink, he propped himself up on his elbow and seized it eagerly. It tasted a bit like blackberries and it was wet. It went down so well, that he wasn't going to question its identity. Then, with a few more words, she took something out of a pot near the fire ring and held it out to him. It was a piece of meat, but blackened with a big bone in it. At any other time he would have accepted it eagerly—whatever it was. This time, however, that wave of nausea again welled up inside him and he shook his head. Falling back onto the pile of furs, he fell instantly sleep.

He must have slept through the rest of the day and the whole night. He could not be sure, but when he awoke it was early morning. Several people were speaking close by. The old woman had been joined by one of the warriors and two younger women. They were obviously discussing him. With a start, then anger, he noticed the warrior wearing around his head a strip of the red cloth torn from his own cloak.

After the warrior opened the door flap and left, one of the younger women came over and looked at him closely. He sat up, embarrassed at her intensive stare. She seemed about his own age. Above two long, shiny black braids, she wore a headband of twisted leather thongs, decorated with beads. Her eyes were very large and dark. What a contrast to Astrid, he thought, and wondered whether her smile would be different. Would she have Astrid's mischievous giggle? But she was not smiling as she held out a small, folded bundle, pointing first to it and then to his torn and dirty tunic. Shyly, she drew back when Harald reached out to take the bundle. Unfolding it, Harald realized that it was a clean tunic meant for him to put on.

Then the old woman came over with something else, some sort of britches made from soft leather. He'd never seen clothes made from that kind of leather. It had a golden sheen to it. Although he welcomed the idea of changing his clothes—after all, he'd been wearing the same ones for days—he wasn't about to do it with all those women in the hut, staring at him. He stood up holding the tunic and britches and motioned for them to go out. After a pause, the old woman nodded and let out a cackle of laughter as she shooed the others out, following them through the door flap. When the flap briefly opened, Harald caught a glimpse of a warrior with a spear standing guard just outside. And that one even had a strip of his cloak's checkered border around his head! So much for any thoughts about escape.

Harald removed his boots and his thick leggings, his broad leather belt with its empty dagger sheath, finally his woolen britches and outer tunic. He still kept on his linen body shift, it wouldn't be decent without it. Drawing on the leather britches and tying them around his waist with a sort of leather thong drawstring, he noticed how comfortable and soft to the skin they felt, much preferable to his heavy woolen tunic. As he prepared to pull the tunic the girl had given him over his head, he stopped in surprise. It wasn't made from leather, as he'd expected. It didn't seem like the tunic he'd seen some of the *skræling* warriors wearing. This tunic felt somehow familiar to the touch. If only he could see it better—the light in the hut was so dim! He took it over to where the rays of sunlight were streaming into the hut from the smoke hole opening. He saw, to his amazement, that it was of dark brown wool, with a small green and red embroidered band around the neck closed by a silver clasp, the same border repeated on the edges of the sleeves, the same loops at the waist to support a broad leather belt. No, it wasn't anything like he'd seen the *skrælings* wear. If not wearing some sort of blanket-like cloak, they were dressed mainly in leather vests of some sort, or shirts of brightly woven cloth. No, this was not a *skraeling* thing. This tunic had come from Norway, he was certain, the wool from Norse sheep.

But how did the *skrælings* come by it? What did it mean? He shuddered as he drew it over his head, wondering if its previous owner had been killed, murdered even. Where was his body lying, rotting somewhere nearby? He wondered if the same fate lay in store for him. Dressed in these strange clothes, he lay back down on the fur rugs to wait.

As the day wore on, Harald grew more and more impatient. Each time he tried to leave the hut, a warrior standing just outside forced him back in with the point of his spear. He caught a glimpse of several more armed *skrælings* not far off. The impossibility of escape was bad enough, but all day long *skrælings* came in to look at him, as if he were some kind of exhibit.

Toward evening, the head man himself came in with the girl who'd given him the tunic. This time they both sat down opposite him on the fur rugs at the other side of the fire ring. Harald wondered whether the girl was the chief's daughter. After the meeting with so many other *skrælings*, it was now possible to compare her with others he'd seen that day, and she was indeed somewhat different, a person of some importance. The head man's daughter? A sort of princess?

Shortly, the old woman brought in some food and served first the chief and the girl, then offered the same to Harald. He felt more like eating by then and actually enjoyed the sweet, yellow cakes and what appeared to be something like the blood sausage his mother used to make back in Telemark. And he was grateful for the pottery jug of cool, fresh water and the black-berry tasting stuff. He wished he could understand everything the chief was saying to him. To be polite, he merely nodded his head occasionally. As they rose to leave, the girl came over to where Harald was sitting, knelt down, and laid his old dagger at his feet. Then both she and the chief disappeared through the door flap without another word.

Harald did not understand what this meant, but he thought of several possibilities. Did it mean they meant to kill him and then bury him in the skiff with all his belongings, like the Viking ship burials of old? A hero's death, but he was not ready for it. Did they mean to kill him and bury him next to the rotting corpse of the man whose tunic he wore? Could it have been Astrid's father's tunic? Or Karlsefni's? It must have been, where else could they have gotten it? He shuddered. Eventually kill him as they obviously did Thorkel and Karlsefni? Keep him here in this village as a sort of pet animal? He'd rather die.

Worse of all, did they intend to marry him off to the chief's daughter? Although, for the moment at least, he felt more secure having his own dagger once again sheathed at his belt, his anxiety increased. He hoped it was not fear he felt. It was not proper for a Viking to show fear. Not to know where he was, not to know what might be in store for him was not the kind of situation he'd hoped for, even though, on this enterprise of King Erik's, danger was only to be expected. Yet he hadn't expected *this*. Yet he'd brought it all on himself.

Or was it Heckla's curse? The curse she'd laid upon Thorkel and Astrid's family? Had the protection rune, *protection from the bird*, which he'd written back at the landing beach not worked? Or worn off? At any moment, Harald expected her to open the door flap of the *skraeling's* hut and enter. More likely, she'd suddenly appear behind the swirling smoke of the fire pit, and point her stick at him. She was coming after him, he was certain of that!

Chapter Eight
Through the Mists

Harald expected Heckla to appear any moment through the swirling smoke from the fire ring. It was his the second night in the *skraeling* hut. Afraid to close his eyes, weaken his guard, he never took his hand off the dagger at his side. Up through the hut's smoke hole he watched the sky continuously lit by blue-white flashes, followed by crashes of thunder shaking the very timbers of the hut and the ground underneath.

The rain swept over the sod roof in sheets. It came through the smoke hole and eventually put out the fire with great hissing noises that sounded like snakes, that sounded like Heckla that first night on the shore—her gray shape against the dark woods, hissing, whispering. Grandfather used to tell an old story about the Norse god Thor, who hurled his thunderbolts when he was angry. The god Thor seemed very angry that night. Harald was sure Heckla was also angry with him. Sooner or later she'd trap him. But hadn't she already trapped him? Escape was impossible. He was doomed.

Sleep was also impossible. Even without the storm, Harald's thoughts would have kept him awake. Propping himself up on his elbow, and clearing away a small space on the bare dirt floor, he traced again the rune charm denying her power, just to be on the safe side. Falling back on the rug, he tossed and turned, his mind full of conflicts. Anger—his father had shown no confidence in him. Guilt—he'd gone against orders. Fear—he couldn't repress it.

Once or twice he did manage to doze off. During those short moments of sleep, he often dreamed of his father, out somewhere in the wilderness. Other times brought confused images and sounds. Toward early morning, he dreamed that a large bird, like the one he'd seen near Heckla's cave above Eriksfjord, swooped down and carried him off in its sharp talons. High above the pine forests they flew, above rivers glistening like snakes, over lakes that shone like liquid silver, thunder booming all around them, until the eagle said something. Harald couldn't hear because of the thunder, couldn't answer. This angered the eagle so much that he let go. Harald fell down, down, down. The rush of air against is face sucked his breath away. The ground rushed up toward him and he crashed into it.

The crash woke him up. He discovered he'd rolled over in his sleep and thrashed around in that terrifying dream until his head hit one of the timbers supporting the hut. The rush of cold air on his face came from outside. The next flash of lightning revealed a small opening in the wall—part of it torn away by the force of the storm, the rush of water washing away some dirt at its base.

Was it big enough to crawl through? Harald took his dagger, scrapped more of the dirt away. The old woman who slept on the other side of the hut called out something. Harald froze in his tracks. Nothing more, she must have been dreaming.

Carefully and as quietly as he could, he dug away at the dirt until it was just big enough to put his head through. Good, the opening was on the opposite side of the hut to where the *skraeling* stood guard outside with his spear. Just beyond lay the woods encircling the village. With a little more digging, he got his shoulders through, wriggled out the rest of his body. He was free—but what next? Where could he go? His skiff, if he could only get to his skiff! That was impossible, he'd have to go past the guard, through the whole village, before he could reach the landing place.

As an afterthought, he reached back in through the opening to pull out one of the fur rugs as a covering against the rain and pulled it over his head. He snaked on his belly through the grass until he reached the edge of the woods. Getting to his feet and crouching down until he was bent nearly double, Harald dashed into the darkness, heavy wet branches slapping against his face, roots tripping him. Stumbling and fighting the branches, he didn't dare slow down. He ran on and on, he wasn't sure where. Then, a sensation of going down hill, the sound of running water.

By the sound, Harald guessed he was on the bank of a stream. And by the feeling underfoot—he was thankful he'd kept his boots on for fear the *skraelings* might take them—he seemed to be on some sort of a cleared path along the edge.

Which way now? His instincts told him to turn right, away from the village. But his brain reasoned that, by going left, he'd come eventually to the landing place where the *skraelings* beached his skiff. That skiff was his only means of escape, of survival. Did he dare risk being seen there, re-captured, perhaps speared to death on the spot? Yes, he had to, no choice. As he ran left down the path, a distant flash of lightning revealed immediately ahead the boat landing below the *skræling* village.

Harald lay down in the wet grass under the fur rug. He couldn't tell whether anyone was standing guard up there. He hoped the storm had covered his escape, that they wouldn't have expected it. But now the storm was passing. Still crawling on his belly through the grass, the fur rug over his head, he crept a little ways up the slope to the where the skiff was turned over on its side. Good, the heavy rain hadn't filled it. His hand touched the mooring rope lying loose on the grass, one oar beside it.

Quietly Harald slid the oar into the skiff and began to inch the skiff down the grassy slope toward the water. Once there he quickly climbed in, positioned himself on the rowing bench, and used the oar as a paddle to move the skiff out into the stream and around the first bend. He paused, listening for someone to raise the alarm. Was anyone following him? Still quiet, only distant thunder. Now out of sight of the village, he dropped the oar pin into the oarlock. But what good was only one oar? He'd have to paddle, but that was too slow. Then his foot touched something in the bottom of the skiff—the other oar. The next moment Harald found himself rowing very fast downstream, away from the village toward he had no idea where.

The dawn brightened. Hanging raggedly over the stream was drifting mist, which gradually changed from gray to rose. Harald tried to calculate how much distance was growing between him and the *skræling* village. He reckoned at least two leagues by now. He hoped he was choosing the right channels as he entered first one stream, then another. He couldn't remember the maze of waterways, even small lakes, which the *skrælings* had taken him through. So much water, so many days ago. He'd lost all sense of time, of direction, and had no idea where he was.

The only thing he had to go on was that the sun was more often than not in front of him. This could only mean he was heading in a southerly direction. He'd gone the wrong way. He should be heading north, back toward the *knorr*. No, that wasn't right. He'd left the *knorr* to join his father's two longboats, and that's what he now intended to do.

He traveled all day, stopping only twice briefly to rest and drink some water from a spring emptying into the river, eat some wild berries he'd discovered nearby. His stomach told him he hadn't eaten for what seemed a very long time. His brain, however, reminded him that food at this point was the least of his worries. Sometime late in the afternoon he entered a main channel and followed it for several hours. When the sun began to descend toward the western horizon on his right hand, he knew he was still heading due south.

Night was falling fast and he had to stop. For fear the *skraelings* might be following him, he dared not build a campfire, not even sleep ashore. The channel had widened out into a small lake. Best sleep in the skiff, let it drift out on the lake and hope the current wouldn't take him too far off course. Wherever that course was.

By noon the next day Harald realized from the location of the sun as well as the few stars he'd been able to sight the previous night that he was veering more toward the southwest. It seemed he was still rowing against the current. Nowhere along the way had he discovered any evidence of his father's group, no sign of a landing or camp. Once or twice, though, he was sure he heard distant drums and strange cries that could only come from a human voice using birdcalls as signals.

The small lake opened up into a much larger one, long and narrow, extending due south. That night he felt far enough away from the *skraeling* village to risk camping on its sandy shore. He wished he could make campfire, although he had nothing to cook on it, in fact, he had no flint stone to make one. A fire would at least have taken the chill out of the night air and provided some sense of comfort. He did have that fur rug, though, and, sheltered in the roots of a large tree, curled himself up in it, hoping sleep would overcome his hunger pangs. Why hadn't he thought to snatch up some of that food left in the hut?

The morning's breakfast consisted of more blueberries and water from the lake. Looking down the length of the lake, Harald wondered how much longer he could keep on rowing. His arms ached, he felt dizzy from lack of food. Bright sun glancing off the water hurt his eyes. Then he had an idea. If he could find a long, straight branch or two for a mast, supple vines, he might be able to rig a sail in the skiff. But what for a sail? That fur rug wasn't very big, but with enough wind it might just move the boat along, and faster than he could row.

The fur rug made a small but still usable jib sail. Now that he had a closer look at it, Harald noticed it was made from the hide of a very large, dark brown animal, with shaggier fur around the shoulders. A strange kind of animal he'd never seen before. He cut off narrow strips of hide with his dagger to make thongs for tying. He tied the mast upright against the rowing bench. If he held one of the oars off the back of the stern seat, he'd have a kind of rudder. With the animal skin stretched as a jib-sail, the little skiff sped along in a strong breeze. Soon he was racing along far out down the middle of the lake.

Here, he thought, *I'm much safer. With the sail I may be able to go faster than any of the skrælings' boats. If they're after me—and they're sure to be by now, maybe I can lose them.*

For one whole day he sailed down the long lake, keeping the eastern shore in sight on the left. As it grew dark, Harald was desperate for rest. By now his whole body ached with the effort of keeping the steering oar in place or adjusting the rigging. His eyes hurt from facing the sun and the stabs of sunlight on the water, and he was weak with hunger.

"Got to make camp for the night on shore," he muttered incoherently. "Got to rest . . . rest." On the shore just off to the left a tall pine marked where a rocky beach came down to the water and he steered the skiff toward it.

It was nearly dark. Harald calculated that by now he'd gone much farther south, since he'd lost the northern mid-summer twilight which continued through the night in Norway, in Greenland, too. Yes, he must now be far to the south of Greenland. Maybe he'd come as far as Vinland. What if his father and the two longboats were actually heading to where they figured Vinland would be? By now they would already be days and days southwest of where they'd left the *knorr*. Maybe they were even turning around, heading back to the *knorr*? But if that were so, he would have met them returning.

But suppose they'd taken a different route? It seemed hopeless. This wilderness had no end, not even an Edge. Harald struggled not to let despair conquer him as he pulled the skiff up onto the rocks for the night.

As he did so, he noticed something strange just at the water line. He snapped out of his daze, not believing. Impossible! A Norse mooring stone, just like the one he'd seen when they'd first landed from the *knorr!* But how old was it? This one seemed to have fresh chisel marks. Someone camped here, and not too long ago. Immediately he started to look around, to see what other evidence he could find.

There were no other traces, other than the charred remains of a campfire, some unused chopped wood stacked beside it, and a few low shrubs with broken branches. Surely that was evidence his father and the longboat crews had spent the night here. His spirits soared—he was on the right trail! He was catching up—they couldn't be more than a day or so ahead.

Then a more sober thought—the *skraelings* might well be following whoever camped here last. They would have tracked the signs, most likely left scouts along the way. It would not be safe to stay here, he dared not risk it. Reluctantly he headed back toward the skiff brought up on the rocks. He'd need to sleep in the skiff again out on the lake, take down the jib-sail, and hope the wind wouldn't cause him to drift back to shore, back into the hands of the *skraelings.*

When morning dawned behind heavy, foreboding clouds, Harald discovered that he'd been able to keep his distance from the shore through occasional paddling with one of the rowing oars. Once again under sail, the skiff moved swiftly through the water until just ahead it seemed that the lake was narrowing. In fact, both east and west shores appeared to come together, melting into one another. The wind died, and now the skiff was merely drifting toward a dead end.

What now? Would he have to leave the skiff and continue by land? And to where, then? It was a dark, heavy morning, the sky thick with gray clouds, mist lying heavy on the river. The weather seemed to echo Harald's discouragement. The sail was no longer of any use, best take it down, he might need the fur pelt later.

As he stood up in the skiff, he saw that the lake did not end. As if by some miracle there suddenly appeared a big river continuing on beyond the lake just around a point of land. Harald rowed straight for it.

Here and there the skiff nudged against sandbars, the first warning that the river mouth was treacherous. Upstream proved little better, for the river twisted and turned, sometimes widening out into almost a lake or narrowing into connecting channels. It was studded with small rock skerries or islands. To make the passage even more difficult, he was rowing against the current, because the river was flowing into the big lake, not the other way around as Harald would have expected.

"Watch out!" he cried out loud, rowing with his back to the bow. Good thing he'd glanced back over his shoulder and seen that rocky skerry just ahead. He pulled hard on the starboard oar to swerve the skiff sharply to the right. It was hard to focus on the way ahead while rowing. If he smashed the skiff, he'd be in deeper trouble than he was.

Coming sharply around the rocks, grazing the side of the skiff as he did so, he faced a smaller branch of the river, partially concealed by overhanging branches. Something—just a little ways in there! What was *that*? Harald rested on his oars, took a second look. A strange sight. An unbelievable sight! He gave a shout. "No, no—it can't be!"

To his utter amazement, the unmistakable dragon prow of a longboat rose up out of the mist. The boat rocked gently in the water, moored by a bowline to a large rock on shore. "A Norse long boat, my father's long boat!" he shouted, standing up in the skiff in his excitement. "Halloa there, Father, Snorri—Svein—it's me, Harald!"

His sudden motion would have tipped the boat over but for the fact that he grabbed an overhanging tree branch and used it to pull the skiff closer to shore. Then he sat down and used one of the oars to guide the boat up onto a partially submerged rock shelf and tied the rope to the drooping branch of a willow tree.

Eagerly Harald jumped out and scrambled along the rocky shore to where the long boat was moored. "Father! Father! Snorri!" he kept shouting. He glanced into the boat as he passed, but there was no one in it. Strange, the oars were not in the boat either. Everything else seemed to have been stripped away, although the storage chest bolted down in the stern was still locked. It took a moment to realize that this was not the long boat in which he'd last seen his father. It was the second one, with Hakon as its captain. But where *was* Hakon? And his men? An eerie quiet hung over everything. The place seemed deserted. Where *was* everyone?

Harald looked around. It was a large campsite, all right, both longboats much have camped here together earlier. He saw the remains of a campfire, the charred wood cold. Suspended over it was a big iron kettle and tripod used for cooking, the remains of some meal still in it, flies buzzing around. Three of the longboat's eight oars he found leaning up against a tree. Several others he thought he saw lying over near a group of thick cedar trees. Idly kicking aside some brush, he uncovered a broken spear shaft. Next to the spear shaft lay a body, face down.

A chill ran down Harald's spine. He felt as if someone had kicked him in the stomach. What had happened here? An attack of some sort. Hesitantly, Harald turned the still form over with his boot. He gasped—the crewman named Ingmar. He recognized him from some time they'd spent together back in Greenland, when he'd helped Ingmar with re-caulking the *knorr*. From the blood on his face and clothes, his paleness, there was no hope the man was still alive. He walked over to a clump of bushes—more bodies there—Kristian, Trygve, and Peik—kind Peik, as young as himself, Peik, who'd listened to his stories about Njal and Skallagrimson! Hakon, whom his father had made captain of the second longboat, lay partially on top of the body of a dead *skraeling*, one hand cut off.

Harald knew he'd find the remaining five scattered around under bushes, under the trees. But where was the other longboat? Why had his father not tried to save these men?

Shocked at the horror he'd just seen and full of agonizing questions, he sat down on the end of a log and buried his face in his hands, his whole body shaking, his stomach heaving. For a long time he did not know what to do. These men had been massacred—if he stayed, they would find him, kill him, too. Yet if he moved on, he would leave these brave men exposed, unburied. That, he decided, he could not bring himself to do.

Throughout most of the day, Harald dragged the bodies, one by one, to a grassy clearing under a circle of cedar trees. The last five he found half-lying in the river, the water eddying around their bodies red with blood. He laid them side by side, Captain Hakon and his crew. There were no weapons to lay beside them, like the Viking burials of old. All the weapons seemed to have disappeared.

Yet there was something Harold felt he could do, some old custom his grandfather had related to him. Scattered among the trees nearby and along the shore were large greenish rocks. It took him several hours of intense lifting, pulling, shoving to gather enough to build a cairn over the bodies, a rocky grave protecting them from the wolves and other wild animals. He would name this site the *Camp on the River Red with Blood*.

It was getting dark early, the heavy clouds all day threatening a storm. Harald knew he had to get away from the spot. First, though, he had one more thing to do. He found some flat, black stones, and placed them on top of the cairn in the shape of a raven, the king's symbol. He found a yellow stone for the beak. He wished he could have done more, but time was running out. The longer he stayed, the surer the danger from any *skraelings* who might return to this spot to recover any booty left, or who might still be trailing the other longboat—the one with his father and Snorri.

But wait! What about *this* longboat, Hakon's? If the *skraelings* found it, they'd use it to pursue his father. He couldn't just leave it here. The quickest solution would be to burn it, but, even if he could find a flint stone left somewhere around the camp, he couldn't risk that kind of signal fire. Maybe he could trying breaking it up with an axe—there was surely one locked up in the storage chest in the stern. He shrugged his shoulders. He'd nothing to break the lock with.

Scuttle the boat? Yes, that was it. He could try filling it with rocks, sink it in the river. That would take time, but was the only solution. It would also mean the boat could be recovered if it needed to be, in the event his father's boat was lost. He hurriedly ran back and forth along the river bank, throwing whatever good-sized rocks he could find into the bottom of the longboat. At last it sank down to the level of the gunnels. Harald was exhausted. There was no way he could lift another single rock.

Then he had an idea. Wading out into the channel, he began to rock the boat back and forth. With each motion, more water poured over the sides and the boat sank lower and lower. Finally, with bubbles gurgling up around it, as if it were alive and drowning, Hakon's longboat disappeared under water. He hadn't calculated the height of the dragon prow, however. Even with the boat resting on the bottom of the river, the dragon's head was clearly visible. It rose up above the water, and looked to Harald like some sort of sea monster about to swim up river.

"Not a bad thing, in fact," he said to himself. "The *skrælings* might think these boats are possessed with demon spirits—maybe the sight of that would keep them from recovering the boat!" Suddenly he remembered the oars back at the campsite. He had to hide them. And so, searching until he found all eight, he hid them under the low, thick branches of a cedar tree.

Harald was much troubled by the horrors of the day and the continued threat of danger. In fact, his mind seemed to be in a kind of fog, not working very well. He rowed upstream until it was so dark that it was impossible to navigate that difficult channel farther. He tied the skiff to a low-hanging branch, stretched out as far as he could in it to get some rest. There was one consolation, and that was that he'd been able to recover some of the food so hastily abandoned in the longboat camp—a few dried pieces of salted fish. Yet they stuck in his throat when he tried to swallow them and made him feel sick. He thought of the man who might have enjoyed that salt fish, who would now never taste it.

    The next day promised to be another dark, dull day, with low clouds and probably rain. Patches of mist clung to the water, swirling here and there in the lazy currents of air. Because of the mist, it was difficult to keep a sharp lookout for rocks or skerries or overhanging branches. And the river continued to narrow, so there was less room to maneuver. Still, Harold did his best to glance ahead for any obstacles and listen for any unusual sounds. Sometimes he got a warning by hearing the current gurgling against rocks. Sometimes the mist cleared. In a strange kind of way, the ducks and wild geese also helped. Because they liked to perch on the rocks in mid-stream, their noise provided warning signals.

    But then came a different kind of sound, coming from the shore on his left. What he heard quite distinctly was the sharp crack of branches breaking near the bank, not far behind him. Then a rustling in the underbrush near the shore, a cry. Was it human or not?

Chapter Nine
Runes Beyond the Edge

"hey –ooo—hu—oo!"

"What was *that*?" Harald glanced nervously over to the bank of the river. Nothing except thick underbrush. Cautiously, he maneuvered the skiff closer to shore.

"Huy—oo—hu—here," more insistent. Twigs snapped and a pale hand pushed aside a few branches. There stood a figure dressed in a dark green tunic and a ragged-looking short gray cloak, trimmed in orange fox fur. Harald gasped. He knew that cloak! The figure emerged fully from the brush to stand at the very edge of the bank. No mistake, even though he was now hard to recognize. His black hair and beard were matted and full of bits and pieces of branches and leaves, his clothes were stained and torn. Part of the orange fox fur on his cloak was ripped off, one legging and boot gone, that leg bare and bleeding from deep scratches. He was a miserable sight.

"Is it you, young son of Bjorn?" the man whined. "Is it really you—*here*?"

Loki! It was the Goth, Ufila, all right! What in the name Loki, was he doing here—alone, and looking as if he been dragged through the woods? For once his appearance matched his true character.

Harald drew closer to the shore, steadied the skiff by wedging an oar between two large boulders. "Ufila," he shouted, "where's my father? You were in his longboat, not Hakon's."

"Your father, young Bjorn? His longboat?"

"Yes. You were with him. Where is he—and the other longboat?"

"Don't know," he shrugged.

"You don't *know*? Come on—how could you *not* know? And what are you doing here?"

Ufila made a few more whining noises, stepped down off the bank into the river, and began wading out toward the skiff.

"Oh, no you don't," and Harald pushed against the rock to move farther out. "Not until you tell me what happened."

"How should I know? Besides, it's none of your business."

"It *is* my business! We are all part of the same commission."

"But, kind, heroic sir . . ."

"Stop your whining, your empty flattery!"

"But, kind sir, no time to tell you, there's no time to lose. We are in grave danger. Those *skraelings* may come upon us any minute. Please, I shall tell you—tell you all, but we must leave this place. Every delay puts our lives in danger. Please, oh please!"

"All right, then, get into the skiff and be quick about it." The wretched man was probably right. Harald already suspected they were being pursued. "And sit there on the stern bench, so I can keep an eye on you—no, not forwards, the *stern bench,* I said*!*"

Ufila was indeed a pitiful sight as he climbed into the skiff. He tried to draw his tattered cloak around him, hide his one bare leg and foot behind the other. He kept wiping his nose and sniffing.

"I'll have the truth sooner or later, never fear," Harald insisted, and he checked to see whether his dagger was still in its belt sheath. He set the oars in motion once again. Best to get as far up the river as he could before he tried to question Ufila. He was certain Ufila knew something about the River Red with Blood and the massacre back there. For certain he had some idea about Bjorn's whereabouts.

RUNES BEYOND THE EDGE

Harald rowed steadily for about a half mile. "Now, then, Goth," he insisted, "speak out." He rested on the oars and waited.

Ufila seemed unwilling to answer.

"We'll not go on until you tell me."

Ufila whined, wiped his face with the torn edge of his cloak.

"Even if it means the *skraelings* catch up with us."

"Well," Ufila began, looking fearfully behind them and all along the banks of the river. "Well, kind sir, since you put it that way."

"Go on."

"Well, you see, the *skrælings*, came upon us."

"Who were *us*? *Both* longboat crews?"

"No, the other longboat had already gone farther south."

"That was my father's. When was this?"

"One day at dawn. Yes, one day at dawn it was. About the second or third day at the camp."

"Why did you stay? You were part of my father's crew."

"Well, yes I was," Ufila stammered. "But you see, I stayed behind with Hakon. I, well I—er—you see, I had some business to do. Yes, some business."

"*Business*? What kind of business?"

"There was some—some smith work." Then, in a rush, "Yes, smith work on one of—one of the—er—swords. And yes, some—er—and some spear heads, yes, that's the business I had to do."

"I thought your business was to be with my father," Harald retorted, suspicious. His explanation did not sound right for two reasons. First, Harald remembered his father had insisted on keeping Ufila with him, under close watch. And secondly, all the weapons, all the equipment had been put in good order before the two long boats left and headed up river from the *knorr*. His father had seen to that. "You're lying—I want the truth from you," he demanded.

"No, no, young sir," whined Ufila. "You see, there was a . . . a . . . a change of crew. It was, as you might say, for mutual benefit," he added with a sly smile.

Harald had enough. There was no point in questioning this creature any further. Harald wasn't sure how he was going to deal with him, but, for the moment, he'd keep him under close watch. Otherwise, Ufila would certainly attempt to get rid of him, steal the skiff. Where he'd go after that was anyone's guess. Serve him right if he simply got swallowed up in this wilderness—or dropped off the Western Edge, if that was a real concept and the earth simply ended, by dropping off far to the west where the sun set.

But, no wait. Then again, Ufila might be useful. So Harald said, "All right. You'll be dealt with later and punished. For now, though, whatever your story is, I demand to know exactly how long ago it was when the first boat left the camp back there."

"What will I get out of it if I tell you?"

"What you will get if you *don't* tell me is *this*!" Harald unsheathed his knife and laid it in the bottom of the skiff under his foot.

Ufila made several more whining noises.

"And I intend to use it."

At last Ufila said, "Well, er—well, if you're going to put it like that." He wiped his nose. "Well, they went, er—they went up stream."

"How long ago?"

"Maybe two—three—four days ago."

"How many days *exactly*?"

"Can't remember." When Harald reached for his dagger, he added, "Oh, yes, let me see, now. Yes, it was three days."

"Why'd they go on, leave the other longboat?"

"Well, you see Bjorn wanted to explore more of the wilderness."

"Why?"

"I don't know. We saw that the land was less forested, more fertile, good for settlers. And food."

"What about food?"

"We were running low. He hoped to find bigger lakes with more fish. Fields with wild grain of some sort. Don't know what else." Ufila was now producing a surprising torrent of words.

"When did he plan to return to that camp?"

"Don't know, " Ufila mumbled with a shrug. "He would never have confided in the likes of *me*."

"Then we will continue up stream until we find out, find my father and the others."

It was just possible they were less than three days ahead of them, at least he hoped so. They probably stayed more than a night or two at one campsite in order to hunt and fish. With that thought, his eye on Ufila squirming on the stern bench, he set his back to the oars and moved the skiff swiftly forward.

As they went up the river, Harald watched the riverbanks closely for any sign that the crew of the other longboat might have camped there. With each bend, around each outcropping of rock, Harald hoped beyond hope there would be some evidence of the first longboat's passage, or, best of all, the longboat itself. But there was nothing, and the day was growing late. Darkness would soon be upon them and they would have to make camp somewhere for the night.

What Ufila reported was true, however. The forests were becoming less dense and the countryside revealed rolling hills. Some of them appeared covered with grass-filled meadows, bright with purple, white, and yellow flowers. Bright, sparkling patches in the distance suggested small lakes. The river they were following began to offer more connecting channels, some of them ending only in swamps. In fact, Harald hesitated several times, uncertain which channel to follow. Mist began to form again, drifting along the banks, in and out of the trees. The river widened, narrowed, then widened again into a series of small lakes, where they had to navigate around skerries. This proved highly dangerous, for mist hung especially heavy over the lakes.

"Not safe to go on," whined Ufila. "You'll wreck the skiff, kill us both. Please, please, heroic sir, I beg you—look for a good camping place for tonight, young Bjorn."

"And let you escape?"

"Where would I go?" He gestured around him. "Consider this. Together we may stand a better chance of survival—both in the wilderness and against the *skraelings*."

There was some truth in that, even though it went against him to trust Ufila. He'd have to stay awake all night to stand guard over him. But he felt exhausted and couldn't go on much farther.

Harald searched the banks on both sides for a place to camp. There was a skerry, a small island just ahead which might do—they'd be protected by the surrounding water. As they approached it, however, he realized he couldn't moor the skiff along its sheer rocks. "We can go on a little more," he said, disappointed, but refusing to give even a hint of hesitation to Ufila.

It was then that he saw it. A plume of smoke rising up from the woods some distance ahead of them. "A campfire!" Harald cried out. "It could be my father." Summoning all his remaining strength, he rowed as fast as he could, mindless of the rocky channel, of the treacherous mist. "Look—that smoke—it can't be so far away!"

"It could also be *skrælings'* smoke," Ufila warned. "If I may be so bold as to say, kind sir, we should keep as close to the river bank as possible until we're sure whose smoke it is."

Well, that made sense, and was something, coming from Ufila. They'd have to be prepared to move quickly out into the main channel to get away if they had to. But because of that Goth in the stern, the skiff sat heavier in the water, and he couldn't make as much speed as before. Too bad he couldn't just throw him overboard, tow him along by a rope in the water until he drowned, like his father had threatened while still at sea.

But, as to that smoke in the distance—if they were in fact *skraelings* over there, not in the middle of river but camping in the woods, they'd probably come overland. In that case, they wouldn't have their birch-bark boats with them. And that meant he might be able to get away in the skiff if he rowed fast enough. But if they were the *skraelings* who traveled in their birch-bark boats, then he'd never be able to row fast enough. He'd be caught for sure. He didn't care about Ufila's fate, but he did care about his own. He stopped this horrific line of thought before it could overpower him.

Through the mist lying low on the water, he saw a good-sized channel appearing on the port bow. It seemed to lead in the direction of the smoke plume. Taking that course, Harald discovered very shortly that the channel opened out into a large lake. Which way now? Still more channels opened out from the lake, it was like a maze! His eye on the rising smoke just ahead, he pulled harder on the starboard oar and turned into the channel marked by an enormous oak tree.

They continued down the smaller channel for several minutes, when it, too, opened out into a large lake with a low, sandy shoreline and a large, rocky skerry in the middle. And that skerry was the source of the smoke.

The smell of meat roasting over an open fire filled the air. It must be them, it must be! "Halloa! Hey!" shouted Harald. Without thinking, he dropped both oars, stepped up on the gunnel, and jumped right out of the skiff into the water.

The cold water was a shock. As he went under he desperately tried to remember how he'd kept afloat that other time, when he'd slid down the *knorr*'s rope after the skiff. He thrashed his arms and kicked his feet, screamed for help when he came up for air, than plunged down again. Water forced its way into his mouth and nose. He panicked. It shouldn't be like this. He'd been able to swim before.

A strong arm caught him, pulling him up, up to the surface. He gulped in as much air as his lungs would hold. The first thing he saw when he opened his eyes was a face wearing a funny, twisted kind of smile.

"Told you, dumbhead! You should've learned to swim. Maybe I'll just let you drown. Then again, maybe the fish won't want you, either. So I'll just tow you to shore."

"Snorri!" Harald gasped. Impossible to believe, against all odds, but, yes, it was him, his black, curly hair falling down over his eyes from the dripping water, his funny smile. This time, however, his usual sarcasm was softened by the twinkle in his deep brown eyes. Harald threw his arms around Snorri's neck out of pure joy—or was it to keep from sinking again?

"Watch out there—you'll drown us both! Come on now, I've got you, let go my neck, just roll over on your back and kick your feet. That's right. See, you're floating, and we're moving toward shore. Just you wait, I've sure got some questions to ask you! And your father will for certain, later!" Snorri half-dragged, half carried him, dripping wet, up over the bank to the campfire.

Snorri's joking had an ounce of bitter truth in it. Harald would sooner or later have to answer to his father. As part of the king's commissioned crew, Harald knew he should be punished for disobeying orders. After all, he'd deserted the *knorr*, endangered its crew by stealing the skiff. He was a traitor, a criminal, no better than Ufila. As he stood, waiting for his father to speak, pronounce his doom, he ducked down his head and braced himself for what was to come. He began to shake, whether from being wet and cold or from fear, he couldn't tell. He waited for the worst. But the worst did not come.

Instead, "Come on, then, let's get some dry clothes on you."

Harald looked up. It was not his father, only Snorri standing there. "My father," he asked, "where—"

"Not here, only myself and Grimm over there. I see he's got Ufila already tied up. Good. I'll explain later. They left a chest full of supplies with us, I'm sure there's a spare tunic, leggings. Here, take off those boots, we'll set them near the fire to dry out."

As Harald and Snorri hunched close to the fire that evening, after a welcome meal of roast pheasant and duck eggs, they talked long into the night. "So much to tell you, Snorri," said Harald.

"An awful lot to tell you, too. Although your story had better be a good one—or your father will—"

Harald had a fair idea of what he was about to say. "Let's not talk about that. I want to hear how you got here, where the other longboat is."

"No, you first."

"No, you."

"Well, all right." And he related how angry he'd been to be left behind on the *knorr*, how he'd taken the skiff and headed out in search of the two longboats in order to be a part of the king's commission. He described the *skraeling* village, how he'd been captured, about the chief's daughter who'd given him the gifts. But his mind turned again and again to Heckla and her evil doings. "She's laid a curse on me, I know it. She's following me. She's still out to destroy me, even though I put out some rune charms against her power."

Snorri laughed. "*Rune* charms? Oh, come on—"

"No, seriously, I'm sure they worked. And they'll work again if I need them, I just know it. I saw her, I really did—more than once, heard her, too. "

"Well, never mind, you can give me those ridiculous details later. You were going to say more about that *skraeling* princess you were about to be married off to. Now that sounds really interesting," and he rolled up his eyes. "Oh, and about your escape, of course."

So Harald once again went over that part of his story, providing a bit more embellishment here and there. He compared the *skraeling* princess favorably with Astrid, even though he knew it wasn't true. Still, he didn't feel up to the part about what he'd discovered the day before at the site of the second longboat camp.

He simply couldn't find the words. In fact, his throat felt dry and his stomach heaved just thinking about it.

"Now your turn, Snorri," he said, desperate to change the subject. "Why are you here with just Grimm? Where's the first longboat and my father—and the others?"

"Grimm and I were left here to meet Hakon and his crew when they arrive. Hakon's longboat remained just where the river came out of the big lake in order to do some hunting, fishing. Necessary to find food along the way, you know. When Hakon and his longboat do finally arrive—and they should be here anytime now, in fact they're already overdue . . . anyway, when they do arrive, we are to tell them which direction your father's boat was taking, and where they are to meet up."

Harald still didn't have the heart to tell him the truth. "Meet up? Were you and Grimm supposed to continue on in Hakon's longboat then, until it reached my father?"

"Yes, and now they'll just have to make room for you and Ufila, too. Then we'll meet your father at what he considers the farthest point of this voyage of discovery. From there, we'll turn around, head north, and eventually reach the *knorr*, then back out of the great inland sea, then back home."

Harald felt a growing sense of despair. It was clear that Snorri knew nothing about what happened back there to Hakon and his men. Should he tell him?

"Your father," Snorri continued, "felt that we'd come about as far as our resources allowed. We've seen enough of the country, mapped it, to make a good report to King Erik, don't you think? Of course, too bad we haven't found those two Greenlanders, Karlsefni and Thorkel."

"But Snorri—I think—" He considered telling Snorri about the strange axe—and the tunic he'd received in the *skraeling* village. But he really didn't know what those things really meant? Were they connected to these men?

"Won't be long before we're all on our way home," Snorri interrupted that line of thought.

"But Snorri—" How was he ever going to break the news?

"Just look at all this beautiful land around here! Good for settlements, just as the king hoped. He'll be so pleased with all this information—give us all big rewards. Say, what do you think you'll ask the king for?"

"That's not important just now. Snorri, listen. There's something I've got to tell you."

"More about that beautiful princess, I hope?"

"No—no. It's serious, terrible news. It's so—" Harald got so choked up he was sure he couldn't talk about it. The tragedy was still so fresh in his mind, the dead faces of the men, the blood, the evidence of a horrible struggle.

"What terrible news, then?"

Harald sat hunched over, his face in his hands. Sensing Harald's struggle, Snorri immediately changed his expression. "Tell me, friend, as best you can." He came over to sit beside Harald, put his arm around Harald's shoulders. "Hearing bad news," he said softly, "is part of our discipline."

Harald was touched by Snorri's gesture. It wasn't like the Snorri he thought he knew. "You see—that second longboat with Hakon," he hesitantly began, "the one you're expecting. It isn't coming. It'll never arrive." And he forced himself to describe the scene as he came upon it, the cairn he'd constructed with rocks over the bodies. But he broke down completely before he could describe how he'd scuttled the longboat.

Snorri listened intently, only a few short intakes of breath betraying the keen emotions he felt. "A horrible loss," he finally said. "Brave men they were, heroes, and fought bravely."

"But what are we to do now, Snorri?"

"We'll just have to go on. You, Grimm, and I will take your skiff, and go down river to the place your father described as the meeting place. When we first camped here, he sent two men on ahead to explore. They came back with the details, the way to get there. I have it in my head—your father made sure I had it in my head, since I was supposed to lead Hakon there."

"What about Ufila?"

"Well, I don't know. Just leave him here?"

"We can't do that. He's got to tell us exactly what happened back there, his part in it. He's got to be properly tried and receive his sentence from the king."

"That's a real problem, all right. I wish we could just sentence him here. He'd sure get what he deserved!"

But Harald had to consider the king's justice. "What about this? That skiff is too small for four men. See those logs over there, chopped down for the campfire? We can take some vines or leather thongs—or something—and tie them together, make a raft, tow it behind the skiff. It'll be slow going, but if, as you said, my father's plan was to wait at the meeting place until you arrived, he must surely still be there."

"Hmmm, that might work," said Snorri doubtfully, smoothing back his unruly hair as he often did while thinking. "Ufila's hardly worth the effort, though. But you know, there's real danger in staying at this campsite any longer than we have to. I'm sure the *skraelings* are tracking you. You know it, too. Obviously they're hoping you'll lead them to the other longboat. We've got to leave first thing in the morning, then make our way south with the utmost speed."

And so they worked through the night to fashion Ufila's raft. The raft turned out to be just big enough for the Goth to sit with his knees drawn up, his hands tied.

"Probably wouldn't float very well being pulled through the water," Harald observed. "Ufila's bound to get soaked. Ironic, don't you think? Almost the punishment my father threatened after we left Iceland." He and Snorri couldn't help laughing at the look on Ufila's face.

It was just before dawn. Harald and Snorri had managed a few hours sleep after building the raft. They lay curled up on the ground close to the dying campfire, while Grimm kept guard over Ufila, lying tied up in the skiff. "Snorri, are you awake?" Harald kicked him gently. No answer. "Wake up, I need to talk to you." Still no response. He kicked him again, harder.

"Uh, what is it?"

"Listen, Snorri. This is important."

"So is sleep."

"I've got to talk to you."

"All right, but say it quick."

"It's about my dream."

"Your dream? You woke me up to tell me about your *dream*?"

"It wasn't only about that—it was—" How could he say it? Snorri had already rolled over again in disgust. "No, Snorri, listen. It's what this dream meant." Well, maybe Snorri wasn't interested, even still awake, but he'd tell him anyway.

"You see, it was like this. I dreamed about the catastrophe back there at the river camp, the loss of Hakon and his nine men. But in this dream, see, everything seemed exaggerated—bigger than life. Bodies everywhere, blood everywhere. It seemed like I was frozen—couldn't move, couldn't do anything to help. In this dream, everything seemed exaggerated—gaping mouths, strange cries from nowhere, blood covering even the trees."

Snorri sat up, touched Harald gently on the arm. "I know it must have been horrible for you. But now, think back. The king probably expected such things on this commission."

"But those men—all lost. Men I knew. And such a death, hardly deserved."

"They'll have fought bravely, you know."

"That's just it. They should all be honored, remembered in some way. But how to honor them—that's what I've been wondering."

"Don't you think that'll happen once we get back to Norway?"

"What if we don't get back? What if no one ever knows?"

"Hmm, I see your point," said Snorri. "Well, we can't do much about it, I'm afraid." He lay back down and rolled over. "Let's get a little more sleep while we can."

But Harald couldn't stop thinking about it. "Those men back, there. Too bad they couldn't be honored according to old Viking custom, in a boat, with all their weapons, set afire and sent out to sea."

Snorri sat up again, clearly annoyed. "Oh, come on. How could you have done *that*? Where's the sea? The boat? The weapons? Didn't you just tell me you'd piled rocks over their bodies, left some sort of sign, marked it with stones?"

"Yes, yes I did that. It was difficult, but that's just what I did. The problem is, no one will never know about it—who they were, why they were killed there." *Marked by stones.* The image brought to mind things his grandfather had told him.

"I just thought of something," Harald added. "Runes—I know I used them as secret charms—and they kept us safe at sea—me safe from Heckla."

"That's what *you* think."

"No, no, I'm convinced. But my grandfather also told me about other kinds of runes. These you could write on stones as some sort of secret message, a memorial to the dead. They could make sure brave men would be remembered, long ages afterwards. The only thing is, I'm not sure I know enough of them to leave that kind of a message."

"Well, you can count me out," Snorri sighed and lay back down. "And don't wake me up again with anymore dreams, anymore stupid ideas."

It was not quite light, just a pale grayish cast to the sky. Disappointed at Snorri's lack of interest, even sympathy, Harald got up and looked around for the storage chest his father's longboat had left behind. In it he found a small axe, a chisel, and a hammer, the last two tools normally used for making mooring stones. .

He went up through the woods cresting the skerry to where there was a small clearing. After some searching, Harald found just the rock he wanted—a large, flat slab, about the length of a man's arm, shoulder to wrist. It was about as wide across as from wrist to elbow and about as thick as his hand with the fingers spread out. *This will do fine, looks like gray granite,* he said to himself, and began to chip off some of the side to make it look more rectangular.

"No wait, have to do something else first." He laid the stone back down, picked up a smaller, smoother one and set to work on it."

"What on earth do you think you're doing?" Snorri appeared before him, hands on hips. "Do you think we've got time for such nonsense?"

"This is important, Snorri. Of great importance. Those men—they should be remembered. Us, too, our whole voyage of discovery."

"Well . . ." He hesitated. "Us as well? If you're going to put it like *that*—"

"And don't forget, people will need to know that we've been here. That we've claimed the land in King Erik's name."

"I see. Well, I guess if I don't give you a hand we'll be here forever. What do you want me to do?"

So while Snorri began chipping away at shaping the large stone, making sparks fly off the axe blade, Harald quickly chiseled the rune charm letters he'd used against Heckla on the smaller one, just to be on the safe side. He hoped they'd also work against the *skraelings*.

"What does *that* mean?" Snorri leaned over to look.

"A charm, something to protect us against our enemies," replied Harald.

"Pah! Bunch of nonsense," commented Snorri in disgust.

Harald paid no attention to his remarks, but quickly buried the rock under the roots of a nearby tree. He wished it were an ash tree, that was part of the rune charm's power, but there were none in sight. Then, brushing off some lichen from the surface of the big, gray rock which Snorri had finished shaping into a kind of rough rectangle, Harald began to cut letters into the upper left hand corner by pounding the top of the chisel with the hammer. "First," he said, "I'm going to say who we are."

ᚠ:ᚤᚯᛏᛘR: ᚬᚬ:ᚠᚠ:ᚼᛂRRᚤᛁᚾ:

"Well, what do you know?" exclaimed Snorri, as Harald finished the last rune. "I'm in there! *8 Goths and 22 Norsemen*—that means me! I'm one of the Goths. Are you going to add my name?" he asked.

"Course not," said Harald. "No time for names. " He continued to chisel, then paused. "How would you describe the king's commission?" he asked. "Voyage of discovery? Voyage for claiming land?"

"Aren't they the same?" Snorri responded. "Doesn't matter, use the shorter word."

So Harald wrote.

ᚬ: ᚬᛒᛃᚤᛌᛏᚴ ᛌᛏ ᚠᚷRᛒ: ᚠRᚬ:ᚤᛁᛌᛏᚷᛌᛒ:ᚬᚠ ᚤᛖᛌᛏ

"Hmm, can't read that," grumbled Snorri, looking over Harald's shoulder.

"It says *on this discovery voyage from Vinland over the West*," Harald answered, scarcely slowing down the chisel. "Now I have to mention the ten men who were killed back there, the ones from Hakon's longboat. Here it goes—but I'm running out of space, I'll have to make it smaller."

ᚠᚷᛌ: ᛂ:ᛘᚷᛌ:Rᚯᛒ ᛏ: ᚷᚠ:ᛒᛌᚬ ᚦ: ᚬᛌ:ᛒᛂᛒ

"Is that all?" Snorri asked. "Come on, we've got to finish this business quick!"

"No," said Harald, "not finished yet. We must pray to the Virgin Mary for them to guide their souls to Heaven and protect us."

Runes Beyond the Edge

ᛆᚢᛘ᛬ ᚠᚱᚮᛏᛁᚴᛁ᛬ ᚮᚠ᛬ ᛁᛚᛚᚢ

"Well, well," Snorri commented dryly. "Her along with all your old Norse gods—you sure are hedging your bets."

The sun had just edged up above the eastern horizon. "Hurry up, Harald!" said Snorri, looking worried. "Not much time, we've got to get off this skerry immediately!"

"Only a little more," Harald answered. "I've got to mention Aiwar, those ten men back up there on the *knorr*. What if something has happened to them?" And so he added against Snorri's protest.

ᚼᚮᚱ᛬ ᛬ᛘᛆᚾᛋ᛬ᚢᛁ᛬ ᛬ᛆᚽᛁᛏ᛬ᛆᛏ᛬ᛋᛁ᛬
ᚮᛒᛏᛁᚱ᛬ᚢᛁᚱᛁ᛬ᛋᛆᛁᛒ᛬ᛁᚠ᛬ᚦᛆᚢᚴ᛬ᚱᛁᛋᛁ᛬ ᚠᚱᚭᛘ᛬ᚦᛁᛋᛁ᛬ᚭᚼ

"Hurry up, hurry up," Snorri was saying. "Now read it to me."

So Harald quickly read off the runes: "*Have 10 men by the sea to see after our ships 14 day journeys from this island.*"

"All right, all right. That has to be it! Time's running out."

"Just one more thing—only one more. We've got to remember the king's plan—his commission to claim the land we stand on. I've got to add the date, and not in those old runes, either. It has to be an official kind of record, in figures all can read."

So Harald took his dagger and hastily cut in the date. " ᚼᛁᚱ᛬ᛁᛋᛁᚠ 1362

Now it says, *in the year 1362.*" After that, he stepped back to admire his work.

"Looks impressive, I hate to admit," commented Snorri. "But we shouldn't leave it just lying here. Here, let's stand it against that bigger rock, put smaller stones around the base. Makes it look more—more official. Wonder what people will say later, when they find it?" He turned to head down to where the skiff was moored. "Now let's go south to find Bjorn, then turn around north to the sea, and then due east. All the way to Bergen fjord!"

Chapter Ten
Distant Drums

Mist was rising above the lake as they pushed off, drifting in thin wisps, hanging over reeds along the water's edge. Harald took the first rowing shift, thankful the current was with him not against him as before. Snorri sat as lookout in the bow, Grimm in the stern on watch duty. Uflia protested loudly at being towed behind on the makeshift raft, the water continually sloshing over his feet, sometimes higher.

The rising sun was already warm on Harald's back, the west wind on his face fresh and cool. "How fine it is on a day like this, Snorri," exclaimed Harald, "especially with the thought we'll soon join my father and his crew. After that—home!"

"Not so fine for *him*," Snorri replied, with a sneer and jerk of his head toward Ufila. "He'll not be looking forward to full punishment, I reckon!"

Harald nodded in agreement. He also suspected Ufila had not confessed everything and was hiding something important.

The skiff rocked suddenly. Grimm rose to his feet and raised his hand. "Stop rowing, Harald! Listen!"

Harald held the dripping oars suspended over the water. Moving forward from its own momentum, the skiff slowed until it simply drifted silently with the current.

Deep beyond the quiet was a sound. Grimm must have heard it first. For a moment, Harald could not identify that *thump, thump,*

thump, dull and rhythmic off in the distance. He'd heard such a sound back in the *skraeling* village. Then he knew. It was a drum.

"Just as I feared," said Grimm.

Harald's heart sank. *Skraelings*! He recalled the scene of death and destruction at the River Red with Blood. Would it be like that for *them*? Were they to fight and die? Who would carve *their* memorial stone? No one would ever know they'd been here.

"What are we going to do now?" Snorri asked. "Those sounds seem to be coming from behind us, and not too far back, either."

"What's ahead, Snorri?" called Harald.

"Looks like two channels leading out of this lake."

"Which one do we take?"

"Bjorn's instructions were to take the one on the left, going due south. That should lead to the meeting place."

Harald hesitated. "But that would bring us closer to the *skraelings*. By now they've reached our last camp, know we've left and are heading south. Most likely they're waiting down along the banks of that left-hand channel, or intending to. They'll for sure attack us once they've assembled other tribes along the river. Those drums must be a signal. No, they'd probably wait until we met up with my father's longboat, attack us there. We'd just be leading them to another massacre, another victory for them. Suppose we took the other channel?"

He brought the oars into the boat, stood up on the rowing bench, shaded his eyes against the sun, and searched the distance ahead as far as he could see. The boat stood quiet in the middle of the lake, gently swaying from the ripples "It looks to me like they're part of the same river, that they divide around a fairly long and narrow island, then meet farther on down."

Snorri shook his head. "We can't be sure of that."

"It's worth a try to avoid falling into the hands of the *skraelings*, leading them right to Bjorn," Grimm pointed out. "Worse comes to worse, we can always portage back to the other channel." He pointed back to Ufila. "And *he* can carry his own raft."

"But if we can elude the *skraelings*, get ahead of them and reach my father before they realize it, then head back another way—"

"Of course that'd be the best plan. Guess we don't have much choice, then," said Snorri. "All right, Harald, let's row as quietly as possible across the lake and enter the right-hand channel. It looks more difficult to navigate. Just look at those narrow, overhanging branches reaching into the water in some places."

"All the more reason to take it," Harald pointed out. "They won't expect it."

That channel proved treacherous. The skiff with the weight of three men—even with its shallow draft—hardly cleared the bottom. Worse still, because the dense forest shut out the sun, the mist was slower to rise. They couldn't always see far ahead, and there were many obstacles like half-exposed rocks or floating logs. The boat slowly scraped and bumped its way through the narrow stream for nearly an hour, twisting and turning now south, now west, now south again. No one spoke. All eyes and hands were focused on getting through and coming out finally into the left channel. That's where they were supposed to be and hopefully well ahead of the *skraelings*. *Boom—boom—BOOM boom*. All ears were strained toward the sound of the distant drum, faint at times, other times dangerously close.

By mid-afternoon they reached a place where the stream divided again into two.

"Now which one, Snorri?" Harald asked.

He shook his head. "Well, looks like only hope we have of getting back to the channel we need is to take the left one."

"No, we've come too far. I see now it was a mistake to think we were going around an island in the river," Harald said ruefully. "We're in a different channel altogether! It'll be impossible to portage across now! We don't know how much distance lies between that channel and us—could be several leagues. What do *you* think, Grimm?"

"Really can't say," said Grimm with a shrug. "It's up to you. Guess you and Snorri are in charge. You, maybe."

Ufila shouted something. "Left channel, oh, please, left channel, kind sirs!"

"Quiet, creature!" Snorri shouted back, "no one asked you. Harald, just take a look at that left channel," he pointed out. "We couldn't navigate it. Don't you see, only a little ways ahead it ends in what looks like a swamp. We don't have a choice, unless we continue on foot."

"That'd be such slow-going, more dangerous for sure. And listen—" Harald suspended his oars for a moment. "Sounds like those drums are keeping up with us, way over there to the east. Even if we tried portaging, tried to rejoin that main channel, they'd be waiting for us—right there!"

"We need to make an important decision, then," said Snorri. "Harald, listen. You came down this way by yourself all the way from where we moored the *knorr*. It seems to me you might have a better sense of how to get through this awful maze of waterways. I have to confess, I wasn't paying too much attention coming down in the longboat with Bjorn."

"What do you propose, then?" Grimm asked.

"Well," said Harald, "it seems to me—well, let me think about it a minute. To make the wrong decision would be the end of us for sure." Could he form in his mind the rune for safety? Would a mental image work the same as a written one? He rested on his oars, squinted his eyes shut, thought hard, concentrated. Yes, there it was, there was that *S* rune. He opened his eyes. And to his surprise, he saw that the skiff was slowly drifting into the mouth of the right-hand channel. More surprising was that the way looked clear for some distance ahead. The rune charm had worked!

"This one," he said, "we'll take this one. We'll still be going south at least, in the same direction as my father." He couldn't express his fears that they would never be able to make contact, that they would end up too far west and too far south from where his father and the longboat waited. He could now well understand how it was that Thorkel and Karlsefni had been lost in the wilderness and never returned. And what if Heckla had once again worked her power, caused him to drift into the *wrong* channel? Suppose she'd worked a counter-rune charm?

By early afternoon they found a small sandy beach on one side of the channel and decided to take a short rest. It was time for Grimm to replace Harald at the oars, Snorri to keep guard over Ufila, and Harald to be the bow lookout. They stretched out on the grassy slope leading down to the water's edge. Ufila was kept out on his raft, his hands and feet still tied, despite his whining protests.

"Hear that, Harald?" Snorri asked, cupping his hand around his ear.

"Hear what? I don't hear anything, except Ufila."

"That's just the point. The drums sound more distant, less often."

"Does it mean we've gotten ahead of them?" Grimm asked hopefully.

To Harald, this was not good news. The greater distance between them and the drums meant they'd veered more to the west. That meant the distance between them and where his father waited was greater.

He imagined a kind of triangle with equal sides, picked up a stick, and drew it in the sand. "Look here, Snorri," he said. "Now here at the top point is our last camp. If we go down to one bottom point, that's where my father and his men are. Now we're at the opposite bottom point."

"Looks simple enough," Snorri commented, smoothing back his hair. "Too simple, maybe."

"So it would look like our hope of reaching him is now slim." It was a sickening realization and hard to admit. "Instead of closing in on the meeting point, we've gone off at an angle deeper and deeper into the wilderness."

"You mean the wilderness of no return? You mean we can never get back?" Grimm asked desperately.

Harald couldn't think of an answer to give him. He couldn't lie by offering the reassurance he lacked himself. He thought of Heckla. Had she planned this all along? He didn't dare mention Heckla to either Snorri or Grimm in this connection. Although Grimm might have been a few years older, at least that's how it was during the voyage in the *knorr*, he now seemed much younger than himself. In fact, how strange, Harald reflected, that he now felt older than even Snorri. Maybe Snorri and Grimm had gotten younger while he'd gotten older. They seemed to be looking to him as their leader. Had King Erik known that all along that this would happen?

Snorri broke into his thoughts. "Well, what do we do now?" He added a half-hearted twisted smile.

"I think," Harald began somewhat hesitantly. "I think we should get back in the skiff and continue rowing." Then, more firmly, "Are you ready there, Grimm? The first thing is to put as much distance between us and those drums as possible."

"Then what?"

"We'll just have to see how far this channel goes, how much longer we can navigate. From what I've already learned about this wilderness, it'll turn into more small lakes, more channels, a maze we'll have to figure out as we go."

"Figure out? For what—to where?"

"Don't you remember how rivers flow, Snorri? Aiwar once told you about that. Watch for the deeper, stronger current—that advice worked for me before, maybe it'll do that again." He got up from the bank. "Come on, let's get moving. Grimm, your turn to row."

For the rest of the day, navigation was treacherous, but not difficult except for low hanging branches. As Harald predicted, once again they were faced with a number of streams issuing out from it in different directions.

"Here we are again," commented Snorri. "The eternal maze. What a country—so far from the sea, yet so full of water!"

"Couldn't we camp here at this lake for the night?" Grimm asked. "In the morning we can see better which channel to take." He didn't admit it, but Harald could tell by his increasing lack of effort at rowing that he was tired and wanted to stop.

"That may be true," answered Harald. "Looks like a sandy beach over there, we'll beach the skiff by that pine tree."

They made camp, tying Ufila to the pine tree, and ate what little food they'd brought from Bjorn's original camp. "I'll keep watch," said Harald. He wouldn't put it past Ufila, with his Loki character, to figure out some way to escape.

That night the stars were clearly visible as Harald sat on the shore, keeping his eye on Ufila, his ears tuned for drumbeats. Although he couldn't help but be impressed by the magnificent sight above him—layers and layers of stars studding a black and moonless sky, it worried him. So many stars weren't visible farther north. This meant they'd come very far south, possibly more south than the southernmost tip of Norway. If only he'd been able to retrieve his astrolabe from the *knorr's* sleeping cabin, if only Awair hadn't been sleeping there the night he left. If only—If only—

He looked up into the sky. With a start he recognized several of the constellations—Orion in the south, *Karlsvogna* to the north. North! The Pole Star! They might be able to find their way back that way! Two constellations pointed to the pole star—*Karlsvogna* and *Lille Bjorn*. Harald located the brightest star on the wagon and the bright one up on the little bear's head, then drew an imaginary line between them as the base of a triangle. He angled the two sides of this imaginary triangle upwards to where they met. That shimmering star at the triangle's apex was surely the pole star. And that was the way north.

Next morning as they prepared to break camp, Harald made a proposal. "Here's my idea. Over there across the lake are a number of channels, some going south, others due west, one going slightly northwest."

"Well, then, we should take the one to the south, keeping the sun at our right hand during the morning, shouldn't we?" Snorri asked. "We still have a hope that way of finding Bjorn and his men."

Harald shook his head. "I'm convinced we've gone too far south for that to happen, and are now too far west to try to go across country. And if you listen carefully, when the wind's in the right direction—from the east—you can still hear occasional drumbeats. At least I did last night. No, my proposal is to take that channel over there, the one which seems to turn toward the northwest."

"Why?" Snorri looked skeptical. "Why *northwest*—the exact opposite to what we want."

"I could be wrong," said Harald. "But I have a hunch that all these channels and all these lakes come off a big river of some sort. At least that's the way geography works in Norway, so why not here? Now listen, if we can just reach that river, then maybe—just maybe—that river flows into the big lake I came down just before coming across Hakon and his men."

"A lot of *maybes*," said Snorri, even more skeptical. He walked a few nervous paces back and forth along the shore. "But just *maybe* it's worth a try. Not that we have much choice. I know what you did onboard the *knorr*. So I'm willing—I guess—to trust your knowledge. As for any instincts, though—don't know much about *them*, being practical myself."

Taking the channel running northwest, they soon found to their disappointment that it was growing narrower and shallower. The skiff occasionally stuck on a sandbar and they had to get out, wade through the water, and push it off. Getting back into the skiff, they discovered leeches attached to their bare legs, and removing them left painful sores. Those small, shrill whining insects which had so plagued Harald his first day out from the *knorr* now attacked them mercilessly.

"Well, Harald," retorted Snorri by midday, "where's your big river now?"

Grimm seemed disappointed, even angry. He said little, became more withdrawn, even sulky. Harald noticed this and it made him uneasy. They had to stay together, defend themselves together, or else—

Ufila, for once, was past whining. He sat on his raft, soaked through, bunched up miserably into a small ball, his head down on his knees. It was as if he'd given up and was simply waiting for the end. That was, however, fine with Harald.

The channel became a small stream, passed through shallow marshes, finally ended in a swamp. The skiff could move no farther. They'd come to the end. At that point, Harald realized he'd made a terrible mistake.

"Well," asked Snorri, folding his arms across his chest, "what now?"

What *could* they do? Peering ahead beyond the swamp, Harald noticed that the land leveled out to low, rolling hills and that most of the forests had given way. The swamp was surrounded by clumps of tall grass. He wondered how difficult it would be to walk through this grass if they were to continue on foot. He still believed that the big river lay just beyond.

"What do we do with the boat?" Snorri asked.

"Scuttle it. If we leave it here as a clue, it'll be for the *skraelings* like a big finger pointing to the way we've gone." He reached into the skiff for the axe. "Good thing we brought along those few tools my father left." It was a hard decision, destroying the skiff. He and the skiff had come so far together. It had saved his life more than once. He swallowed hard as he handed Grimm the axe. "Here, Grimm, set to work, and Snorri, see if you can submerge the pieces under rocks and among the reeds. We dare not leave a single trace. I'll wade through the rest of this swamp and have a look at what's ahead of us."

Grimm grumbled as he began to destroy the skiff. Ufila had come back to life and was protesting being left on the raft. "No, Ufila," shaking his axe at him, " you just stay right there until we decide what to do with you." He clearly hated the man.

After about an hour, Harald returned. "It's mostly grass out there, very tall grass, seas of grass, a few trees. Some big shaggy-looking cows grazing—we might be able to kill one for food." He recognized them as the same animals as the pelt he'd taken from the *skraeling* village. "Glad to see you've still got your bow and arrows, Snorri. They'll be useful for hunting. We've only got enough food in that bag for one more day."

"They're my only weapon, you know that."

"What about me? What about me?" Ufila whined. "Are you going to leave me here to die? Please, oh please, I couldn't stand that. Please, kind son of Bjorn, kill me first, put me out of my misery."

"We'll just have to take him with us," said Harald with a sigh. "Another problem, but we can't leave him here. Grimm, untie his feet, get him off the raft."

"I'll hide that raft," Snorri said, and pushed the raft through the shallow water until it was hidden deep inside a clump of reeds.

With that, the four of them began to make their way through the swamp, sometimes wading and trying to avoid dead tree stumps, sometimes walking on soggy strips of land. Every once in a while they had to pull off leeches. It was slow going, and tiring. Harald realized they had to find some shelter for the night and rest.

"That clump of trees over there," he said. "Let's make for them. I'll check our course by the stars tonight, we'll get an early start tomorrow." No one disagreed.

The next day's march was not difficult. They tramped through what seemed endless oceans of grass, broken occasionally by clumps of brushy trees, a few pines. It was to Harald, in fact, like walking on the sea, flat as far as the eye could see, the wind causing the grass to look like rippling waves. By mid-afternoon of that second day, however, it was a different matter.

"That hot sun," complained Grimm. "It never lets up—not a cloud in the sky!"

"It's the wind, that's the worst," Snorri added. "Good thing it's sometimes at our backs, otherwise we'd be going backwards for sure."

But for Harald, the main problem was lack of water. Ironic, he thought. They'd just come through so much of it, now the goatskin flasks were empty, and his mouth felt like it was stuffed with wool. He was concerned that their march through the prairies was becoming slower and slower. Even Ufila had to be dragged along by the rope which Grimm kept attached to his belt.

Suddenly Snorri was shouting. "Look, look over there! Water!" In the near distance was a small lake surrounded by a grove of poplar trees. It meant fresh water, cool shade, a brief rest. He ran on ahead, whooping and leaping through the tall grass. Then he stopped to allow the group to catch up. Under the dark shadow of the trees at the edge of the lake something was moving. "Some deer! I'll try to get a shot at one—we'll have water *and* food tonight! Careful now, don't scare them off."

But as they came closer, they saw it was not deer but rather a group of people. *Skraelings!* Maybe six or seven of them. Harald drew his dagger, unsure of what do. The odds were certainly against them. Then he noticed that two of the *skraelings* were women, in the act of drawing water in large clay jugs from the lake. They screamed, dropped their jugs, and ran to hide behind some trees. Two *skraeling* men rushed at Harald, raising their bows as they did so. The third actually hurled a spear, which dug into the ground just at Snorri's feet.

"No, wait!" cried Harald. "We mean you no harm." It seemed to him these *skraeling* warriors were quite different from the others. They were taller, the men were naked to the waist and wore a sort of leather loincloth elaborately decorated with beadwork and quills. One of them wore a headress made from an animal head with huge horns, the same animal as the ones they'd seen grazing on the prairies. The warriors seemed to be getting impatient, their hands tightening on their bows.

Thinking quickly, Harald unslung the leather bag containing the very last of the salted fish and held it out toward them. The men hesitated, but did not lower their weapons. What else could he do? "Snorri—Grimm, put your weapons down on the ground, then sit down."

"Are you crazy?" demanded Snorri.

"We've got to stand and fight," Grimm insisted.

"No, we'd have no chance. We have to try it this way." He sat cross-legged on the grass, laid his dagger down beside him. Reluctantly, Grimm and Snorri did the same. Ufila collapsed on the ground beside Grimm, the rope still attached to Grimm's belt.

Although the three *skraeling* warriors hesitated, still suspicious, they lowered their bows a degree or two. After some talk between them, they sat down opposite, staring at Snorri's sheaf of arrows which he carried on his back. "An arrow," said Harald. "Give them one, they don't have iron arrowheads, they use flint." Snorri grumbled that he couldn't spare any, but at Harald's insistence, pulled one out and handed it, feathered end first, to the largest of the three warriors. They examined it eagerly, ran their fingers along the edge of the arrowhead.

When Harald offered the leather bag of salted fish, the second warriors took it, opened it, then showed it to the others. They seemed more interested in the bag than the fish, because the bag was one of those provisioned by the king, with the royal crest painted on it in right shades of red, blue, and gold. They excitedly exchanged a few words amongst themselves, then, to Harald's surprise, one of them reached into a pouch slung over his back and offered Harald something wrapped up in a piece of animal skin.

Harald bowed his head in a gesture of thanks. "Should I open it?" he asked Snorri.

"Well, since they opened their gift, that seems to be the right protocol."

Harald unwrapped the package. Inside the leather covering was a series of large leaves, inside them some of the blood sausage type of thing he'd eaten back at the *skraeling* village.

"Say, look at this, will you?" he gasped, holding up the piece of animal skin. It was cut from a similar provision bag as the one they had, except that the fragment of the design still left looked slightly different, its colors faded. "What do you make of it?"

"Hmm, looks like part of an animal—part of the head."

Harald took a closer look. "No, look! It's a dragon, part of a painted drawing of a dragon's head, like the ones on our boats." What could this mean? The surprise rendered him speechless. "Do you think," he finally managed to say, "do you think this might have something to do with Thorkel or Karlsefni?"

At the word *Thorkel*, one of the *skraelings* said something excitedly to the others. He pointed to the piece of leather Harald held in his hand, to the pouch Harald had given him.

"Thorkel?" Harald jumped to his feet. "Thorkel? Do you know this name? Do you know where he is?"

"Toor—kul—Tor-kul—" One of the warriors repeated the name several times, pointed to Harald, then to Harald's yellow hair, to the fragment of the pouch, then to the western horizon.

What did this mean? If only Harald could understand. "Oh, help me, Loki," he muttered. He made signs with his hands, tried to describe the motion of a boat going through water, pointed north, brought his hand down to point at his feet. "Help me, Snorri," he pleaded, "help me communicate. We've got to find out more about Thorkel." There were more exchanges of words and gestures, the name repeated several times, as well as the name *Busse*. After another question or two, the warriors simply shook their heads and got up from the ground.

It was hard for Harald to hide his disappointment. They knew no more than before. Was Thorkel dead or alive? From what he could understand, Thorkel was dead in the wilderness far out to the west.

He thought of Astrid, back in Greenland. As brave a girl as seemed to be, it was going to be difficult to tell her his father was gone forever. That is, if he himself ever got back. He now doubted it.

The *skraelings* called to the women, still hiding behind the trees. They came timidly out and retrieved their water jar, looking suspiciously at Harald's group all the while. Then, placing the jars on their heads, they joined the warriors. The group left walking—or rather gliding, for that was how it looked to Harald—quickly south through the endless seas of grass. One of them seemed to lag behind, trying to catch up. The grass was so high, at times over their heads, that the group of *skraelings* was quickly swallowed up.

It was a strange encounter, leaving more questions than answers. "Well, at least we can fill our water flasks," Snorri commented. "About that blood-sausage looking stuff they gave us—well, I'm not sure about that, have to be really desperate before I'd eat it."

"It's really not too bad," offered Harald. "Food, anyway. But come on, let's be on our way because we've no time to lose. Although those *skraelings* were different from the others—the ones with the drums—we can't be sure we won't be attacked by another band. And we've got to reach the river, the long lake as quickly as we can."

"Well, what good will that do?" Snorri asked. "No skiff, no longboat. What do we do, *swim*? I wouldn't vouch for your swimming ability, in that case." For once Snorri seemed utterly despondent and unable to smile at his own joke.

"Snorri, there's something I haven't told you. There's just a chance, a slim chance—"

He stopped. Better not to mention the scuttled longboat back at the River Red with Blood. Suppose they weren't able to come out of the prairies just at that point? Better not to raise false hopes. Things were bad enough.

Suddenly Grimm raised a loud shout. "Ufila! Ufila! He's gone!"

"What? Gone?" Snorri cried.

"What do you mean *gone*?" Harald couldn't believe it! "He can't have just disappeared!" Then he thought of Loki—now Loki could have disappeared into thin air like that. He shivered. Suppose he *was* Loki, all along—trying to trick them, deceive them? Hadn't he tried to send them down the wrong channel? And hadn't he seemed to make his raft heavier, harder and harder to tow with the skiff? Harald could only conclude that Ufila was Loki in disguise and one of Heckla's agents. What form would he take next?

Chapter Eleven
The Mysterious Stranger

"I don't know what happened," confessed Grimm. "We were just sitting there with the *skraelings*, Ufila's rope tied to my belt. Unless—"

"Unless he managed to untie the rope while you weren't paying attention? You knew he had tricky fingers that could pick locks, steal. You should have been paying attention. It was your duty to guard him." Harald tried not to reveal how angry he was. Showing anger wasn't good for a leader.

In one way he was glad to be rid of the man. Ufila had been a problem from the beginning. But to allow him to escape the king's justice like that! For Grimm to be slack in his duty! Harald wondered whether Ufila could be one of Heckla's agents through his Loki-like ability to shift forms. Where might he appear next? They had to consider every possibility.

After Harald's stinging rebuke, Grimm shifted his eyes and lowered his head. Although he said nothing, Harald noticed he was clenching his fists—not a good sign.

This proved to be the case. During the night, Harald awoke to some sounds he couldn't quite identify—scraping, rustling, a movement of some sort. "Who's there?" he cried. The sounds stopped. Probably only some prairie animal in the grass. He could hear wolves howling off in the distance. He rolled back over on his side. Just as he was drifting back to sleep, the sounds began again, closer. Fully awake this time, Harald sprang to his feet, felt for his dagger. It was not in its sheath. "Who's there—speak up!"

Laurel Means

The faint light from the moon and stars revealed Grimm, crouching beside Snorri, Harald's dagger poised over him. He'd slung Snorri's bow and sheaf of arrows over his shoulder.

"Stop—what are you doing? Snorri—watch out! Grimm—"

"Uh, what's happening?" Snorri mumbled, half asleep.

"Wake up, Snorri—watch out for Grimm—he's going to—"

"Grimm? What's going on—Grimm—what are you doing?" Snorri leapt to his feet and jumped for Grimm. In that fleeting second Harald recalled the time Snorri had done a backwards somersault on the docks back in Bergen.

With Snorri on his back, Grimm fell to the ground. Twisting and turning, he slashed out with the dagger. Snorri gave a cry of pain, put a hand to his shoulder, fell back, lay still. Harald knew Grimm would go for him next. Before Grimm could get to his feet, though, Harald fell on top of him. Together they rolled over and over through the grass. Harald forced down Grimm's left hand, but Grimm still held the dagger in his right and slashed out wildly. Harald got a hand on Grimm's throat, causing him to choke and gasp. If only I had a weapon, Harald thought, the man's too strong for me—can't do much with my bare hands.

Grimm regained control and kicked Harald off. As Harald fell backwards, Grimm jumped him and struggled to pin him down. He raised the dagger, ready to plunge it into Harald's heart. Just at that moment, the strap holding Snorri's sheaf of arrows snagged on the branch of a nearby low-lying brush and checked him. In that slight distraction, Harald managed to draw his knees up, and, with all the force in his body, pushed Grimm off with his feet.

"Ooomphh!" Grimm cried, as he turned slightly sideways in the air, fell to the ground with a loud thud, and rolled over face down. He lay motionless.

Harald got shakily to his feet. In the pale moonlight, he saw blood gushing from the side of Grimm's head and oozing onto a large rock lying beside it. "Snorri!" he called. "Snorri, are you all right?" He hoped beyond hope that Grimm had not killed him. To be left all alone out here in the wilderness—what chance for survival would he have then?

To Harald's relief, Snorri staggered to his feet, holding his shoulder and obviously in pain. "What happened?"

"Grimm—I've killed him!"

Snorri came over to look. "No—nooo, I don't think so. Unless you threw this rock at him—that's what killed him, crushed his skull when he fell."

Harald was relieved. He'd never killed a man before, although he knew that's what warriors did. "We must bury him," he said. "Can't leave him for the wild animals, the wolves". A glint in the grass showed him where Grimm had dropped the dagger. "I'll start digging with that, see what you can find to help."

By the time dawn arrived, they'd finished the shallow grave near the bushes where Grimm had fallen. "Well—will you look at that?" Snorri remarked in surprise. "My own arrow sheaf caught in that bush. Where's the bow? Ah, I see it—Grimm fell on top of it." He started to pull it out from under Grimm's body. "Oh, no! It's broken—useless now." He threw the broken pieces into the grave in disgust.

"Grimm was planning to take what weapons he could, kill us both. I don't know whether he even knew how to use a bow or not. It was clear he knew how to use a dagger—and on me."

"Why?" Snorri asked, still in a half state of shock.

"My guess is he blamed me for getting us lost out here, for failing to meet up with my father and the other longboat. Maybe he was going to try to find them on his own, probably thought that was his only way back to the *knorr*."

"If that were the case, he'd sure have some fancy explaining to do to Bjorn. Obviously Grimm disliked Ufila, resented the guard duty. I suspect he would have tried to kill *him*, sooner or later."

With that thought, Harald wondered whether Ufila had poisoned Grimm's mind against him. Could he have twisted it in such a way as to make him go berserk last night?

"How about a memorial stone?" Snorri asked.

Harald wasn't sure whether he was serious or not. "What do *you* think?" He turned to the shallow grave they'd dug. "All right, Snorri, let's cover his body with this sod. We've got to get moving. Sun's already up."

Just before they headed out once again through the grass, Harald stopped to roll the rock, spattered with Grimm's blood, onto the grassy grave. "That'll be memorial enough," he said.

The sun grew unbearably hot by mid-day. From time to time Snorri put his hand to his shoulder, grew tight-lipped. Harald knew the knife wound bothered him. The water cask was empty and they'd eaten the last of the blood-sausage gift from the prairie *skraelings*. They looked desperately for another source of water. Without his bow, Snorri could only hope to set a snare for a rabbit, some other small animal, and that would take up valuable time.

Suddenly Snorri gave a shout. "See way over there—about a quarter of a league away?"

"That group of three popular trees? Could mean another pond or lake!"

"That and—something else, Harald. Look, under the middle tree!"

"Can't see anything—or just barely." He shaded his eyes against the sun, looked very hard off into the distance. Then he saw it. A tall figure, standing motionless, looking like he was watching them. Hard to tell, though, because a headdress of some sort covered most of his face.

"What'll we do?" Snorri asked. "Without my bow, we don't stand a chance, not even against a single warrior like that one. And see, he's got a long spear. He sure doesn't look like someone interested in exchanging gifts."

"No, besides we don't have anything to offer—we could try your arrows again, but I won't give up my dagger. Suppose we just wait here, see what he does. If he makes a rush for us, well, I guess we'll have to stand and fight."

The figure did not move. The sun was getting hotter, and, combined with a hot wind from the east, waiting was becoming unbearable. "We've got to do something, Snorri. We might as well face him. Come on, take out an arrow—you might be able to stab him with that if you can get close enough."

They headed toward the trees. The figure still stood motionless in the shade beneath them. Snorri and Harald stopped, waiting for him to make the first move. They were now close enough to see him more clearly. What Harald noticed first was the figure's headdress—an enormous animal head like those hundreds of animals they'd seen grazing on the prairie, its horns menacing, its face replacing the man's face. In fact, the man seemed to have no face. He was dressed, not like the *skraeling*s they'd just seen, but rather in something black and leathery, with a glitter of red and silver beads across the chest, the yellow gleam of something woven slung over his shoulder. His huge fist enclosed the wooden shaft of a spear with a spearhead of glittering quartz.

"Come—in—peace," he said, in a deep, halting voice.

Harald was speechless. To hear words he understood from a *skraeling*? How was that possible?

"Come," he continued. "Water behind me. Thirsty. Drink." Hesitantly, Harald and Snorri walked around him to the spring. Would the warrior spear them to death as they knelt down to drink from the small pool which formed just below the rocks? Harald thought of Ufila—Loki. "Safe, no harm," the warrior said, as if reading Harald's mind. "Drink."

After they could gulp down no more water and unsure what to do next, they sat down beside the pool and waited, Harald keeping his hand close to his dagger. The stranger seated himself opposite.

He placed the spear at his feet and slowly lifted off his heavy headdress. Harald gasped. He was an old man with long, white hair and a white beard and moustache, his skin darkened by the sun. Thick eyebrows overshadowed his eyes to the extent that they looked like holes in his face, a skull-like face. Harald couldn't tell where he was looking. "Names?" he asked. "Why have you come?" Although the words came slowly and with a strange accent, they were in Harald's own language, the language of the Norsemen.

Was this man a *skraeling* or not? He seemed neither Norse nor *skraeling*. Like a lightening bolt, the thought struck him—he was Astrid's father! Lost so many years in the wilderness, he'd forgotten his own ways, become like *them*. "*Thorkel!*" he shouted. Yet no sooner had he called out the name when he realized this man could not be Thorkel. He was too old.

"Thorkel?" the stranger answered. "No, I am not the one you name." With that, he turned to open the yellow basket pouch he'd worn over his shoulder and took out the same, blood-sausage type of food which they'd tasted before. "It is called *pemmican*," he said, breaking off several pieces. "Eat! It gives strength. Eat. We walk far."

Throughout the rest of the day they walked through endless seas of grass, the stranger untiring, Harald and Snorri lagging farther and farther behind, the stranger growing more and more impatient. At last he stopped and waited for them to catch up. "Hurry! No time," he said. "Do you not hear them?"

Harald and Snorri listened intently. "I hear nothing, sir," said Harald.

"The drums," the stranger said. "The drums along the river. You hear nothing because your ears have not learned to listen well. Come, we will walk more quickly. As we walk, I will speak." He moved ahead, with the strange, gliding movement of the *skraelings* back at the small lake where Ufila had disappeared.

Harald and Snorri struggled to keep pace, especially difficult for Snorri. "Shoulder," he moaned several times..

"Those drums pursue the yellow-haired people with the monster boats," began the stranger. "It is believed the yellow-haired people will take this land, these hunting grounds. The drums intend to put an end to their journey. The beaters of those drums have already killed one of the dragon demon boats, destroyed its warriors. Now they seek the second one."

Harald knew he referred to the massacre at the River Red with Blood. He wondered how the stranger knew of it and also of his father's longboat after it had rowed south. The man had a power of knowledge about him, a strange mysteriousness. He thought of Loki, Loki leading them right into a trap!

"Come," the stranger ordered. "We must travel north until darkness falls, camp tonight in a circle of pine woods on top of a tall hill."

As they lay out under the stars that night, Harald could distinctly make out Charles Wagon, Little Bear, and the triangle pointing to the pole star. How did the stranger know about reading the stars? Why were they camping here? And where were they going? His feelings were mixed up. Glad to be still alive, glad to be heading north—for surely this was in the direction of the *knorr*. But what was happening to his father? Had the *beaters of those drums* already discovered him, killed him? Who was this stranger, was he friend or foe? And where was he taking them?

"Snorri," he whispered, "the old Vikings of old sometimes captured people they used as slaves. Do you think that's what he plans? Let's make a break for it while we can. He seems to be asleep—we can crawl out of these trees, then start running, get a far distance before morning."

"I'm with you," Snorri whispered back, "although with my shoulder, can't make very good time. Feel kind of dizzy. But I'll try by best. Come on, let's go!"

They hadn't gotten more than a spear length's beyond the pine trees when the stranger stood tall and menacing before them in the pale moonlight. "Go back," he demanded, "or I will make you unable to walk—or even crawl."

That morning, while the stranger handed them a meager breakfast of several mouthfuls of *pemmican* and a skin flask of water, Harald came to a decision. He would demand to know the facts from this stranger, even if it meant his life. And it looked like the stranger might do just that without any hesitation at all.

"If you are not Thorkel, sir," he began, "then who are you? If you are a *skraeling*, how is it you know our language? How did you come to find Snorri and me? Where are you taking us?"

"Too many questions. You will know in due course," he answered sharply. "Enough talk—we must reach the meeting place of five rocks by tonight's moon rise."

That night Harald heard a strange bird call. Although it sounded like the hooting of an owl, the calls were in different patterns—long, short, long again. The stranger quickly rose and walked out just beyond the rocks. As if out of thin air, two warriors appeared beside him. They engaged in talk for several minutes, all three gesturing, pointing.

"What do you suppose they're talking about, Harald?" Snorri asked. "Not about doing away with us, I hope."

When the stranger returned, he motioned for them to lie down and sleep. "I shall tell you this much," he said. "When the sun rises next morning, we must then turn at our right hand and go to where there is a *tonka* skull on a pole by a dead oak tree. There we will meet another messenger, a warrior named Blackhawk."

"Well," Harald later whispered to Snorri, "I guess that's all we're going to find out for now."

"What's a *tonka*?"

"Not sure," Harald whispered back. Might be that animal we see all over the prairie—stranger has the head of one for a headdress. Really huge kind of shaggy cow—fierce looking, too. You'd have to be a great warrior to kill one, specially with the kind of flintstone arrows they have."

During the night Snorri tossed and turned in his sleep. "Burning up," he moaned, "shoulder." Harald realized he was feverish, that the wound was festering. And he could do nothing about it.

Next morning they turned toward what Harald assumed, judging by the position of the sun, was eastward. Because clouds were beginning to form, Harald worried that he soon might lose all sense of direction. He needed to know approximately were they were, and things were already uncertain enough. The stranger walked on relentlessly, and yet the going seemed somewhat easier. Not only was the air cooler but the grass less tall, and the stranger skirted around areas of dense woods. The flat prairie was giving way to low, rolling hills. Harald's heart gave a bound. Wouldn't that suggest a river valley ahead? And they'd turned due east. Could that mean they were nearing the big river he'd been seeking, the one leading into the long lake?

The distant sound of drums. Snorri heard them, too, and seized Harald's arm. The *skraelings*," he hissed, "the stranger's taking us back there—to that village you told me about. No telling what they'll do with us there! I'd rather die right here, it'd be an end to my pain."

Harald had never seen Snorri so miserable. "No, Snorri—what kind of a man are you? Where's the king's warrior now?"

"Take out your dagger—you'll be doing your friend a great favor—friend to friend, blood brother to blood brother, like back in Greenland." He collapsed on the grass. "Let's say good-bye for the last time."

Come, come," said the stranger. "Stop—get up! The *tonka* skull ahead, Blackhawk waiting." He prodded Harald with the point of his spear, and with his deerskin boot nudged Snorri as he lay on the grass. Then the stranger walked on ahead and was soon engaged in conversation with the *skraeling* named Blackhawk. The stranger pointed to Harald, to Snorri, then back the way they'd come. There were gestures which Harald did not understand, but he did recognize the fact that Blackhawk kept pointing to the east, then toward the north, then toward himself

"Looks like you won't have to use your dagger on me or yourself, Harald," Snorri ruefully remarked. "They're going to do the job for us."

At that point the stranger's manner changed. His whole body seemed to tensed up as he looked far off toward the way they'd come. He placed a hand on Blackhawk's shoulder, said something, and they both began pointing south. Then the stranger threw off his heavy headdress, dropped his spear, and began, not gliding in that direction, but *running*.

Harald strained his eyes against the sun, but could make out only faint specks on the horizon. He tightened his grip on the handle of his dagger. "Could be our chance, Snorri," he said. "Want to make a run for it?"

"Not yet. That warrior Blackhawk has an eye on us. See, he's fitting an arrow into his bowstring. Couldn't get very far. Besides, more warriors coming—look down there, the stranger's meeting up with them. They're probably planning to drag us into their village in some kind of victory procession."

The group on the horizon grew more distinct. As they approached, it became clear that it was not a large company of warriors, but only four men. "They're *skraelings* of the plains," Harald said. "See—look—even at this distance I can tell by their clothes, the *tonka* headdresses they wear. No, three of them, anyway. The fourth has a black thing on his head."

As Harald and Snorri watched in some amazement and not a little anxiety, three of the men quickly melted into a small birch forest just below a slight rise in the land. The remaining figure began to run toward the stranger, waving his arms. As they met, both men threw their arms around each other, slapped each other on the back, stepped back to look at each other, then laughed and embrace once more.

"What does all that mean?" Harald asked Snorri.

"No idea. Do you think it's better to be captured by hostile people or crazy people?"

"Maybe they're the same," Harald answered.

The stranger and the *skræling* exchanged a few words with Blackhawk. Harald noticed the stranger offer Blackhawk something—a small bag of some sort. Blackhawk accepted it, touched his hand to his heart, and turned away to glide back the way they'd come.

"At least we're not under attack—yet," commented Snorri.

"Do you have any idea what's going on?"

"No, but now that he's closer, I've a feeling that other man is not what he seems."

"Is not—what?" Harald's uneasiness was growing.

Snorri did not have time to answer, for the stranger and the fourth *skraeling* were coming toward them. He wore a black fur cloak, the hood made from a bear's head, its upper jaw and teeth concealing most of his face. "What am I, then?" he asked.

"You—you speak our language, too?" Harald asked in utter confusion.

The man threw back the bear's head hood to reveal a mass of yellow hair and laughed. "Of course—slightly different speech as a Greenlander—but maybe you'll excuse that!" He was younger than the stranger, had a yellow moustache but no beard.

"This man is Thorkel, the one you were seeking," said the stranger. "He is Thorkel, the son of Lief Thorkelson of Brattahlid."

Harald could contain himself no longer. "Thorkel Liefson!" he shouted. "Oh, sir, oh, sir." He seized Thorkel's hand, both hands, then stepped back, embarrassed at his boldness. "Thorkel, Astrid's father! Heckla has lost!"

"Yes, that's who I am," Thorkel replied. "Do you know something of my daughter? Of my family back there at Eriksfjord? And what is it you're saying about Heckla?"

The stranger interrupted. "There is no time, we must be on our way."

"Yes, that is very true," said Thorkel. "The *skraelings* from the northern villages have launched their canoes down the streams to the south. They intend to join their brothers in pursuit of the second longboat. So I have been informed by scouts from the *skraelings* of the prairie, who are their enemies."

"That second longboat, sir," Harald began, "my father and his crew."

"Your father's name?"

"Bjorn Erikson, also known as "Fierce-as-a-Bear."

"And this is his son, Harald," Snorri added, "although he doesn't have that kind of a name yet." Despite the pain from his shoulder, he smiled his funny, twisted smile. It had been a long time since Harald had seen that smile.

"And you, young warrior—a Goth, I take it, by your accent."

"Come, Thorkel," the stranger said emphatically as he took Thorkel's arm. "No time for introductions, idle talk. If we do not make haste toward the river, no tongues for talk later."

"How far, then?" Thorkel asked.

"Blackhawk informs me about an hour's march from here."

"My scouts tell me," said Thorkel, "that the camp down the river—one where a stone with strange writing was found—"

Harald gasped. The rune stone memorial—they'd discovered it. "The runes," he began, "they were—I did—"

"Ah, so that was it. The northern *skraelings* were very angry when they realized you'd eluded them through another channel. It wasn't long before they found out which one. After that, it was easy to trace your passage all the way to the edge of the prairie. You destroyed your skiff there? They found that, too, along with a raft. At this very moment they are tracking your path through the prairie. Although they are not *skraelings* from the plains and unfamiliar with this part of the land, you can be sure that hardly a broken blade of grass, an overturned pebble will escape them. That is why we have no time to lose."

"You already know, Thorkel," the stranger said, "that they will be sending *canoes* from the long lake up river to the camp where there was a massacre of the other longboat crew about eight days ago. They will hope to retrieve any weapons they can find."

Harald gave another gasp, a sharp intake of breath. So this stranger knew about that. "How did you—" he tried to say. But the stranger simply shook his head and motioned for silence.

"No," Thorkel continued, "I knew only of the massacre." He gave Harald a searching look. "Your father—let us hope . . ." He did not finish, but Harald knew what he'd intended to say.

Sir," Harald pleaded, "we must reach that campsite first!"

"Why?" The stranger asked. "My intention was to reach this end of the long lake as soon as possible. My brothers have placed a large war *canoe* there for us. Then we will paddle north until we reach the great in-land sea, then cross the straits from Markland to Greenland."

"A *war canoe*?" Thorkel shook his head. "Hardly seaworthy enough for that. A treacherous sea, there, strong winds. We could never make it."

"We must try," the stranger replied. "Our only chance."

"Sir, but sirs . . ." Harald began.

"No time for talk," the stranger said, and to reinforce his words, he strode past the *tonka* skull and descended down a slope on the other side. "Come!" he shouted back, "make haste if you value your lives!"

As they hurried on toward the bottom of the long lake and what they hoped was their one means of escape, Thorkel was striding alongside Harald. "You are puzzled at all this, are you not?"

"Yes," Harald answered. "But there seems to be no time for questions—or answers, either."

"I can give you a few answers now—perhaps more later. We will have one night's camp along the shore of the long lake before we reach the great in-land sea. Then perhaps you will hear more of the stranger before we look for the big war *canoe* left for us."

"But, sir," Harald broke in. "That's what I was trying to tell you—and the stranger." He hardly knew what to call him—no name had ever been mentioned. "I'm trying to tell you, if you'd only listen, that there is already a more sea-worthy boat at the river-mouth landing place, a big *knorr*. And also that there is another—"

"A *knorr*? At that place on the in-land sea? Is that where you—and the two longboats—came from?" He sounded incredulous.

"Yes, a *knorr* with ten men from our original crew of thirty. I only hope they're still there. They could already have given us up and sailed home. My father—" He could not go on, so overcome with emotion. Not befitting, he well knew, but there was no help for it. It was obvious by now that his father would never reach that *knorr*. Even if he'd eluded the *skraelings* heading south toward where his longboat waited for Hakon and his men, he still had to make his way north to reach the *knorr*. He would have been surrounded by bands of *skraelings* who could have ambushed him at any moment. The thought, the hopelessness of his father's situation, the certainty that he would never see him again, made the ground below Harald's feet uncertain, the way ahead a blur. He would have stumbled had not Thorkel caught him by the arm to steady him.

"I understand," Thorkel said kindly. "What my own family has suffered back in Greenland, not knowing—two years—but we shall not speak of these things. I, too, landed there, years ago—I have now lost all track of time. But now, tell me what brought you here?"

"King Erik of Norway sent us, commissioned for a voyage of discovery and also to find . . . to find—"

"Ah, I might have guessed," Thorkel said. "And so you have. We can only hope that this is not the end of that commission."

"If I may ask, sir, how was it that you found *us*?"

"You see," he said, "and you will excuse me if my words don't always come easily—it's been so long since I've spoken our language. You see, I was originally captured by the northern *skraelings*, and after a skirmish which killed my companions, I was held captive in one of their villages—a large one on a wide stream."

"I know that place," said Harald. "I escaped from there in the *knorr's* skiff."

"The skiff you finally scuttled? I tried to escape several times, never succeeded. But then I can't say they treated me badly. I was useful to them."

"Useful?"

"I'm a barber-surgeon by trade—although I also went out with Brattahlid's fishing fleets, since we needed every able-bodied person to survive. After what seemed to the *skraelings* a few magical healings, merely in medical terms minor surgical operations, they held me in some kind of awe. I began to teach them a few things."

"You are a man of medicine?" Harald asked excitely. "My friend here has a wound in his shoulder—he's suffering but won't admit it. Do you think you could—"

"Yes, I'll have a look at it when I can . . . tonight when we camp. I've learned much from the *skraelings* about healing, the use of herbs and such—probably more than they learned from me."

"Thank you, sir," Snorri said, overhearing this conversation. "I do need to heal, to go on. But please tell us more."

Well, to make a long story short, during a raid by a hostile tribe I was captured, moved to another village, eventually sold to another and still another. Before too long I had no idea where I was and eventually found myself far to the west in a village of the prairie *skraelings*. Very different people, but yet so far from where my boat entered this land that I despaired of ever finding my way out."

"Why did they let you go, then?" asked Harald.

"Did you run away?" Snorri added.

"No, my lads," Thorkel replied, "didn't have to. I was set free, even given an escort to track you to this place. And you can thank that man—another Goth I think he was."

"A Goth?" Harald asked, incredulous.

"A *Goth* in a prairie *skraeling* village? Surely you're joking!"

"No—his name was—was—Well, I've forgotten, a strange name."

"Ufila! Was that it? Did he have a low, shifty look?"

"A green—a green tunic with a short cloak of sorts—bordered with mangy-looking orange fox fur?" Snorri added.

"Yes, yes, he answers to that. How he got there, I've no idea."

Then Harald remembered. "Snorri, think back—back. Remember that meeting with the *skraelings* just before Ufila disappeared? Remember that group of *skraelings*, the women with the water jars?"

"What about it?"

"When they left, I noticed one of them lagging behind, trying to catch up. I thought it was one of the women. Now I'm sure it was Ufila."

"Yes," Thorkel said. "I think that's the name I heard. From what I understand—after living among them for over two years I've picked up much of their language—this Goth convinced them that he knew how to work iron. Now the *skraelings* have been very interested in that since they've come into contact with our weapons and other things. I'll never know exactly how or why there was an exchange of him for me. How it happened, why such a man as this Ufila—that's what you say his name was—would do such a thing, give his life up for another's."

Harald didn't know the reason, either, but he could guess. It was to escape the king's final justice. In order to escape what lay in store, anyone—even Loki—would try anything.

The stranger was waiting impatiently for them to catch up. "Blackhawk's instructions were not very clear on the location of the *canoe*, which his people left on the shore of the big lake. I only hope we find it before we are caught."

"Was he reliable? You don't think it was a trap?" Thorkel asked.

"One can never be sure. Relationships between these tribes are very complex, as you yourself have discovered."

"I need to tell you, sir—" Harald was getting desperate to say something about the scuttled longboat.

"What if we have to walk?" Snorri interrupted.

"Far too slow. It would take five or six days at least, through dense forests, marshes."

"Oh, no!" Harald had to speak. "The *knorr* might not still be there! But I have to tell you about another—"

The stranger broke in. "What did you say? A *knorr*? Where?" After Thorkel explained what Harald had told him about the *knorr* and King Erik's commission, he said, "What a miracle that would be indeed, to find such a vessel!"

"Please, sir," Harald now felt bold enough to say. "There is another boat which may be closer. I've been trying to tell you this, but—"

"*Another* boat?" The stranger and Thorkel in chorus.

"That depends," Harald said, "on where we're going. Will we come to the River Red with Blood?"

The stranger looked surprised. "You know that name?"

"It was my name, after seeing the massacre at the first longboat's campsite, after trying to bury the ten men."

"You were *there*? You did that? Strange, you used the very same name the *skraelings* use for that river. That campsite was much used by them, situated as it is on a rich hunting ground. Many battles were fought there over possession of that location." He paused. "But listen! By the sound of the drums, the *skraelings* are not too far from there now—some may already be returning from their pursuit to the south. We must now go a long way around, circle westward, then come out at the very river's mouth into the lake. But you have spoken of another boat near there. How can that be? The longboat left at that site disappeared, according to my scouts."

"Well, it did sort of. It disappeared under water," Harald explained. "I couldn't destroy it, so I filled it with rocks and scuttled it. The oars I hid in the underbrush."

Looking at Thorkel, the stranger said, "What an unbelievable piece of luck, if what this lad says is true." He walked up to the top of the hill in front of them, peered ahead. "We may be only a half league or so from the river—down that slope and through the willow trees at the bottom. I cannot be sure whether we are above or below the camp. Let us hope we are above, to the north. Remain here until I give a signal."

After what seemed a long time, Harald saw something flashing through the willow branches. "That's the signal," he said. "Good thing the sun's come out, it's reflecting off his dagger blade—or that quartz spear head. It must be safe."

The three of them rushed down to the line of willows. Sparkling here between the leaves in the noon-day sun was the river, the River Red with Blood.

"The campsite is down to our right, just past that overhanging rock," said the stranger. "Move along this bank cautiously, now. There may be men hiding in the underbrush—hiding anywhere."

As they crept along the bank, the mist drifted up and dissolved into the sunshine. There, just ahead of them, the dragonhead of the second longboat rose up clearly and proudly out of the water. There was no other sound save the lapping of the water against the bank and the soft breeze fluttering the leaves above their heads

Their next task was to cross the river and raise the boat. After some discussion, Snorri stepped forward. "I have an idea."

"An idea, young Goth?" Thorkel remarked. "At this point, we must be willing to consider anything. The day is passing quickly."

"I can see a sandbar in the middle of the river, dividing it into two channels. The longboat rests down in the deeper, swifter channel. Now the sandbar on this side looks like it slows down the current a bit. If I can swim across that channel first, then rest a moment on the sandbar, then swim up to where I can grab hold of the dragon head, then use it to grab hold of some of those low-hanging branches to pull myself ashore—well, then I think I can make it."

"But your shoulder—"

"Don't worry, I'll manage."

Harald remembered something. "Those oars," he said, "they may be long enough to lay across the narrowest part of the channels, like a bridge. The rest of us can get across that way."

"You come across with me. You've got to find the oars," Snorri insisted.

"I can't swim."

"This time you've got to. No time for lessons."

The stranger nodded. "Once we're all across, we should be able to raise the boat with only four men."

To his surprise, Harald made it across both channels, although Snorri half supported him across the first. They soon recovered the oars and laid four across one channel, four across the other. Thorkel and the stranger made their way across, taking up the oars behind them as they went.

"To get out the rocks, now," said Harald. He and Snorri jumped back into the water and began heaving up the rocks that Harald had thrown down into the bottom of the boat. Harald hadn't realized there were so many until his arms ached and his head seemed full of water. He knew Snorri, with his wounded shoulder, must be in far greater pain.

"Now then," said Thorkel, "we'll wade in and help you raise the boat." It took their combined strength to raise the longboat up through the water and tip it sideways enough to drain out a good part of the water. "It's floating now—see whether you can find a bucket or something to bail with."

"No," protested the stranger, "no time for that. "Bail as we move. Get in, take an oar. With four rowers, the current with us, the wind behind us, we should be able to faster than any *canoe*."

By the time they exited the mouth of the river, they were indeed moving very fast. Harald recalled coming down the lake in the skiff, his *tonka* pelt as a sail. "A sail!" he shouted. "There should be a spare sail in the storage chest, if only we can break the lock."

"Here, try this," said the stranger, and he handed Snorri his spear. "The blunt end—if you hit the lock sharply enough, it may shatter."

The big square sail was soaked, but began to dry out almost as soon as it was hoisted. Within moments, the longboat seemed to fly through the water as swiftly as the sea gulls screaming above them. Freed from rowing, Thorkel took the bucket he'd found and working on bailing.

Suddenly the stranger pointed over to the eastern shore. "Keep well out in the middle of the lake," he shouted to Harald, who sat at the helm to work the rudder oar. "They're over there, following us."

Harald peered intently in that direction. To his horror he saw several *canoes* moving through the water close to the shore. Looking beyond them he spotted some lighter shapes against the dark woods. The *skraelings* were tracking them.

"Thorkel, you take one oar, I'll take the other. Snorri look after the sail, and Harald, keep to the rudder. Now we must really fly!"

Harald hoped they would fly fast enough to reach the *knorr* in time, that they would find their way back out of the great inland sea, that he would be able to bring Astrid's father back to her. But what about his own father? King Erik would most certainly declare Bjorn Erikson a hero, but there was nothing heroic about a mere memory, nothing at all.

That night they camped on the western shore of the long lake. Thorkel examined Snorri's shoulder, where Grimm had made an incision about four fingers long. "It's inflamed," he said, "but fortunately not very deep. I'll see what I can find to ease the pain." After looking briefly around the woods, he returned with the leaves of a plant Harald didn't recognize. "We'll just make a paste of these with water, apply them to Snorri's shoulder. If I wrap his belt around them, they should stay on long enough to do their work."

Later, as they sat around the campfire, Thorkel said, "There is still great danger. The *skraelings* of the north could cross the lake and come up by land. We must be constantly on guard, listening for the slightest sound—a twig snapping, an unusual ripple in the water."

Harald shivered. Although he admitted to himself it was from cold—the fire was confined to a few branches, lest it become a signal to the *skraelings*, his inner-self confessed to fear. Those first few moments after retrieving the longboat from the river, after sailing full speed with the gulls overhead and foam dashing against the sides of the boat, were indeed glorious moments. But now reality had set in. There was still some distance to go, still dangers along the way, still the possibility the *knorr* had already cast off for home. And his father—dead.

The mysterious stranger had walked down to the shore to keep watch. Harald was disappointed at losing the opportunity to find out more about him. He avoided revealing anything about himself, and Thorkel was no help. The stranger had obviously been living in the Western Edge for some time, knew the land and the ways of the *skraelings* well. If it hadn't been for him and his contacts with the prairie people, the meeting with Thorkel could never have happened. For Astrid's sake, he was glad of that.

By noon the next day, the wind had dropped and the longboat sail went limp and useless. All four took to the oars. Without a helmsman, it took great effort to steer by means rowing maneuvers. With such slow going, the stranger became even more anxious. During the night, he'd heard distant drums coming from *both* shores of the lake. That meant they were being pursued by more than one tribe. No one spoke. All efforts were concentrated on getting through the lake to the river issuing out into the great inland sea.

"There it is!" cried Harald. He recognized the spot where he'd camped with the skiff, where he'd fashioned a sail from the *tonka* pelt. That meant they were getting close.

"A good thing the river's current will also be with us," said the stranger. "Make for that entrance there, but watch for rocks where the channel narrows. Harald, be our helmsman again—you have great skill. Thorkel and I will continue to row, and Snorri—keep a careful watch in the bow. There are sharp turns, rocks, some sandbars—and rapids ahead."

It wasn't long before Snorri shouted, "Rapids ahead!" Harald knew the longboat was too heavy to portage. He wondered how his father and Hakon had managed on their way south, unless they'd taken a different channel.

"Harald, we'll need you in the boat to steer. Thorkel, you, Snorri and I will get out to lighten it. Then we'll edge it around that shallow channel off to the side. The current is weaker, because the channel wanders around through a marsh. Careful, now!" Holding onto both sides of the boat, they waded through the channel until it joined the river about a half league downstream.

Harald hoped there would be few such setbacks. Already everyone showed signs of exhaustion. And no one, not even the stranger, knew exactly how much farther before they reached the mouth of the river where the *knorr* had been moored.

Just after the third set of rapids it happened. This time the only way around was through a swamp, the longboat's passage continuously obstructed by rotted tree stumps, floating logs, and water plants which wrapped themselves around their bare legs and cut into their flesh. The water was so shallow that even Harald had to get out and help push the boat forward. He remembered the leeches at the time they'd scuttled the skiff. He hoped that leeches could not live this far north. After the first needle-like sensation on his right leg, he knew they did, in fact, live here. Anxiously he looked ahead to see how far it was before they'd gone around the rapids and before the swamp led back into the river.

At last here was the main channel again, the water slowed down to a gentle movement. "All right, now," said the stranger. "Back into the boat. Since the river widens here, we will make better time. Thorkel, you and I to the oars again, Snorri—change places at the helm with Harald. Rest your shoulder."

At the bow, Harald pulled off a second, then a third leech from his calf, and hoped there would be no more. The bites hurt, but Thorkel had given him a poultice from some mud and weeds he'd found along the bank.

"Harald!" called the stranger. "Watch out for rockfall as we go through these two overhanging cliffs."

As the longboat came out from the shadow of the cliffs, Harald instructed Snorri at the helm to steer sharply to port, for just ahead a narrow strip of land reached out into the river like a finger. To his complete amazement, there was a man standing on it, waving and shouting as the boat approached. "Ufila!" Harald blurted out. "It's him again, Loki again!" He turned back to the others. ""No, don't stop, keep rowing. This time he'll destroy us for sure!"

"It can't be Ufila," said Snorri, "impossible." Then he let out a cry of recognition and began to laugh. "Harald—dumbhead! Have you totally lost your mind? Don't you recognize your *own father*?"

Chapter Twelve
That Pile of Whale Bones

Just as the sun set, the dragon prow of a longboat pushed out of the river mouth into the great inland sea. A shout from the bow.

"Look! It's beyond belief!" cried Svein, one of the Bjorn's four surviving crew members. "The *knorr* is still moored out there!"

"We made it back—and in time!" cried Harald.

"Yes," added Bjorn as he stood up on the stern, "it *is* beyond belief. We are indeed on our way home!"

The longboat grated against the rocks as Harald used one of the oars to beach it. There was a rush of three or four men along the bank to meet them.

"We almost gave you up for lost, Bjorn," Aiwar cried as soon as the men began clambering out of the boat the instant it beached. He embraced Bjorn, looked around in disbelief at Harald, Snorri, Svein and the others. He stared in amazement at Thorkel and the stranger, at a loss to say more.

"It is indeed good to see you, Aiwar," said Bjorn, "and the crew left here still safe."

Aiwar seemed to have some difficulty recovering his voice. Finally he said, "A terrible decision we had to make, sir. We were running out of supplies and there isn't much game here. After so long a time, we were convinced the longboats and all of you were lost. So by today there was no alternative. This very evening we were loading up the last of the water casks. Tomorrow we'd have pulled up anchor!"

"It would have been the right decision, however hard," Bjorn said. "But what a welcome sight to see all of you, especially big Ole cooking something in his big iron kettle over there at the landing sight." Ole laughed his big belly laugh, which seemed to relieve the heightened emotions of the moment.

"Where are the others?" Aiwar asked, anxiously looking around. "Is the second longboat coming just behind you?"

"I'm afraid not," Bjorn replied sadly. "They were brave men and gave up their lives in the king's service. We nearly did not make it back ourselves."

"What happened?" By this time Ole and the others had gathered round.

"We left Hakon at a campsite to hunt and fish for a few days. We ourselves continued south, leaving Snorri and Grimm at the next campsite to guide Hakon and his boat down to a meeting place at our farthest point south. When they failed to come after several days, and we knew the *skraelings* were on our tail, I had to make a terrible decision as well. We found a channel leading west, took that, several more, until we found ourselves out on the edge of a vast prairie. It was impossible to turn back, try to return by water. We abandonned the longboat and turned north through the prairie on foot. But this story is too long for now—"

Harald had heard his father's story in the longboat after they'd picked him and the other men up. The stranger did not seem surprised to hear that they had been guided up through the prairie by a series of *skraeling* warriors. He'd heard something of this from Blackhawk, but not knowing the outcome, was reluctant to raise false hopes. Bjorn told how they'd been taken in a *canoe* up another river, running parallel to the long lake, then across to the river where they were told a dragon boat would soon pass. The wait on the finger of land had seemed endless, for he had no idea when—or if—the longboat would pass that way. The sight of it— with Harald in the bow—was indescribable. Yes, it had indeed been a *near thing* for all of them

As they prepared to set sail early the next morning, Bjorn assigned Snorri as helmsman in the longboat, with Awair as captain and Einar, Helgi, Johan, and five others crew to make up the necessary ten oarsmen. He assigned the remaining men to the *knorr*. Harald thought how sad it was that, out of the original thirty men starting out, only sixteen would return. To Thorkel, Bjorn said, "You will be my guest aboard the *knorr*. We have much to speak of."

"What about the stranger, Father," Harald asked. "To which boat?"

"Neither boat."

"But—but—" Harald began.

"He has chosen to remain," Bjorn said. "That is his decision."

"Why?"

"He has made his decision, that is all I will say for now. There is still much to do before we leave at dawn. I believe your task was to make sure all oars were in place."

Although Harald was disappointed not to be in the longboat, his father's argument that he was needed on the *knorr* to guide them was some consolation. "That map thing you drew on the storage cabin wall," he said. "If you can interpret it for us, it may save time and get us safely out of the inland sea. And now that you have your astrolabe, we may very well need it."

All things considered, though, it was wonderful to be alive, heading eastward. Harald knew that up ahead they would come out of the great inland sea, then sail down the channel to where the coastline jutted out into the sea marking the entrance to Eriksfjord. At the very end of that fjord he would see Astrid again and bring her father back to her. It was no less a miracle that he'd found his own father alive. That they'd fulfilled the king's commission—claimed the land beyond the western edge, recovered Thorkel at least—was another miracle for sure.

Or were they miracles? He was convinced his rune charms against Heckla's power had everything to do with it. Her evil menace had followed him since that first encounter on the cliffs up above Brattahlid. Why? Because, Harald realized now, she knew all along that he'd try to release Astrid's family from her curse. Those charms he'd left against her power—rune symbols scratched with his dagger on a piece of whale bone and buried it under a stone back there near the beach where they'd left the *knorr*, or that night in the *skraeling* hut where he'd traced it in the dirt floor. It was just possible that Grandfather's knowledge of the old Viking ways had worked. If not, then best keep his guard up. No telling what she might do to them—to everybody—once they reached Brattahlid.

"What do you think, Snorri?" he remarked as they loaded the last of the oars in place on the longboat to which Snorri was assigned. "What do you think it'll be like once we get to Brattahlid?"

"Decent food?"

"Come on Snorri—more than that!" He was thinking of seeing Astrid, bringing back her father, of learning more about the old Viking settlers. "And what about Bergen? Coming before King Erik and telling him about all our adventures. Just think of all his rewards!"

Snorri smiled his weird smile. "Just getting back all in one piece—that'll be our greatest reward."

Harald didn't know what to say to that. There wasn't any question about the truth of what Snorri said. But somehow Harald hoped for—well, he wasn't sure what. *Name any gift you wish and it shall be yours.* Didn't kings ask heroes that in fairy tales?

They had set sail in mid-June, now it was the end of August. The voyage through the great in-land sea and across the straits to Greenland went smoothly, without the treacherous winds they'd had before and without lost time turning into the wrong channels or going aground. Harald's charcoal-drawn map was a great help. As the *knorr* and longboat entered into Eriksfjord, Harald could see that trees on the hillsides above the fjord already showed signs of autumn.

"Look!" shouted Svein, part way up the mast to trim the sail. "I can see it—the church tower!"

The light-colored rock and log buildings scattered around it grew more and more distinct and Harald's excitement grew. The boats were nearly there. Ingve and Karl lowered the great square sail all the way, and Bjorn was commanding Ole and Tomas to prepare the mooring ropes.

"Look at that big crowd," Ole remarked, "and listen to it. Must have recognized us far out there—the king's emblem on the sails, I guess."

"I can see old Lief Thorkelson, hobbling down the main road to the docks," cried Harald. "Let Thorkel know." And so the first person to step out onto the dock was Lief's son, whom he had years ago given up for dead.

"Can it be? Can it be?" Lief exclamed in absolute disbelief. Thorkel rushed over and caught him just before he fell to the ground.

"Yes, Father—I'm home," said Thorkel.

Lief held Thorkel at arm's length, embraced him again, and again held him at arm's length. There were no more words between them until Lief slowly realized that they were not the only two people standing on the dock. Reluctantly he let go of his son to turn and courteously greet Bjorn and the others.

Harald could no longer wait for the *knorr's* mooring rope to be twisted around the dock capstan. He made a big leap for the planks, almost missing them. He hoped Astrid was not watching, for she would surely be among the crowd and laugh at him. He'd only just picked himself up when he heard Svein's stern voice. "Back aboard, young man. Look after that sail tackle, if you please!" After that he had to help unload the *knorr*. He did manage to steal a glance up at the cliffs above town, to see whether he could locate the Heckla's cave-house. He didn't see it, but a cold chill went through him all the same.

As soon as the boats were secured, Lief accompanied Bjorn, Svein, and Thorkel to his house. "We have much to speak of," Bjorn said. "Many questions to answer."

"What do you think they're going to talk about, Snorri?" Harald asked, as they were stowing ropes in the *knorr's* storage cabin.

"Don't know, but there sure is a lot to talk about. And a lot of questions to answer. Like, who was the stranger, and why he stayed. Any idea who he might have been?"

"Don't know, no one ever said, not even Thorkel—which strikes me as odd. As if there were some secret about him, something they don't want people to know. I have an idea about him, though."

"What's that?" Snorri asked.

"I think he was Karlsefni. Don't you remember? He was the other Greenlander who went with Thorkel—the king mentioned them both?"

"Karlsefni? That doesn't make sense. Surely Thorkel would have said so. And why would he want to stay in the wilderness? Why not return to Greenland, to his family? No, he had to be somebody else"

"You're probably right. Someone will know—my father, for sure, and I intend to find out. There are just too many unanswered questions out there."

The celebration for those who'd returned from the Western Edge was held that evening in the market place at the bottom of the church steps. No one in town had a house big enough for all the people or the ten spits roasting geese, chickens, pork, and elk meat. Cod fish lay baking in the coals, while the trestle tables set out were loaded with breads, cheeses, smoked sausages, sliced cucumbers in vinegar water, boiled carrots, honey cakes, currant cakes, jugs of milk and whey, and casks of ale. Father Marcus came out from the church in white and silver vestments to give his blessing to the food and all those at the feast. It was hard to know what was being celebrated more—the arrival of the sixteen survivors or the miraculous return of Thorkel Liefson. The man seemed to have come back from the dead.

"Come, Harald—celebrate with us!" Thorkel invited Harald to join him and his family at one of the long tables. "After all—I wouldn't be here, if it hadn't been for you."

Harald was embarrassed. It was only partly true. There'd been a whole series of things, Ufila being one. And although Harald enjoyed the attention, it disturbed him that Astrid acted so distant. She seemed different from before, and he couldn't account for it.

During the three days it took to provision the *knorr* and the single, remaining longboat for the long voyage back, there were a number of private meetings between Thorkel, Lief, and Harald's father. "What's all this about, Father? Is it something I should know?" Harald asked, as the men emerged their next to last day from Lief's *fire room*. They'd been in there talking a long time and looked serious.

"You will know in due time," his father replied, and promptly dropped the subject.

Later that day Astrid came down to the *knorr's* mooring where Harald was checking over the water casks. "I've brought this for you," she said. "I made it myself, because I know you lost yours." It was folded into a small square, but when Harald shook out the folds, he gasped in surprise. It was a new, red wool cloak, very similar to the one he'd lost when captured by the *skrælings* but without the black and white woven border. "See, around the hood—I've embroidered a black and white design of leaves around the edge to remind you of the wilderness." She draped it around his shoulders, fastened the silver clasp under his chin. He liked the feel of her cool hand against his skin. "But, oh, I wish I had more time," she sighed. "I could have made the border all the way around. Maybe later."

Harald was puzzled by this last remark. It was true, she'd had little time to work on it during his short stay. Not much time for him, either. She claimed her family was very busy. Now their time together was almost up and he felt devastated. He would likely never see her again. And there had been that *fóstbræðralag*, a blood bond between them—all of them—made high up on that bluff by Heckla's cave.

Heckla's cave—Was the witch still holding her spell over Astrid? Was she seeking revenge for Thorkel's miraculous return? Astrid's family seemed to be in some sort of trouble, he wasn't sure what. He'd noticed regular movements of chests, furniture, other things in and out of Astrid's house. Astrid herself seemed moody, tightlipped. Maybe the spells against Heckla which he'd scratched in runes weren't the right ones. What if he'd written the wrong ones and actually given her more power?

His questions about Astrid were answered the last evening in Brattahlid. Lief held a farewell party—a very special celebration, he announced. Thorkel and his family were invited—Astrid, her mother, Karen, and little brother, Njal. But before the meal was only half finished, Harald sensed the event was not exactly a celebration. For one thing, Lief's wife, Gudrid, kept wiping her eyes and often disappeared along with Karen out into the kitchen.

"What's wrong with them?" Harald asked Astrid in a low whisper as they sat together on the bench along one side of the table.

"You'll see," she replied solemnly.

Just as they'd finished the last of the apple dumplings, Lief rose from his seat at the head of the table. "Now then, my dear family and my new friends," he said. "I have something important to say, as this will be our last meal together." Protests were heard from around the table. "Yes, I'm an old man and the sea is too wide to grant many more journeys. I shall live out the rest of my days here in Brattahlid beside my loyal wife, Gudrid." Gudrid modestly bowed her head, but Harald suspected she was trying to hide tears.

"First of all, we must mourn the loss of Gudrid's brother, Thorfinn Karlsefni. A brave man, sent on the king's errand beyond the Western Edge. He has chosen to remain there, among those he now calls his brothers. He has chosen to impart to them our ways, our knowledge. Now let us drink to his courage and his memory!"

As everyone raised their mugs, Harald's mind was in a whirl. So the stranger *was* Karlsefni all along.

Lief continued. "As I said, this is our last meal together—you, Bjorn, Harald, young son of Bjorn, my own son, Thorkel, and his wife, their little one who's the namesake of one of Iceland's brave heroes—and also my dear granddaughter, Astrid. Now we shall drink to them!"

Surprised at his words, Harald looked at Astrid sitting beside him. She glanced quickly back at him, smiled shyly, then lowered her gaze. What did this mean?

Lief continued speaking. "I wish all of you a safe voyage back to Norway, I wish you a long and happy life back where our families were born, several generations ago." He turned to Astrid's father. "Leave this house, now, Thorkel my son, and get a good night's rest. Rest for you, too, Bjorn and young Harald. You will need to prepare for the long voyage home. Yes, I can still say *home* . . ."

Harald could hardly wait to ask his father the many questions flooding his mind. The first opportunity came only as they were preparing for bed in the little stove room just off the kitchen. "Father," he began. "What did Lief mean? Are Thorkel and his family going somewhere? What's happening to them? Are they leaving their home here in Greenland?"

"Yes, my son," Bjorn answered simply. "They are going back to Norway on the *knorr* with us."

"With *us*?" Harald felt a surge of joy, a rush of excitement. Could it be that Astrid wanted to be with him? "But why, father? They have their home, their family here. Why would they give up all that? Maybe they'll change their minds, once they realize that tomorrow."

"There are many reasons for them to leave." Father yawned and turned over. "Many reasons. Too complicated to go into now. Just go to sleep."

"I need to know," Harald protested. "Please, I need to know. It's so important."

"Well, I"ll give you one and only one of the reasons. The night is getting shorter all the time—we've got to leave with the ebb tide, even before it's light. Now listen, for here is that one reason. One reason for Thorkel and his family to return to Norway is the obvious, official one. He needs to appear at the court in Bergen, to report to King Erik what he has discovered about the lands and the people beyond the Western Edge. He has learned more than I, he must report for both himself and Thorfinn Karlsefni. It must all be recorded in the king's books."

"But why the whole family?" Harald insisted. "And why . . . why . . . Astrid?"

Bjorn yawned again. "Because Lief, his father, thinks it best," he replied. "Now that makes *two* reasons. Go to sleep." Harald felt cheated. His father hadn't really told him what he wanted to hear.

Harald's chance to find out more did not occur until after they were well out to sea the next day. Snorri was assigned to the longboat crew under Aiwar's command, and they followed in the wake of the *knorr*. In fact, Snorri was made chief helmsman, boasting about this several times to Harald's dismay. Aboard the *knorr*, Astrid and her family were given Bjorn's private sleeping cabin, while Harald and his father shared the sleeping quarters of the rest of the crew.

It didn't look as though Harald would have much chance to talk to his father alone, to ask about Astrid's family, about the stranger, who'd stayed behind with Lief's family in Brattahlid, and this was disappointing. The crew's quarter were crowded, and his duties about the ship would keep him continuously busy. Then, too, he didn't have Snorri to talk to, either. But it could have been worse. He remembered all too painfully those anxious nights sleeping in the bottom of the cramped skiff, or out on the cold prairie sod.

In between duty watches, Harald was grateful for the chance to stretch his legs by walking around the deck. Late afternoon on the second day out, gave him an opportunity—not to speak to Bjorn alone, but to Astrid alone. He could hardly believe his luck.

He and Astrid were leaning over the rail, watching the water rapidly speed past them to leave a foaming wake. The west wind was at their backs and filled the big square sail of the *knorr* and the slightly smaller sail of the longboat following. Because of the strong westerly winds this time of year, Svein predicted a much faster voyage home than they'd had coming.

"Astrid," Harald began, uncertain how to approach the subject, but he just had to know.

"Yes, Harald?" she said absently. She seemed to be more interested in watching the foam trail or some whales surfacing and spouting off in the distance. "Hmm, did you say something?"

"Yes. It's important."

"I'm listening," she said, turning away from the rail to look at him.

"Well, here it is. I've got to ask you this, however much you might say it's none of my business. Can you tell me what the real reasons are that you and your family are leaving Greenland? And with close kinfolk still there?"

Astrid did not answer right away. She turned back to look at the whales with a more serious, thoughtful look. At last she said, "Yes, you probably should know. There are good reasons why my father—all of us—are returning to Bergen with you."

"Of course," said Harald. "He must report to the king, as my father must do."

"No," Astrid said. "That's important, of course, but not the only reason. No, there's another reason, more family related, more personal." She paused, looking out over the sea as if deep in thought. The whales had disappeared, but she still gazed absently in their direction.

A-ha, thought Harald. *Here it comes. She's going to say it's because of me.* He leaned eagerly toward her, expectantly, smiling.

But when it came, Astrid's answer was very different from what Harald expected. "Did my grandfather Lief ever tell you about what is happening to the western settlements in Greenland? About more cold weather, the difficulty of growing crops, about the *skrælings* up farther north?"

"Yes," replied Harald, "a little."

"Well, my grandfather is afraid for our future if we remain. He wants to be sure we will be safe, survive. He wants our family line to continue—after all, we, too, have some famous Viking blood in our veins, heroic feats to our record. We still have family down near the Oslofjord, and we'll join them there."

"But what about—what about—" He was going to say *me*, but then checked himself. Perhaps Astrid did not have the same feelings as he. Maybe she wasn't ready to say what he wanted her to say. Perhaps, just perhaps, she didn't know *what* her feelings were. He'd best change the subject to something easier to handle. "What about *Heckla*, then?" he asked. All along he'd suspected that Heckla was one of the reasons for the family's leaving Greenland. "Are you still afraid of her? Her evil spell?"

Astrid laughed and laid her hand on Harald's arm. "Don't worry anymore, Harald," she replied. "And now I'll tell you why. It's a very strange story. You didn't know Heckla disappeared?"

"What?" asked Harald, incredulous.

"Yes, even my grandfather could not explain it. Father Marcus, either. You see, Grandfather said that it was about a week or so after you'd all sailed for the Western Edge, although he couldn't be sure. One Saturday, several people spotted Heckla up there on the cliff in her doorway. She hadn't come down in her donkey cart to market to barter for food, as she usually did. No one thought much about it. After all, her ways were so strange. But later, when she wasn't seen anywhere on the cliff, and didn't come down the next market day, several townsmen decided they would go up there to investigate."

"Did they find anything?" Harald asked, with growing excitement.

"That's the puzzle," she answered. "You see, they found nothing. Only a large pile of whale bones, mixed with some eagle feathers and some charred wood chips just outside the door. The dirt on the pathway was scrapped into strange little lines. Her door stood open. The cave was empty, the fire in the stove out, the ashes cold, and there's been absolutely no trace of her since. Grandfather Lief ordered the cabin destroyed, so men went up there with pickaxes and collapsed the cave around it. The cabin, everything in it now lies crushed under the rocks."

Harald did a rapid calculation in his head. When was it that he'd buried the charm he'd scratched on the whale bone? The one on which he'd scratched with his dagger Heckla's bird name in runes to undo her power? Could it have been about the same time as Heckla disappeared? "Do you think there's a connection with—with . . ."

"With what?" Astrid asked.

Harald was sure Astrid would think him crazy, or silly at the most, maybe even stupid if he confessed about the rune charms. "Well, never mind," he replied, shrugging his shoulders. "You wouldn't believe me, anyway." But in his heart he believed that he, Harald—along with the runes, of course—had been the cause of Heckla's losing her power over himself—hadn't he survived against all odds, hadn't he found his own father? Then Heckla lost her power over Astrid's family—hadn't her father, Thorkel come safely back? But, most important of all, Astrid was returning to Norway with him. They would be back in Bergen and together.

Harald's elation, however, soon gave way to fear. Several days later, their boats were becalmed in a dense, cold fog, and most of the men, including Harald, were set to the oars. The big square sails flapped forlornly from the masts, begging for the slightest breath of wind. The two boats seemed to hang suspended in time and space.

For a whole day they rowed steadily, hoping that they maintained an easterly course. "Too bad we can't use your astrolabe now because of the fog," Bjorn said to Harald. "We'll just have to go by our sense of direction, the way the current moves." He called up to the lookout on the mast, "You, Svein, up there—keep a sharp lookout for Aiwar's longboat behind us. We don't want to get separated!"

Nevertheless, they did get separated during the night. By early evening the wind picked up. It dispersed the fog and filled the sails until they snapped and boomed. Harald was glad when he was able to replace his pair of the *knorr*'s long, heavy oars inside the boat. His arms were tired and his shoulders ached.

"Go on down into the crew's sleeping cabin," said his father. "Get some rest. You'll need it before your next watch."

As Harald lay curled up on the narrow plank along the inside of the bow which formed a berth for three men—end to end, foot to head and head to foot, he could sense the increasing movement of the boat. It rolled and pitched, sometimes throwing him rudely off the plank. The boards of the boat creaked and groaned as if they were being torn apart. It was impossible to sleep, but at least he got some shelter from the wind, the sea spray, and the chilling rain. He wondered how Astrid and her family were managing in their cabin, where they'd been ordered to remain for their own safety until the storm passed.

At midnight Harald was called up to his watch on the deck, relieved that it was not at the mast, spinning and gyrating from the motion of the sea. At the helm, the pressure from the wind and waves required two men on each steering oar. They had to keep the boat steady and headed into the waves so the boat did not slide broadside into the trough between waves. Once that happened, they'd be quickly swamped. In seconds, the boat would roll over and sink.

During the night the threat of destruction was so great that Bjorn came up on deck to oversee the handling of the rudder and adjustments to the rigging. Harald had to admit that he was glad for his father's presence. Each violent roll of the boat spelled a possible violent end to the king's commission—and to himself.

When dawn came, it was hard to believe what they had just been through. It was as if the storm, the rain, and the violent winds had never happened. The big square sail billowed out with just the right amount of wind. The *knorr* skimmed gracefully over an aquamarine sea. Waves sparkled rose-colored here and there from the first rays of the rising sun.

"Look, father," Harald cried as he left the steering oar to Tomas and prepared to go below to rest before his next watch. "Oh look—there's the sun rising just before us. We're still on course. And there's the morning star—I'll try to get a reading to see if we're about where we should be. Then I'll signal the longboat."

But, looking back behind the *knorr* for Aiwar's longboat, he saw only the gentle waves of the sea. Surely they were still following. He scrambled up the mast to get a better view. All around him the full circle of horizon was empty. The longboat, with Snorri at the helm, had gone down in the storm.

Chapter Thirteen
King Erik's Justice

Even far out in Oslo fjord, Harald recognized the sounds. As the *knorr* came closer to Bergen harbor, cries, shouts—a great wave of sound borne by the wind filled the royal sail. Harald had waited for this moment. And now, when it finally came, it seemed unreal. The sights, the sounds came over him, as he stood in the *knorr*'s prow, like a great wave of impressions, all mixed up and striking his eyes and his ears in enormous confusion. His whole body shook with emotion, and, for once, he made no effort to conceal it.

"There they come!" came from one of the king's lookouts from up above on the rocks.

"Look! See out there! They've returned!" cried another lookout. From a large ox horn slung over his shoulder on a golden cord he blew three long blasts. The blasts echoed around the mountainsides and all down the fjord. Then, cupping his hands around his mouth, he shouted, "Ho la, ho la, below! Alert the dock men, get up to the castle and inform the king!" All at once the bells in the tower of Bergen cathedral began to ring. Their deep sound boomed against the cliffs, first on one side of the fjord, then the other.

A small fishing boat sailed up alongside the *knorr* and followed it toward the harbor. "Welcome, welcome home!" shouted one of the fishermen. "Thought you'd be dead by now, eaten alive by who knows what over there!" Shading his eyes against the sun, the man searched the open sea in their wake. "Where's the other longboat?" he asked.

"Is that you aboard, Bjorn?" shouted the other fisherman. "What happened to the others?"

"Can't expect much else, going out that far into the unknown, can you?" Harald heard him say. "Fool-hardy voyage in the first place, if you ask me." He paused a moment to trim the small sail so as to keep a steady distance from the *knorr*. "You're the lucky ones."

Yes, I'm the lucky one, thought Harald. *Not Snorri.* And the realization of his loss at what should have been one of the happiest moments of his life changed that moment into one of regret and sadness.

By this time other fishing boats had joined them, forming a large flotilla which advanced in the brisk breeze, closer and closer to the main docks of Bergen. Arrival after an absence of nearly five months was truly a great event, marked with even more noise and excitement on land than their return to Eriksfjord in Greenland with Thorkel.

What a contrast to the grief Harald felt. Snorri was not there to share it. He'd lost a true friend, a companion in arms, a bond-brother. During the *fóstbrædralag* up there on the cliffs above Brattahlid, the blood from Snorri's veins had flowed into his veins. They had shared all the horrors of the Western Edge. No one in Bergen who could claim that, not even back home in Telemark. Harald leaned out over the rail and looked intently at the waves, lest anyone suspect his true emotions. Snorri—gone!

And they had scanned the ocean every single day since the storm for some sign of Aiwar's longboat, some trace of debris— an oar floating in the water, a plank from the boat. Nothing. Even if any of the crew had managed to climb onto some of the icebergs he'd seen floating to the north, they would never have survived the cold. When Bjorn had been forced to sail on, he'd asked about the missing boat in Rejkavik, where they had to take on more provisions. None of the Icelanders had seen or heard anything. Yes,

Snorri was gone, and Harald hoped the king would honor his memory in some way. Surely it was up to the king to provide for Snorri's aged father, Jonas Arneson. If that failed, though, Harald was determined to do it. He would adopt Snorri's father as his own—or perhaps, given his age, as his grandfather. Not at all like the one who'd taught him all about runes, but as someone who probably knew other kinds of old stories—other kinds of charms. He had that look about him, for sure.

Harald recalled the last time he'd seen Snorri, little suspecting he'd never see him again. They were about to sail from Brattahlid. "You've more than proven yourself, Snorri Jonason, my lad," his father had said, laughing, as they were preparing the two boats, the *knorr* and the remaining long boat. "Don't you remember I once asked you if you'd ever had any experience at sea? And you admitted it had only been on a *fishing* boat—as a *passenger* at that? Ha, ha, you've had enough voyaging experience now for a lad twice your age." He placed a firm hand on Snorri shoulder and, with the other, tilted his face upward, for Snorri was much shorter than Bjorn. Looking directly into Snorri's eyes, he said, "We've lost Ingmar, one of my best helmsman, and now I need you as helmsman on the long boat. I know you'll bring her safely back to Norway."

Yet in that terrible storm, whatever ability Snorri possessed proved of little use. All these thoughts now so totally overcame him that Harald raced down into the darkness of the crew's sleeping cabin so no one would see it. He especially did not want Astrid to know it. She and her family were up on deck, eagerly awaiting their arrival. "Oh, Snorri, Snorri," he cried, burying his face in his hands. "My blood bond-brother, "how I'll miss you!" If only he'd been able to make a rune charm for his safety. If only he'd known the secret runes for that, Snorri would be there to share their glorious homecoming.

But this was no time for sorrow, no time for wishful thinking. His father was shouting up on deck for all crew to take their stations, and Harald heard his name mentioned more than once. Rushing up on deck, he was met with, "Where were you? What were you thinking of? Take charge of the mooring ropes! Don't make me have to layout your duties again, do you hear?"

After his father's stinging rebuke, Harald forced himself to concentrate on docking the *knorr*. He knew careful maneuvering was now essential, for the big sail was dropped and they were moving only with the boat's own momentum and the use of the steering rudder. No sooner had the boat nudged the dock than swarms of townspeople mixed with the crews, making their landing and descent from the boat difficult. Hardly aware by that time of what he was doing, manipulating the mooring ropes automatically as if in a daze, Harald somehow found himself stepping off the boat onto the dock, moving through the streets with the crowd, climbing up the hill to Grandmother's house. After that things seemed even more unreal.

And there was still more unreality that night as he sat in Grandmother's little parlor, crowded with Astrid and her family and Snorri's father, Jonas. To be together again—all except one. How painful it was to see Jonas's grief over the death of his son. "All I have," he kept repeating, "all I have, there is nothing more."

Harald's sister Anna appeared to have grown much older since he'd left. Maybe that was the new way she was wearing her hair—thick braids coiled around on top of her head like a crown. And she had a woman's white apron-like thing over a pale green *kirtle*, white lace sticking out around her neck, set off by a silver broach. She was sitting quietly off in a corner, taking it all in. Was she betrothed yet? Harald wondered. Wouldn't be surprised. Better finish her dower chest soon. Yes, that was probably the one thing that could make him feel like he'd actually—truly—come home.

Suddenly his grandmother's high, shrill voice broke in. "Oh, how could you have broken that pickled beet crock?" she complained. "One of my best! How will I ever replace it—it belonged to my mother ... the big brown crock, made the best pickles!" No, Harald definitely was not dreaming. He had indeed come home.

Reality also intruded in the form of a loud pounding on the door. A grandly dressed page from the court entered, wearing a tabard with the king's royal intertwined ravens on it. With a sweeping bow, he removed his felt hat, topped with an enormous ostrich feather. "By royal command," he announced in a loud official kind of voice, "you, Bjorn-Fierce-as-a-Bear, and you, Harald son of Bjorn, and you, Thorkel Liefson, are hereby summoned to appear at his majesty's castle at noon tomorrow. At noon, not a moment later." He bowed again for emphasis. "And furthermore," he added, "you, Thorkel Liefson, and your family are hereby commanded to accompany me back to his majesty's castle. His most generous majesty wishes to extend his royal hospitality for as long as you care to remain in Bergen. Come, there is a traveling wagon awaiting you just outside the door."

Hurriedly Harald, Snorri's father, and Bjorn helped Thorkel and his family gather their few belongings together and climb into the wagon. Disturbed, Harald stood watching the wagon's twinkling lantern disappear as the wagon lumbered down the steep path to the town below, lurching dangerously whenever the horse stumbled on loose rocks. How disappointing to see Astrid's family leave. What opportunity would he have later, before they left for their family estate on the Oslofjord?

As he went back into his grandmother's house, Harald's thoughts turned from Astrid to the castle, from the castle to the king's great hall, from the great hall to the prospect of an audience with the king tomorrow. He recalled that first summons—it seemed so long ago, he seemed but a mere boy then. He'd been so afraid, so over-awed by the size of the great hall, the size of the king himself. But now—well, he'd sure been in far worse dangers, fought off enemies and evil spirits, survived a wilderness bigger than thousands of kings' halls all put together.

Still, it was a fitful and restless night for Harald. He tossed and turned, the old difficulty about sleeping when he was troubled. This night, however, sleeplessness was hard to understand. Here he was, he and his father safe at last, his most earnest wish—his wildest dream—come true. Here he was in the familiar little sleeping closet up in Grandmother's loft. Astrid and her family were probably being treated like royalty. Now if only Snorri were happily reunited with his father out in the caretaker's cottage. Grandmother said that Jonas had been such a help and comfort to her. She wanted him to stay on after Harald's father, Anna, and Harald returned to their farm in Telemark. Yet Harald thought Snorri's father somehow now belonged to him and he would find it very hard to leave him in Bergen.

Well, that was one problem. There was another, and it was Astrid. Leaving Bergen also meant leaving Astrid. Yes, Astrid—that was the worst part of it. There must be something he could do, there must surely be something. He waited eagerly for the dawn to come when the busy demands of the day would distract him.

The next day did arrive. The big cathedral clock was tolling twelve noon. This time Harald and his father were not kept waiting in King Erik's ante-chamber. The guard bowed as he approached. "Come with me, sirs," he said. "No, you need not remove your weapons. His majesty does not fear men such as you."

Entering the crowded hall, the guard announced their presence in such a loud voice that all fell silent. When Harald and his father knelt together before the throne, the massive king himself arose to greet them.

"So, you have come back safely, Bjorn-Fierce-as-a-Bear, and you also, Harald son of Bjorn," he proclaimed in his booming voice. "You are most welcome to us, most welcome of any in this kingdom." Motioning for them to rise, he beckoned to one of the courtiers. "Fetch Thorkel Liefson here," he commanded. "He waits in the armory room." When a few minutes later Thorkel came to stand beside Bjorn, the king said, "We have heard something already of your voyage, we have heard how you have fulfilled our royal commission. We know much of the success of the expedition, and certainly, the fact that Thorkel Liefson now stands before us, alive and well, is one proof of that."

Bjorn and Thorkel bowed in acknowledgment. Harald bowed, too. Hadn't he played an important role in this expedition? Yes, he—Harald son of Bjorn—had played a larger role in the success of this expedition than the king would ever know. And he could never know, because, in order to do that, Harald had disobeyed orders, made a whole series of mistakes, and relied upon the power of rune charms. That confession would never be made.

"So, Harald, young Bjorn," the king boomed, "although we shall never know your exact role in the success of this expedition, this is also a great moment for you, is it not?" There it was again—the king's uncanny ability to read his thoughts. He tried to force his mind into a kind of blankness, and bowed hesitantly.

"Now then," the king continued, "we have much to speak of. Our scribes must record all you have seen, the exact distances you have traveled, the precise measurement of the lands you have traveled, maps you must draw. We must know of the claim you planted—the very words you used, the date. These must all be written down, recorded and preserved in the great parchment rolls kept in the castle's records room."

Oh, no! Harald thought at the king's last remark. Could he remember all he'd written in runes on that memorial stone? He would have to ask for Snorri's help, but Snorri wasn't here. What if the king wanted to hear them now, this very moment, before all the court? He felt his head begin to swim, his throat tightening up.

"Do not fear, young man, for you need not say them now," the king said, as if reading Harald's thoughts again. "There is a banquet being prepared to celebrate your return, but first we will go in procession to the cathedral for a service of thanksgiving to mark your safe return—a return bringing even more back to Norway than we had hoped! Then, afterwards we'll go to the records room, where the scribes will take down your report."

The day passed in a kind of blur. There was so much ceremony, so much talk. It seemed to Harald they spent hours and hours in the records room of the chancery. The five scribes, sitting at small desks, quills in hand, with big sheets and rolls of parchment paper before them, were becoming tedious. Harald sighed repeatedly. Every word had to be exact, descriptions accurate. It was very difficult to remember details. His father and Thorkel droned on and on. They were recounting everything, even describing in great detail—sometimes actually drawing pictures of plants and *skræling* clothing and weapons.

Finally the scribes came to the subject of the memorial stone. Harald gave what he hoped was an accurate version, but immediately the scribes protested. "Futhark is no longer used," they claimed. "Those runes belonged to old, pagan times."

"But, sirs," Harald began, "my grandfather—"

"Yes, yes," one of them answered, "some country folk, a few old-fashioned people living in the past, may use them for charms and the like—but here, in his majesty's chancery, is no place for them!"

Finally they agreed to translate Harald's words into Latin and write them down in regular letters. Harald did not really trust them, wondering whether they would really get it right. He had no intention of mentioning the other *futhark* charms he'd used, the *sikkerhet* charms for safety, and the *fugl* charms against Heckla. For sure they'd deny the charms' success, too.

By the end of all this reporting, Harald's brain was reeling. He could hardly wait to get out of the stuffy chancery. He ran all the way back up to Grandmother's house, eager to tell her and Anna about everything that had happened at the castle. He burst through the door. The house was empty. "Grandmother! Anna, are you here?"

No answer. How disappointing. Then he heard voices outside coming from Grandmother's small garden, sounded like Anna talking to Snorri's father, Jonas. Rather cool to be just sitting out there on this late autumn day, almost winter it seemed. Of course, they were bringing in some of the root vegetables for winter storage. He pushed open the small door in the back of the kitchen. Anna was sitting on a wooden bench along the garden wall, just where ivy vines grew up to overhang it like a canopy. Someone was with her. They stopped talking the instant they saw Harald.

"Oh Harald, Harald," Anna cried. "He's here!"

The figure beside her rose and came toward him, smiling. At first Harald didn't recognize him, but as he came closer Harald recognized the smile. Snorri's smile! Familiar or not, Harald knew he was seeing a ghost. It had to be a ghost. Snorri had drowned. Yet wasn't Anna seeing this ghost at the same time? Now the ghost came closer, a little hesitantly at first, then made a kind of leap in the air and threw his arms around him. "Harald, you old sailor, you! Harald, my bond-brother! And look at that moustache, will you! " Suddenly he dropped his arms and stepped back. "Oh, my," he said. "I must smell like fish—and you know what your father once said about my sailing experience on a fishing boat!" He smiled again, his funny, twisted smile.

Harald could not speak. He just stood there looking at Snorri. Smell like fish? It was really and truly Snorri! Yes, he did smell. Ghosts wouldn't smell like fish, would they? How did that happen? How did he get here?"

"Come, you two," said Anna, taking Harald by the arm. "Come inside by the fire—the late afternoon's getting too cool to stay outside. Come, Harald, Snorri!"

Around the big fireplace, with Snorri warming his feet against the grate and drinking the hot whey-milk Anna had prepared, Harald listened eagerly to his story. "After we got separated in the big storm," he began, "we kept a sharp lookout for your boat.

We must have been driven backwards awful far, for we never did see the *knorr*. That was a real worry, for we'd sprung a leak near the forward bow and were taking in more water than we could bail out. Boat kept getting lower and lower in the water, the dragon head finally plowing right through some of the bigger waves. We knew we were lost. Even for a swimmer—which none of us were, except for me, of course—it'd be hopeless out there. Water freezing cold, who knows what hungry monsters might be down there in the deep." He paused, took another sip of the whey-milk, looking disturbed at the re-telling.

But Harald wanted to know more. "What then?"

"Well, after about a day and a night, the boat began to break up. I managed to hang onto a piece of the deck. I made a sort of raft and pulled up Aiwar onto it with me. Don't think any of the eight others survived. There we floated for a day or so. I lost all track of time, freezing cold and dying of thirst at the same time."

"Aiwar—what happened to him?"

"I'm sorry to have to tell you. Aiwar died during the night. Couldn't do anything but push him off the raft for the waves to take."

Harald remembered Aiwar well. He'd been left in command of the *knorr* after his father took both longboats into the wilderness. And Harald had betrayed Aiwar by deserting with the skiff. He must have had a horrible death. He didn't deserve it.

"Well," Snorri continued, "I'm not sure what happened after that, being in a sort of daze. First thing I knew, a rope was being tied around my middle and I was being pulled off the raft up into another boat. At first I thought it was yours—you can imagine how happy I was at that. But then I realized it wasn't you and the *knorr*. In fact, it was the smell of cod which made me come to."

"Cod?"

Snorri gave one of his snorting kind of laughs. "You see, it was an Faeroese fishing boat, bringing a big catch back here to

Bergen. And so, to make a long story short, here I am. Ummm, yes, I guess I sure do smell. Is there a washing room where I can take a bath?"

"Oh, yes," said Anna eagerly. "I'll heat some water!"

All that evening and throughout the next day Harald and Snorri ate, exchanged stories, ate again, and remembered together the many adventures they'd shared. Harald had to make a trip back to the king's castle that afternoon to provide a few more details for the king's scribes. He returned with more court gossip, more details of what he'd related for the account they were writing.

Although she seemed a little preoccupied that evening, Anna listened politely to Harald's account of the day's events. Snorri, however, seemed to grow increasingly impatient. At last he broke into what Harald was saying. It was just as Harald was describing the funny way one of the scribes looked, his head bald except for a fringe around his ears. Harald thought Snorri would appreciate the image.

"Stop, Harald," Snorri interrupted, "no more of that gossipy stuff. I've something more important to ask you, to tell you."

"Yes, brother," Anna said, "it's most important. Snorri and I have been talking."

"Well, of course, you sure have. My sister is a great talker, and you, Snorri, aren't far behind! Probably talked each others' ears off!"

Harald was unprepared, however, for what Snorri said next. "You see," Snorri continued, "your sister Anna and I—well, we've become good friends, isn't that right Anna?" Anna was intently studying the ground at her feet and said nothing.

"In just one and a half days? Harald asked incredulously.

"What I mean is," Snorri said, looking genuinely embarrassed for the first time since had known him, "you see, we'd like to become better friends. We'd like to—" He stopped, began again. "We have so much in common and . . . and . . . and after all, you know, you and I are sworn blood-brothers."

"Well—what does all that mean? What are you driving at?"

"It means—" Anna suddenly looked up. "Yes," she said, "it means—it seems to have been planned all along—brothers—it seems—like fate—"

Harald was completely astonished. Snorri and Anna—and in so short a time? Of all things! What did this mean? What would his father say? What would his father say about him and Astrid, for that matter? Suddenly a light dawned. Himself and Astrid—had that been planned—fated—all along as well?

Well, the matter of Anna and Snorri was one thing. The matter of himself and Astrid was another. Greatly troubled, he resolved to bring up the subject with his father that same evening.

They sat before the fire in Grandmother's parlor after everyone else had gone to bed. Father absently stroked Flossi the cat as he did when his thoughts were in many other places. Harald was glad in a way that Astrid and her family were staying at the castle. He needed time away from her, time to think.

"Astrid and I—you see—well, I'm thankful she's not back in Greenland. She's—well, you see, Father, I'd like to be more than friends. I'd like it to be—" He couldn't go on. It was too painful.

"Well, my son," commented Bjorn with a knowing smile, "this is hardly a surprise. I sensed your friendship with Astrid might lead to more than that. I sensed it from the beginning. Sometimes one knows these things without being told." Harald couldn't believe what he was hearing. "But you must realize," his father continued, "that you both are too young even to consider marriage. Her father would agree with me, even though I know he thinks well of you."

Harald's hopes were shattered. "Father," he protested, "I know so many who've wed at a young age—why, you yourself and Mother!"

"That's true, you have me there. But you know, your mother and I belonged to a different generation. We married earlier then—

although not as young as you and Astrid. You see, our generation didn't expect to live as long as yours does now. Times have changed."

"And then there's Anna and Snorri," Harald found himself blurting out. He'd intended to let Snorri speak for himself, and wished now he'd held his tongue.

"What about them?"

Harald explained as well as he could what he thought Snorri and Anna had been trying to tell him, that they wanted to perform the betrothal ceremony. "They're still young, too," Bjorn replied when Harald had finished. "They've known each other such a short time. Yet . . . they're both of age, and I must confess I've come to have great respect for Snorri—I haven't forgotten that he saved your life at least twice. I'm grateful to Jonas, his father, too, and how he's helped your grandmother."

He fell into thought, then, coming to a sudden decision, stood up, causing Flossi to slide off his lap with a protesting yowl. "I'll speak to them, Anna and Snorri. Of course to Astrid's father and mother as well. But don't forget, all of you must also have the king's permission. That may be difficult. I'll try to have a private audience with his majesty tomorrow before the big ceremony to honor us. It'll be a very important day. But the next day, we'll return to Telemark, so I'll see what I can do to speak to the king."

Although Harald was nervous about the formal ceremony, he was more nervous about what his father would say concerning his possible betrothal to Astrid. Whatever gifts the king might bestow—well, that seemed unimportant just now. More important was his future—Snorri and Anna's too, for that matter.

He waited in a small sitting room off the great hall, pacing up and down across the stone floor. From time to time he looked absently out the narrow window. He could see many boats down there in the harbor, including the *knorr*.

It seemed an eternity before a page announced that he was to be conducted into the great hall. The king had been in a private meeting with Bjorn and Thorkel. Now his majesty was ready to receive all of them formally before the court. Would the king be just in his rewards? Harald wondered. He'd learned from his grandfather that royal justice could be arbitrary, uncertain, even unfair.

Entering the great hall, Harald was struck by the size of the crowd. With difficulty, the page nudged him forward to a cleared space at the end of the room. Where was Astrid? And his sister and grandmother? And Snorri, his father, and Jonas? They'd all been invited to this formal ceremony, too, but because of the great number of people he couldn't find them.

A hush fell over the crowd as two trumpeters and a drummer announced the arrival of the king. King Erik Thorgeirson briskly entered the hall through the small door behind the throne, causing all the men to bow, the women to curtsey very low. The king was followed by Bjorn, Thorkel, and Svein. As captain of the first long boat, Svein would also be honored. All considered only a miracle had saved him and Bjorn from being forever lost beyond the Western Edge. The three came to stand beside Harald.

At that very moment, Harald spotted Astrid with her mother and little brother. They were just at the edge of the crowd, over to his left. Astrid was beautifully dressed in clothes he'd never seen before—a dark purple gown trimmed with black fur, silver ornaments all down the front, a white veil-like thing covering her hair and neck, topped by a large black fur hat. She looked beautiful and grown-up. The sight took his breath away. He dared not look any longer and quickly glanced away. He wondered whether she'd noticed the new outfit his grandmother had prepared for him. Grandmother outfitted him with some of his grandfather's best clothes, still kept in an old chest in her room, although Harald had insisted on wearing the red wool cloak Astrid had made for him. He was shocked to hear the king's guard hiss something into his ear. He'd been thinking about so many other things that he'd forgotten to kneel.

"Today we honor brave men," the king boomed. "We recognize the bravery and courage especially of these two men—Bjorn Erikson and Thorkel Liefson—who have led our royal expeditions far across unknown waters. They have risked untold dangers in a wilderness that knew no boundaries. They have expanded our kingdom. They have prepared the way for our children and our children's children. And now we honor them with royal gifts, which they and their children and children's children may have and hold from this day forward." He nodded and raised his hand. "You may now stand."

The king's guard then escorted two pages before the throne, each carrying a small brass chest. The guard ordered the chests to be set down and opened before Bjorn and Thorkel. From among the gleam of many gold coins which filled them, the pages took out a parchment roll.

"In those chests," continued the king, "are the deeds to several estates. You will each receive 200 hectares of land as *hersir*. For you, Bjorn, an expansion of your farm in Telemark to extend it from the coast on the east to the mountains of Rogaland. Your *hersir* will also include what was once the Bergson farm north of Bergen. As for you Thorkel, your *hersir* will include five farms forming the Upland province to the south and east of Bergen, and the Vastberg estate south on the Oslofjord. Also in those chests you will both find gold *kroner* enough to do as you wish, to support your title and responsibilities as a *jarl*."

He beckoned to another page, who then held out a smaller chest to Svein. "Svein Johanson," the king boomed out, "for your part in this expedition, we award you two hundred gold crowns and the title of *jarl*. You may purchase whatever freehold farm you wish." Svein looked surprised, falling to his knees in gratitude. Clearly he hadn't expected such a generous reward.

Harald was struck dumb with amazement. So much land, so much wealth, and the noble title of *jarl*. What would his father do with it? Snorri and Anna—surely father could spare them enough hectares for a prosperous farm, with pastures and orchards and wheat fields. But the most wonderful thing of all was that Astrid and her family would now hold land of their own and it would be not be far from his father's estates. Would that the king would now grant him his own wish—

"And as for you, Harald, son of Bjorn—" With a start Harald realized the king was speaking to him. "What wish will we grant you?" Again the king read his thoughts! "Well, speak up now, you have our permission to get up off your knees and approach the throne."

Harald's earlier courage deserted him. His knees seemed too weak for support. Here was the king, saying exactly what he wanted him to say, what he had always imagined he would say. *Name anything you wish*—just like in fairy tales. So embarrassing that the little page had to help him to his feet. He could not find his tongue. He knew what he wanted to ask for, but the thoughts couldn't seem to convert to words. "Your majesty," he began, "I—I—"

"Yes, yes, my lad," the king said, bursting into his deep roar of a laugh. "So your father has spoken, the lady's father, too. And so it shall be. Come forward, Astrid Thorkelsdattir, and take Harald Bjornson by the hand."

The whole room seemed to swim before Harald's eyes, weakness rising up from his knees to his arms to his head. Then he knew Astrid was standing beside him, felt her cool hand firmly take his own.

"Now, receive these rings," said the king, motioning the page to hold out to them a green velvet cushion on which lay two gold rings, each set with a ruby. "Wear them as a pledge of your betrothal to one another. But you cannot marry yet. You must wait until you are of age. You must prove yourself, Harald Bjornson, prove that you are the true son of a *jarl*. In three or four years we shall see. If the lady still wants you then, we shall receive you once again in this court and honor you both together."

There was a big celebration at his grandmother's house that evening, the house too small to hold all the guests. Many had to spill out into the garden, even into the caretaker's house where Snorri and his father would live until Snorri and Anna were married in the big cathedral the following month. Then they would travel down to Telemark with Grandmother and take over the management of one his father's newly awarded estates.

Harald slipped away in the midst of all the festivities to go out to the storage shed in a corner of the garden. It hadn't been used since he and his father had sailed for the Western Edge so many months ago. It smelled musty, and there wasn't much light. He brushed away the cobwebs from Anna's dowery chest, her *heimanfylgja*. Yes, tomorrow he would finish it. He had only to add the date in runes, *Year 1362 October.*

And then he would begin a wedding chest for Astrid. Three years was a long time, an eternity, but the king had spoken. The king had granted him the very gift he had hoped for, but not the justice behind it. Real justice would not have demanded such a long wait or further proof of his courage and valor. Surely he'd already done enough. Nevertheless, since it was so, he would prove himself worthy of the king's favor. He would win honors in his own right.

Meanwhile, he would now have time to make an ashwood wedding chest for Astrid. Not exactly a *heimanfylgja*, since she'd already left her home in Greenland. No, it would be something to remind them both of the Western Edge. The Western Edge had brought them together. On the top and sides of the chest, he would carve on it some of the things he'd seen in the wilderness—leaves of strange trees, prickly orange flowers on the prairie, wild animals, especially the ones called *tonka*. He didn't think he'd use *futhark* for her name and the wedding date, though. Those old runes had served their purpose—at least for the time being!

Historical Note

Harald's story is based on historical fact. In November of 1898 a Swedish immigrant farmer named Olof Ohman was clearing his land near Kensington in west central Minnesota with two sons, Olof and Edward. As he tried to pull out the roots of a tree which he'd just cut down, ten-year-old Edward discovered a large, gray stone underneath. It looked like the stone had been covered over by earth many years before, with a tree later growing over the spot and wrapping its roots tightly around the stone. Edward had to chop the roots away with his axe in order to get the stone out, not easy since it measured thirty by eighteen by four inches and weighed over 200 pounds. Father and sons recognized that it was no ordinary stone. It had strange writing chiseled into the face and along one side. Experts were called in and discovered a message in runes, a form of old Scandinavian writing called *futhark*. The message said the stone had been left there by an exploring party of eight Goths and twenty-two Norwegians in the year 1362, and that ten of them had just been killed. How could this be? Vikings so far inland into North America, and in the late Middle Ages? The stone must be a fake, thought the experts.

That the stone was some kind of hoax was the theory all during the past century. Very recent discoveries, however, have concluded that the so-called Kensington stone is not a fake, but just what it claims to be: a memorial stone marking the site of an encampment made by Scandinavians on a voyage of discovery. We now know that there was a real reason behind the 1362 voyage, because history records that in the year A.D. 1354 King Magnus Erikson of Norway commissioned a Norwegian named Paul Knudson to lead an expedition to explore the lands west beyond Greenland. Iceland had already been settled by Erik the Red in A.D. 870, Greenland several years later, and some explorations continued to the coast of North America, areas the Vikings named Markland, Halluland, and Vinland. Archaeologists uncovered the remains of a Norse settlement at Anse-aux-meadows ("Jellyfish Bay") on the northeast coast of Newfoundland, a Viking colony of about A.D. 1000. History records that about the year 1360 King Magnus attempted to trace the whereabouts of two Greenland explorers, lost several years before into the North American continent. History also records that, for political reasons, the king needed more land and wealth in view of an aggressive campaign on the part of King Valdemar IV of Jutland (Denmark) to acquire more territory in Scandinavia and beyond to the west.

As well, other discoveries support these historical records. We now know that Olof Ohman was incapable of writing what was recorded on the stone. He was "functionally illiterate" with only six months of formal schooling. He could not possibly have known about the unusual runic letters and words on the Kensington stone found only in the dialect of fourteenth-century Bohusland, which had strong connections with Gotland. Other evidence comes from archaeological finds in the area: a Norwegian fire iron, a spear head, and mooring stones of Norwegian workmanship. Biological evidence examining DNA among the Innuit and Mandan Indians suggests inter-racial connections. Finally, chemical and geological tests made as recently as 2001 proved that the stone was cut and its writing chiseled in before the stone was discovered by Ohman, in fact *long* before there were any white settlers in the area. Geological finds have also recently proved that the land where the stone was discovered was indeed once an island in a lake, just as the message claims.

The story of sixteen-year-old Harald Bjornson, then, has its origin in fact. His account attempts to recreate those events which may have led to the rune stone's carving: a group of thirty Norse on a voyage of discovery, sailing from Greenland through the Hudson Straits, along the southern shores of Hudson and James Bay, up the Nelson River to Lake Winnepeg, up the Red River which empties into it, and finally into the Detroit Lakes area of west central Minnesota. It also suggests how inter-racial traces between early Europeans and native Americans might have come about. More than that, Harald's story suggests the human drama behind the stone's mysterious message.

The following provide more information about Harald Bjornson's world and the Kensington Stone:

Elliott, Ralph W. V. *Runes. An Introduction.* 2nd ed. Manchester: Manchester UP, 1959.

Hall, Robert, Jr. *The Kensington Stone: Authentic and Important.* Forum Linguisticum. Lake Bluff, Illinois: Jupiter, 1994.

Jones, Gwyn. *A History of the Vikings.* Rev. ed. Oxford: Oxford, UP, 1984.

Nielsen, Richard, and Scott F. Wolter. *The Kensington Rune Stone: Compelling New Evidence.* N.P.: Lake Superior Agate Publishing, 2006.

<www.runestonemuseum.org>

Appendix

NORSE WORDHORD

bjorn	(pronounced "bee-yorn") bear
dattir	daughter
draugar	ghost
fóstbrædralag	sworn kinship through exchange of blood
fugle	bird
futhark	runic letters and numbers
fylgja	fetch, a personal spirit accompanying someone, sometimes taking the form of a bird
hamrammer	shape shifter, a person who can leave the body and change into an animal or bird
heimanfylgja	a woman's dowry, the property or possessions that follow her to her new home, represented by a carved chest
hersir	holder of land granted by king
jarl	aristocratic title, lord or earl
Karlsvogna	Charles' Wagon. The Big Dipper or Big Bear constellation
knorr	Viking cargo boat with a deep draft and large hold. Length thirty to fifty feet, width eight to ten feet; single masted, with a large, square sail.
landnáma	land-taking, colonizing
landvættir	guardian spirit of the land

LAUREL MEANS

Lille Bjorn	Little Bear. The Little Dipper constellation.
Loki	Old Norse god of communication, deception
Odin	Old Norse god of war
rune	ancient form of Scandinavian writing, differing slightly in Norway, Sweden, Denmark, or Gotland. The runic letters and numbers in this story derive from southwestern Norway of the fourteenth century.. Named *futhark* after the first six letters of the alphabet (like ABC's), it had 24 characters and 19 numbers made from a combination straight lines and circles. It was used mainly for charms or memorials inscribed on stone, wood, or bone.
seiður	magic spell, written or spoken
sikkerhet	safety, security
skræling	native people
stallari	steward, high-ranking official in the king's court, responsible for preparations for war
storgaard	large, royal castle
valhalla	Old Norse paradise, reserved only for slain warriors

RUNES BEYOND THE EDGE

RUNIC ALPHABET

f	ᚠ	g	ᚵ	s	ᚼ
u	ᚢ	h	✳	t	↑
th	ᚦ	i	ᛁ	ü	ᛉ
a	✕	j	ᛄ	w	ᛉ
r	ᚱ	l	ᛚ	y	ᛑ
k	ᛉ	m	ᛘ	æ	⋈
b	ᛒ	n	ᚿ	œ	⊕
d	ᛑ	o	ᚮ	å	✖
e	✝	p	ᛔ		

RUNIC NUMERALS

1 2 3 4 5 6 7 8 9 10 11 12 13 14 15 16 17 18 19